DEATH AND THE GOOD LIFE

RICHARD HUGO

 AVON
PUBLISHERS OF BARD, CAMELOT, DISCUS AND FLARE BOOKS

My thanks to Deputy Sheriff Jim Doxtater
of Plains, Montana, for his generous help

Five chapters of this book originally appeared in *The Montana Review*.

AVON BOOKS
A division of
The Hearst Corporation
959 Eighth Avenue
New York, New York 10019

Copyright © 1981 by Richard Hugo
Published by arrangement with St. Martin's Press
Library of Congress Catalog Card Number: 80-21622
ISBN: 0-380-59840-x

The St. Martin's Press edition contains the following
Library of Congress Cataloging in Publication Data:

   Hugo, Richard F
     Death and the good life.

     I. Title.
   PS3515.U3D38   813'.54   80–21622

First Avon Printing, July, 1982

CRITICS CALL *DEATH AND THE GOOD LIFE* ONE OF THE MOST ORIGINAL AND SATISFYINGLY CONVOLUTED MURDER MYSTERIES TO COME ALONG IN YEARS

"Al Barnes is a strikingly new kind of detective. He is soft-hearted (but by no means soft-headed); such is his warmth, humor, and humanity that not only do suspects and witnesses open up to him willingly, but the reader would like to do the same."

James Dickey,
Author of DELIVERANCE

"Straight, sharp, and nasty—a promising first case in a hard-boiled but...un-clichéd mode."
Kirkus

"A good read what with several ax murders...a little softcore porn, a lot of big money, fancy cars buzzing about the Pacific Northwest countryside, and a complex plot with more twists than the coastline."
Library Journal

"Like all good men Richard Hugo is a bit crazy...Having achieved deserved prominence as a leading American poet, he has reached out—up, down, aside, who knows?—and written a detective story that puts him up front in that class too. I hope he is crazy enough to write another one."

A. B. Guthrie, Jr.,
Author of THE BIG SKY

For Defense Attorney Ron Talney
and Detective Jim Fleming
both good poets too

ONE

1

I imagine the three men having a good time. I imagine them singing.

We know they'd had beer for breakfast at the Hammers' house, and we know that Lee's sister, Lynn, had served pancakes and ham. By six A.M. they were off to catch the early fishing at Rainbow Lake. It was mid-September, and at our altitude the nights were already cold. Sedge was receding in the lake now that the surface water was cooling, and the big rainbows were coming up. The three men expected to catch fish, and they felt festive.

That's why I imagine them singing on the eleven-mile drive to the lake from Plains. They'd had beer for breakfast, they expected trout and they felt festive. I never checked with Lee Hammer or Robin Tingley afterward to find out if they actually sang on the way.

Lee and Robin told us they took the boat they'd hauled there out from the south shore of the lake. Ralph McCreedy, the third man, wanted to fish from shore. He got too cramped in boats, he had said, and besides, he liked fishing from shore with bobber and worm. So Lee Hammer and Robin Tingley trolled, and Ralph McCreedy made his way east on the south shore until he found a spot he thought looked good. He set up the lightweight folding lawn chair he'd carried, rigged up, baited his hook and cast out. He then sat down comfortably in the lawn chair to watch his red and yellow bobber drift from left to right in the slight wash of wind from the west. The rest of what happened to Ralph McCreedy I imagine, now that the facts are in.

I imagine that around ten A.M., with two rainbows smaller than he'd anticipated, which we found on his stringer, McCreedy was still studying his bobber. The boat with Hammer and Tingley was not in sight. I imagine McCreedy imagined the boat with his two friends was down near the dam at the far-east end of the lake, around

8

the small headland that hid that part of the lake from
him.

I imagine McCreedy heard a noise and thought: bear.
He looked around but saw nothing that might have made
the noise. The sound could have been a snap of a twig or
a cottonwood leaf cracking underfoot. I imagine he heard
it a second time and turned again, and again saw nothing.

I imagine the last time he turned he must have been
terrified to see the enormously tall woman with wild gray
hair who cackled as she brought the axe down on his head.
I imagine he was trying to understand what was happening and that he murmured "why" just before the second
blow came. I imagine he remembered a lake long ago and
a girl he saw there and that he heard some old music
before he had the briefest sense of pain and black took
over forever.

If you want a good
detective on the case, at least an experienced detective,
you're lucky I'm here. A crime like that is virtually unheard of in Plains, or anywhere else, for that matter. Sanders County, Montana, just doesn't get many murders. Probably because Sanders County doesn't have all that many
people.

I spent seventeen years on the Seattle police force, the
last ten of them as a detective, mostly in homicide. I said,
if you want an experienced detective, you're lucky I'm here.

But if you want a tough cop, you've come to the wrong
place. My name is Al Barnes, and for years on the Seattle
police force I was known as Mush Heart Barnes. I may be
the softest cop you've ever seen. When I was a rookie, they
first put me on traffic detail, chasing speeders. In one
month, I turned in fewer arrests than anyone in the mod-
ern history of the force. I set a new record for not giving
speeding tickets. My boss, a sergeant named O'Brien, ate

my ass out twice, but still I couldn't help myself. I fell for every sob story I heard.

Finally, they took me off traffic and gave me a sort of beat. I cruised around with a partner in a patrol car, hoping always to find things in order. One day we chased and caught some bank robbers. I felt so sorry for the one I held at gunpoint, I felt like letting him go. It struck me at the time that, after all, it was only a system that was out anything, not some individual.

The fact that I'd studied for three years at the University of Washington, majoring in creative writing, of all things, didn't help me when it came to ragtime with my colleagues. I bore their jibes fairly well and went on in my spare time trying to be a poet. The only reason I became a cop was, it was the only job I could find at the time, and I was desperate.

Finally, fed up with my weakness, they gave me a job lecturing to grammar school and high school students on the value of the police force to the community. I did OK in public relations work, but a big shake-up in the administration and a new chief who wanted his cops well-rounded found me again in a patrol car.

This time I lucked out and helped solve a series of murders that took place in the Broadway district where we patrolled, my partner and I. I made it into homicide as a beginning detective as a result. And finally, I found something I could do. I was pretty good. For one thing, I don't like murder, and I don't like it even more than most people don't like it. To solve a murder, I could find some toughness in me I could never find with most other crimes.

And I found I had a special gift. I don't know where it came from. People tell me things, and I don't know why. For some reason, people trust me. I must look sympathetic and understanding. It's a handy gift to have when you're investigating a murder. Because most murders are solved by information given to the detective by witnesses, or relatives of either the victim or the killer, or friends of either the victim or the killer—just tips. Most murders are solved because someone tells the detective who did it, in one way or another.

Once a woman told me her husband couldn't have sex without first eating cashew nuts. She said she'd never told anyone that before. Another time a high school teacher told me he had been a homosexual years before that was acceptable. Not only could it have cost him his job, it actually made him a suspect in the murder case I was investigating. My favorite example is the black guy who admitted he'd gotten away with a string of drugstore hold-ups twenty years before in Dayton, Ohio. I didn't bother to report it. He was living a good life now, had four children, and the information had nothing to do with the murder under investigation. But I asked him why he had told me, and he said, "I don't know, man. You just got the face."

Anyway, as long as the new chief remained, I got shifted around. Narcotics: no arrests in two months. Burglary: three arrests in six weeks. Robbery: one arrest in nine months. So it was back to homicide where I already had a good record. And before I could get shifted again, another shake-up and a new chief and a new policy. I stayed in homicide.

One day I arrested a nice little old man we wanted for questioning. He asked me not to handcuff him, please. His circulation was poor and the cuffs might cut it off entirely, he said. So, true to my nickname, Mush Heart, I told him OK. He asked if he could use the bathroom before we left, and I told him sure. I'd frisked him and knew he wasn't armed. But he was armed when he came out of the bathroom, and he shot me three times.

I just barely made it to the hospital in time. Someone had heard the shots and called the police. They discovered me on the floor amid a lot of my blood. I was in the hospital for seven months; then I took the medical discharge they offered. I was in fairly good shape, but I thought I'd had it with police work. Seattle had gotten bigger and bigger during my seventeen years as a cop, and the work was getting bigger, too. More people, more crime. I got tired of the city, almost as much as the police work there.

But I was forty, and I couldn't do anything else. I had given up trying to be a poet long ago. One cop I liked very much, a big guy named John Mrvich (you had to put a *u* between the *M* and *r* to say it right) had also been interested in writing, and he had kept at it. But years before, he had moved to Portland, something to do with his wife's family, and so my best buddy was gone. Even though my record was good and I had the respect of my colleagues now and was seldom called Mush Heart anymore, staying on didn't appeal to me.

I used the insurance settlement and my old car to buy a new car, and I set out to find some peace and quiet. I'd never gotten married and so at forty was free and feeling adventurous. The pension wasn't really enough to live on, and I needed to do something. I loved Plains, Montana, the first time I saw it.

Plains has just one main street, more or less. On the east side of the street are the shops, cafés and bars. On the west side is an old railroad station and the tracks and, beyond the tracks, most of the homes, and south of those the large lumber mill that supports the town. It looks like the ideal small town, at least it did to me more than a year ago when I first saw it. I didn't see one house built to impress others. They all looked like they should be lived in.

Then I found out by asking around that the new sheriff, Red Yellow Bear, who was headquartered in Thompson Falls about twenty-five miles away, was looking for a deputy. I drove over to Thompson Falls. The new sheriff was an impressive man, though the first impression I got was one of absurdity. He was five feet seven or eight, weighed about 280 pounds and his ears stuck out. His nose, wide as a pound of butter, looked like someone had used it as a dart board for years. His hair, raven like most Indians', lay flat on his head as if he had just removed a tight cap. And his voice sounded the way I imagined a bear's voice would sound, though I couldn't recall ever hearing a bear's voice, not even during my visits to the Seattle zoo.

But as we talked, my impulse to laugh at him melted away. He was very impressive in other ways, too. His growly raspy voice didn't hide the fact that his questions were sharp and to the point. There was both charm and a no-nonsense quality about the man that became evident during our interview. Then I thought, he must have had something to be an Indian and get elected sheriff of Sanders County, Montana. I didn't know much about Sanders County, Montana, at the time, but unless it was Eden, it probably had the same bigotry one finds anywhere. Red

Yellow Bear must have had something special going for him.

Later I found out his first name was Redfern, hence the nickname. He hired me almost on the spot and assigned me to Plains after I'd indicated that I liked Plains very much, what I'd seen of it.

"Sometimes I'm going to have to switch you around, you understand," he growled over his cigar, "but for most of the time you'll be in Plains. A guy with your experience, you'll learn fast enough. It's not all that different, anyway, I suspect."

It was all that different, though. It was a hell of a lot nicer. I'd been there for a year and a little more, and during that time I'd helped quell three married fights (same couple three times); got involved in a case where a man shot a cow thinking (he said) that it was an elk; run out of town a stupid derelict from L.A., who tried an obvious con game over the phone, to save him from the local citizens; talked about fifty thousand high school students—well, it seemed like fifty thousand—into quieting down when they'd had too much to drink; talked a farmer into not burning down his farm for the insurance; written three traffic tickets and given about two hundred traffic warnings (Mush Heart to the end); and never turned up any stolen fishing or hunting equipment, though there was quite a lot reported. The only time I'd come close to danger was one night in Orney's Bar; I'd had to take a knife away from a guy who was threatening to cut up everyone in the joint. I took the knife from him as soon as he had passed out on the floor in the middle of a wild threat. Oh, I loved Plains, Montana.

And shortly after I took over as deputy of Plains, I met Arlene Orney. She owned one of two bars in town, a homey, down-to-earth drinking hole with a nice old oak bar; big western-style mirror in back of the bar—the kind that someone breaks in John Wayne movies; lovely stuffed heads of mountain goats, mountain sheep, bears, deer, elk and one antelope on the wall; and an old potbellied stove near the rear that had not been used since she'd had central heating put in but had been left there for the effect. It was my kind of bar, another home. A lot of other people in Plains felt that way, too.

She was some woman, the best I'd ever known. She had great hips and thighs and at least enough bosom. Her bottom was near glorious. She was slightly on the fleshy side, which I like in a woman—I don't care for those thin fashion model types who look like they live on two ounces of granola a day—and she was both tough and tender in the right ways. Her hair was long and brown, and her eyes were as green as spring grass. But, as someone observed, sex lies in the personality, and it certainly did in hers. She was as warm and willing a woman as I'd known, a real positive force in the universe. I mean she was warm and willing with me, which is exactly the point.

Her husband had been dead for two years, and one brief love affair had ended some months before I got to know her, ended when she found he wasn't all that single and his wife in Missoula was getting suspicious of his frequent trips to the country. She was free and easy just as I came along, equally free and easy. Not that about half the town wasn't trying, including two high school boys who knew a good thing when they saw it. I was the lucky one. She had a couple of kids, both girls in high school, but she had been a smart mother and they didn't depend on her much anymore and didn't take a lot of her time. They were good girls, too, lively and fresh and fairly innocent. I liked them, and because I was their mother's lover and was good to their mother, and because when it came to dealing with teenagers I displayed my mush heart in all its glory, they liked me, too.

So I had it made—a wonderful woman, a relatively easy job, a pension from another job, time to do some fishing. I was sure it was smooth sailing from here on out. I put on twenty pounds in fourteen months or so in Plains and settled back into a life of peace and quiet.

That's what I thought.

3

I was having coffee at the Hammers' new house a mile out of town. Lee and Lynn Hammer, brother and sister, had saved this town of Plains shortly before I'd arrived on the scene. The mill had been about to go under, and about one hundred people would have been out of work. The future of Plains looked bleak.

Then Lee Hammer purchased the mill. He and Lynn were loaded with money, having inherited Hammer-Index Plywood Industries when they were in their mid-twenties. Both were divorced, and Lynn had one child, a big, handsome, dark fifteen-year-old boy named Mike, from her brief marriage. I knew this because they joked about it so much, the brevity of both their marriages. I'd only seen the boy once. He usually stayed in Portland.

That's where the Hammers lived, eight months of the year. But every June they came to Plains and stayed through September before going back. Summers are usually great in Montana. Lee talked with the mill bosses he had put in charge: Robin Tingley, plant manager, and Ralph McCreedy, who was chief accountant and a sort of treasurer. Together they studied the mill operations, made plans for the future, suggested possible ways to cut costs, all the things businessmen do. McCreedy and Tingley had been with Lee Hammer for years in their Portland operations, which now included three plants and a downtown office.

I liked the Hammers, though I didn't know them well. They were both approaching forty, and both were unpretentious and not at all impressed with their own importance, though the people of Plains thought them very important. The only thing I thought strange about them was the fence they'd built around the few acres on the bank of the river. That and the gate with a guard they had

posted. It was unlike them and even more unlike anything
in Montana. Mycroft, the servant they'd brought from
Portland, stood guard on the gate when Lee was home and
said things to would-be visitors like, "Whom did you wish
to see, sir?" It seemed unreal, this tall man of some former
time when dignity was in style, peering down his nose at
you in your car, his wide nostrils seemingly dead in their
rigidity and his kinky white hair immaculately combed
and brushed. Needless to say, Mycroft was a standing joke
in the bars. The mill workers held contests to see who
could imitate Mycroft best, the loser having to buy the
next round.

We were being frank and candid as always. It seemed
Lynn's only style. So I asked her about Mycroft.

"That's Lee's doing," she said and poured me some coffee
while I studied her behind, which wasn't being down-
graded by her tight silk slacks. "He says he doesn't want
any interruptions when he's working, and Montana people, sweet as they are, have the habit of just dropping in.
I suppose it's just that there are so few people, they don't
think anything about it. So Lee had the fence built when
we built the house and put Mycroft at the gate. He's been
with our family forever. I suppose you saw the phone?"

She had turned, so I looked at her face. "Yes," I said.
"I take it he phones in when somebody comes and finds
out if you want to see them."

"That's it. I'm sort of against it all. I know Mycroft is
a local joke—the whole damn bit is so unheard of here,"
she laughed. She was a brunette with a short nose and a
round face and dark eyes. She looked a lot like her brother,
and both looked a little like Eskimos. She was also very
good-looking, in a more forbidding way than Arlene. Arlene was a good-looking woman I liked to look at, and she
obviously liked my looking at her. Lynn Hammer was the
sort of good-looking woman I like to look at briefly and
then look away, as if her looks ought to be rationed. When
she went to the range again to get more coffee, I doted on
her shapely rear. I was doting on it when the phone call
came. It was Arlene.

"Jesus, Al. Someone's been hurt up at Rainbow Lake.
Red's been trying to get you for an hour. Everyone's up
there."

"I've got to run," I said.

"Can I ask you something before you go?"

"Sure," I said, putting on my hat.

"Do you like my bottom, after your lengthy and sneaky appraisals?"

"I and your sneaky way of spotting my sneakiness should bring blushing back into style," I said.

"Some days I wish that Arlene didn't have you in a cage," she said, laughing. I liked her. Nothing too heavy. I'd missed some of that easy cavalier city manner in Montana.

4

I kept the siren open all the way to Rainbow Lake. I was the last to arrive. There were two sheriffs' cars on the spot already and an ambulance, plus a dozen or so civilian cars, all parked in the campground under the big ponderosas.

A woman sitting in a blue Plymouth was nearly out of control. I could hear her moaning, "Horrible," over and over. I stood next to her car, feeling a bit helpless.

"Can I do anything, miss?"

"Horrible," she said and pointed down the lake shore.

"Will you be all right?"

"I don't think so," she said. Her answer told me she would be all right. I headed down the lake.

The fifteen or so people who had stopped to see what was going on were subdued.

No one talked above a whisper. Yellow Bear said to me very quietly, "Where the fuck have you been, Al?" It was said in such a way that I suspected he hoped with his tone of voice to preserve civilization. His voice lacked its usual good-natured growl. When I got my first look at Mc-Creedy's body, I knew why.

"What the hell," I muttered involuntarily.

McCreedy's head was so mutilated one could not say for

sure it had ever been human. It was pulp. I assumed the
gray was brain matter, the white splinters were bone and
the red glob that encased the gray and white in some
utterly formless way was blood and flesh. Some blood had
splattered on the rocks and dried. His worm can had fallen
over and the worms had crawled away. In their place in
the dirt that had kept them alive, one of McCreedy's eyes
that had come loose stared blindly at the sky. Except for
the remains of a black narcotics dealer years ago in Seattle, I'd never seen a more hideous corpse. It seemed unreal, with the sun dazzling off the lake and two lovely
deep-red rainbow trout floating on McCreedy's stringer.

Lee Hammer and Robin Tingley were sitting on rocks.
Tingley looked like he was in or near shock. Lee looked
grim, almost angry.

Tingley normally looked relaxed. He was the plant
manager, and his manner usually suggested that if there
was a problem, just bring it to him and he'd solve it. His
broad, open face seemed to carry few secrets, and ever
since Lee Hammer had brought him up from Portland to
run the mill, he had been popular with the men and women
who worked there. Now he looked like a gray little boy,
trying to find a response that was too deep to locate. He
stared at the water as if obsessed by the lake, as if the
water might divert his attention forever from the gro-
tesque sight a few yards away.

Lee Hammer angrily stamped out a cigarette. "Son of
a bitch," he muttered. He seemed to be calling whoever
had killed McCreedy just that. I'd never seen him look this
way. His eyes were normally friendly. Now they were hot
with desire for revenge. He looked like a man who detested
any break in the natural order of things, who would resent
forever this monstrous act that had taken the life of a
friend who had been doing nothing more harmful than
fishing. Lee usually was as fluid and warm as his sister,
at least when he wasn't preoccupied with business matters.
Now he looked like a resolute primitive, like a stone that
had suddenly experienced rage.

Even Manny Sanderson, another deputy, was shocked
into decency by the murder. That was something new for
him. Sanderson is one of those cops who make other cops
ashamed they are cops. He had soft blond hair and a

straight thin nose and blue eyes like the eyes of an Alaskan husky, sort of crazy.

Manny Sanderson also had the reputation for brutality to prisoners. He had once beaten a high school boy nearly senseless, trying to make the boy confess to something he was not only innocent of but ignorant about. I knew that was true; I'd talked to the boy later, and the kid was too scared to lie when he told me.

Sanderson had also been known to shoot people, at least that was the story I got from the kids in Plains, and I could believe it. He was bigoted, too, and when he had had a few drinks, he wasn't too willing to hide the way he felt working for a "goddam fish spear." I think Red Yellow Bear knew Manny Sanderson's feelings. In fact, I think Yellow Bear knew a hell of a lot about a lot of things. I think he kept Sanderson with him in Thompson Falls to keep an eye on him and maybe to win him over ultimately. Indians, like a lot of other minorities, know the value of patience when it comes to the individual bigot.

A doctor from Thompson Falls, Margeboin, had checked out the remains. (In Sanders County the sheriff is the coroner.) He suggested sending the body to Great Falls, where a pathologist might find something that would help us. Attendants loaded the body in the ambulance. Red Yellow Bear ordered the crowd to keep back while we went over the ground for physical evidence. We didn't find anything that might help. The crowd—twenty people constitute a crowd in Montana—was making its way back to the cars.

"Ever see anything like this in Seattle?" Manny Sanderson asked me.

"If I did I'm not proud of it," I said. I tried to have as little to do with Sanderson as possible. To tell the truth, I was a bit afraid of him. I have always found people with so little civilized restraint frightening. I walked over to Hammer and Tingley.

"We found him," Lee said with some bitterness. "Nice fishing trip. The end of a perfect day."

"We got seven," Tingley said. "One goes four pounds." Then he caught himself. "I'm sorry. I don't know why I said that." He looked embarrassed.

I touched his arm lightly. "It's really normal. Really it

is." It is, too. People often leave subjects they can't deal with for those subjects they can. Once, a guy whose wife had been murdered and was still lying in the front room tried to show me some pictures of a farm he wanted to buy.

"Al. Hey, Al." Now that the body had gone, Yellow Bear's voice was getting some of its old growl back.

"Chief?"

"Don't call me that. I'm a brave," he said. Not so much snap had returned that his favorite line, one I'd heard before, came through with the same zing I'd gotten used to, if you can hear zing in a growl. Next to him was a little guy who looked beat up from the night before and who seemed to think his condition normal to the human race. You see a few like that in Montana.

"This is Toby. He works on a ranch outside Thompson Falls. Toby, this is Al Barnes."

"Glad to meet you," Toby said, shaking my hand.

"Toby's got a story to tell you. Might be something for us. Tell him, Toby."

"Well, I'm on my way back from Missoula. I got drunk there last night and got in a fight. So I had to stay over to get patched up in emergency in Saint Pat's. Then I slept at a friend's place. So I'm comin' back this morning, and I stop in Dixon—hair of the bitch and so on, you know— for a beer. Just to feel a little like living again. And there's a guy there, sorta drunk. A little guy like me. And he tells me—we're the only guys there except for the bartender— that he just saw this woman with an axe here by this lake. Big mother, he said. Big. So I took the back way, just bumming around, you know—I often take the back way into Plains 'count of I like to drive through Camas Prairie, you know. Thought I'd like to get a look at this big woman with the axe. Sounded like nothing I ever seen. Shit, I'm sure glad now I didn't run into her. Christ. Who wants his fucking head chopped up?"

"Al. Why don't you run over to Dixon and see if you can find this guy there? You remember his name, Toby?" Yellow Bear looked at the beat-up little guy.

"I don't think he ever told me. But he was the only guy there when I left. He's flying already, and he's probably still there."

"I'll get going, Red," I said. "Thank you, Toby."

"Yeah, Toby. Thanks," Yellow Bear said. "Hey, Al, keep that fucking siren off, will you? What in hell were you running it for on these damn roads? Trying to warn the deer to stay on the shoulders?"

It struck me as funny and dumb that I'd used the siren on a road with so little traffic. It had probably taken over an hour for the few cars that had stopped to collect. This was my first murder in Sanders County. I must have thought I was back on the streets of Seattle.

5

I took the dirt back road down to where it bends left and shoots straight across Camas Prairie. I was alternately disgusted by the memory of McCreedy's remains and mildly excited about the possibility of an eye witness. Camas Prairie looks like a bit of eastern Montana that mistakenly found itself west of the divide. It is spacious and bare. Behind me now, to the west, sloped hills covered with pines and larches rose slowly. Ahead of me, bare hills bordered the east side of the basin that, if you looked at it closely, dipped somewhat like a very gradual trough. When I hit State 382, I turned right and sped along the two-lane road. As usual, I was the only car in sight. I passed the loneliest-looking school in the world and a couple of minutes later had left the prairie and was winding through a canyon with low rocky cliffs on either side. I emptied out of that just above Perma. The Flathead River ran below the bridge I crossed, strange salad-green water that ran slowly but suggested undertow and power, even now in late September when it was low. I turned left on 200 and started for Dixon. By now I was thinking more and more about the possible eye witness and less and less about the bizarre remains of McCreedy.

When you see Dixon you feel as if, had you lived there all your life, you'd be either more interesting than you are or you'd drink more than you do, or both. Everything about the place is charmingly the wrong color, or the wrong size, or in the wrong relation to the other things. The library is too small and painted a sort of off-aqua. The general store is too big proportionately to the other buildings. The houses, at least most of them, don't seem to be in a particular order. The bar is just the right size for the town but too close to the road. Across the road from the bar was a small building, long run-down, that must have been a garage before cars outgrew it. There was only one car parked at the bar. It had a Missoula County license plate.

I'd never been inside the bar but had passed it a few times on the way to Missoula. My first impression was that it was as homey a bar as I'd ever seen. The green plaster on the walls, the three tables against the wall, the short bar with maybe ten stools, even the light invited you to come in and relax. I never saw a place that was more unpretentious, that asked less of anyone. It struck me as a fine place to drink your life away and tell the world to go to hell. That's just what the only customer seemed to be doing. The bartender was reading the *Missoulian*. He didn't even look up when I came in. When he did, my uniform seemed to impress him about as much as the death of Jean Harlow.

I approached the only customer. I had a terrible urge to sit down and get drunk with him. It would have taken some concentrated belting to catch up. He looked drunk enough for 10 P.M. It was 12:34, according to the clock on the wall.

The only customer wore a Havana shirt under a green zipper jacket. Despite his state, there was something civilized about him, almost refined. "Officer," he said, throwing his head to make sure the words came out, "have a drink." His accent was unmistakably eastern U.S., but I couldn't place it. His yellow eyes weren't quite in focus. He had a gray, short-billed hat pushed back on his head. With his pixie face and the hat pushed back, he reminded me of the breezy reporters in movies from the thirties that I'd seen on TV. I guessed he was in his late twenties.

"Deputy Barnes," I said. "Sheriff's office, Sanders County."

"You have a splendid organization, sir. Just splendid. Doesn't he have a splendid organization, bartender?"

The bartender went on reading. I had the feeling drunks were nothing new in his life.

"Bailey, sir. Shelly P. Bailey, of Missoula, Montana. Formerly of Butte, Montana, and before that the ski slopes of yesteryear." He brought his left hand slowly down an imaginary ski slope. "Swooooosh."

"Mr. Bailey, a man at Rainbow Lake said you had seen a big woman in that vicinity this morning."

"Ah, indeed. The big girl of the tundra. Was she tall? Shit. Come to the table, Deputy Beamers." He picked up the double shot glass that still had some whiskey in it and the beer that he was using for a chaser. We moved a few feet to the table against the wall. "We can talk here," he said. It was obvious the bartender could hear us just as easily from where we were now. "Let me buy you a drink, copper." He tried to say it in Jimmy Cagney's voice. It wasn't close, but he was amused by his effort. "How about it, copper?" He was still no closer to Cagney.

"It's Barnes, not Beamers, Mr. Bailey. And thanks, but I can't join you right now in a drink."

"Shelly. Please, sir. Shelly, as in Percy Bysshe. Imagine having a name like Bysshe, for Christ sakes."

"Can you tell me about the woman you saw, Shelly?"

"Tall. Real tall. Jesus God, was she tall. Six eight, maybe. Six fucking eight. You're not a Finn, are you?" His eyes were about as focused as those of a dead fish. His profanity seemed odd, almost an act, as if he never swore when sober.

"No. I'm not. Now, Shelly, if—"

"Me, neither. Never see many Finns around here."

"The woman you saw."

"In Butte. Lots of Finns in Butte. More Irish, though."

"Shelly, the woman? Six feet eight?"

"At least. Shit, was she tall. Came up right out of the woods there when I was passing the lake. She was carrying an axe, a fucking axe. Barnes? English, maybe?"

"I think so. Tell me, Mr. Bailey, if I have this right. You were driving past Rainbow Lake and saw a very tall woman coming up from the lake carrying an axe? Did she come from the road that leads down to the campground?"

"Right out of the trees." He started to laugh. "Right out of the trees. Like the first primitive. That's a good one. Right out of the trees. First day feet on the ground. Oh, shit, that's good." He howled with glee. Tears of good humor ran down his face.

He finished his whiskey and poured some beer after it. I signaled the bartender. The bartender brought another double shot and beer to Bailey. I paid.

"A gentleman and a sheriff. How about that?" Bailey said, recovered from his joke.

"Did she have a car parked anywhere?"

"Barnes and Bailey, those two funny people. And here they are, those two funny people, Barnes and Bailey. Tah tah tah tah ta."

"Mr. Bailey, please try to concentrate. A man has been murdered."

"No shit." His eyes came into focus for a minute. "Murdered. Boogie. Boogie." He waved his hands in a gesture of mock horror. Maybe I needed a laugh after seeing McCreedy's body. I damned near burst out laughing at Bailey. He seemed so funny, all of a sudden. I fought back the urge to laugh, just barely successfully.

"Now about this tall woman, what time was it?"

"What time was what?" He was holding two fingers in the form of a V, one on either side of his nose.

"What time did you see the tall woman with the axe?"

"Right after Plains, Rainbow Lake—right? Plains, my second stop on my tour drunk."

"Tour drunk?"

"I take tour drunks every so often. I hit as many bars as I can, driving away from Missoula. Wherever the last place is, that's where I stay the night. Next day I start back and hit all the bars again. After this bar, I hit Ravalli, Arlee, Evaro, the bar at the cutoff to I-90, and whoosh, I'm home. Left Thompson Falls this morning. Hate the Great Falls run. Too long between bars. You could be German. Probably not."

"Do you think you should be driving?" I asked, genuinely concerned. He seemed too nice a guy to end up early in a car wreck.

"Too drunk to walk, officer," and he laughed at the dated joke. "Never had an accident yet. Not no way."

"Could it have been ten or maybe ten-thirty when you saw the woman?"

"Had a beer in Perma after."

"Ten, maybe ten-thirty when you saw the tall woman?"

"Got the wrong road. No bars between Plains and Perma that way."

"Ten or ten-thirty?"

"Yeah, must have been. I passed out last night in Thompson Falls. That's the trouble with this fucking booze. It'll kill you. Got up early, had breakfast and whooosh, on my way. Back on tour. Took the wrong road out of Plains, and there she was at Rainbow Lake."

"Did the tall woman with the axe have a car?"

"Didn't see one. That's why I offered her a ride."

"You offered her a ride? You mean you spoke to her?"

"Sure. There she was. Right out of the trees." He started to laugh again. "First day, feet on the ground. First day, off of all fours. Now hernia becomes a risk, right? Oh, shit." I waited for his convulsions to die down. "And there she was. So I stopped. I thought she wanted a ride. So I stopped and said, 'Shelly P. Bailey offers you a ride, my lady.' And you know what? She called me an Egyptian. Can you imagine that? Do I look like a fucking Egyptian, for Christ sakes?"

"An Egyptian. Are you sure you heard her right?"

"Sure. Old Shelly P. Bailey got ears. She said something like, 'Get out of here, you goddam Egyptian, or I'll give you the same.' Imagine that. Me an Egyptian. The Egyptians aren't even up. No one is Egyptian, specially your friend and mine, Shelly P. Bailey esquire. Not at ten fucking whatever. You're not, are you? I mean Egyptian. I didn't mean any offense if you are."

"Can you describe her?" I was getting excited now. "I mean, I know she was tall. But what about her hair, her eyes, her mouth? How old was she?"

"Old. Gray hair. Wild fucking hair. But her face was almost pretty. Yeah, she was pretty. I remember I thought she was the prettiest old woman I'd ever seen. And she had green eyes; I remember because they made her look like a cat, a great big pussycat. They sort of glowed. Only, when she called me an Egyptian and swore at me, she didn't seem so pretty anymore."

"What do you do for a living, Mr. Bailey?"

"I teach."

I took his home address in Missoula. I didn't want to try and pull any more out of him. I liked him, but it is exhausting talking to a drunk when you're not drunk, too.

"I may be down to see you again, Mr. Bailey."

"Please."

"Can you tell me something? Were you frightened at all?"

"Why should I be?"

"Well, here was a tall woman who seemed hostile, and she had an axe. Didn't that scare you?"

"No. I figured she was a forester."

On my way out I checked with the bartender.

"He got here about eleven or a little after. The bar at Perma called and warned us he was on the way. He's been here before, and I don't mean just yesterday. He really takes 'em. The tour drunks he told you about. He's sort of nice."

"Maybe you ought to try to talk him into coffee before he drives off. Or maybe get him to eat something. I'm afraid he'll kill himself."

"I've already thought of it," the bartender said.

As I was going out the door, Bailey yelled at me, "Hey, Barnes. If you see any of those fucking Finns from Butte, you tell them Shelly P. Bailey isn't afraid of a goddam one of them." He was slapping the table and giggling when I closed the door.

6

When I got back to Plains, Arlene was busy with several customers. Everyone was talking about the killing at Rainbow Lake. Several customers asked me if we'd found anything, but I put them off.

"It's great for business," Arlene said, "if too many don't

get killed. But there must be better promotional schemes. Jesus, Al. I heard it was awful."

"It was, for sure. It made me all the more thirsty for some more life. And my plans include you—all night."

"I've been thinking the same thing. Listen, the bunch is up at the Hammers'. Red and Manny, that creep, and the Hammers and Tingley. Red said to tell you to come up."

When I arrived, the others were showing the numbness that often follows shock and revulsion. It was especially unusual for the Hammers. The few times I'd seen them together, they'd always been lighthearted, except when Lee was working. In fact, they were often childishly good-natured when I'd been around them, kidding each other and putting everyone else at ease. They were not only the saviors of Plains, they were a prime social force in the community during the four months they spent there each summer, June through September.

It turned out McCreedy had a brother and mother in Portland, and the Multnomah sheriff's office had already been notified. Some poor deputy was probably on his way to give them the rotten news right now.

Red took me aside, and I told him about the meeting with Bailey. He said we'd better have a meeting that evening.

"This is my first murder as sheriff," Red said. "I'm glad you're on the force, Al. I think I can use your experience. We all can."

Lee and Lynn were off in a corner, talking to Manny Sanderson. Tingley, still looking a shade grayer than normal, sipped a drink and looked out the window and thought his own thoughts. I wondered how Lee and Lynn liked our number-one brutal cop. I supposed Manny had some social grace somewhere. At least, Lee and Lynn seemed interested in whatever he was saying. But, of course, Lee and Lynn Hammer were pretty classy people. They wouldn't show bad manners, not even to Manny Sanderson.

It was a joyless hour I spent there. I was glad when we left, Red and Manny to drive back to Thompson Falls and me to go back to Plains, where right now Arlene Orney was being relieved by the night bartender, and we could

have an hour together before I went to Thompson Falls for
the meeting. I didn't plan to use that hour to eat dinner.
I wanted Arlene right now. I was hungry as hell at the
meeting.

7

All six deputies were
there. Manny Sanderson, a guy named Jones I hadn't gotten to know very well yet and a guy named Scott I knew
even less. They were Thompson Falls' deputies who
worked directly under Red Yellow Bear and under Sheriff
Pop Powell. Deputy Oborn worked out of Hot Springs, and
Deputy Butz worked out of Noxon. Pop Powell was an old
hand and so nice that people tended to behave just so they
wouldn't offend him. Red Yellow Bear got started right
away. Night was beginning outside. The street was empty.
It wouldn't get much fuller, this being a week night.

"I've got something, I think. There's been three murders
in the past few years like McCreedy's. One on a dirt road
outside Cottonwood, Idaho, in 1974. Some guy with no
surviving relatives. His name was Ben Hazel. I guess he
was a kind of bum. He had no job. But it was the same
deal. His head was pulp and bone. Then, in 1975, we had
two. One outside Saint Regis, Montana—that's close—in
the woods. A logger who was unemployed; well, actually
a gyppo, I guess. The guy was named Melvin Johnson. The
other guy was a Wyatt Popling. He got it near Riggins,
Idaho, along the bank of the Salmon River. All out in the
country, none in or near town. All men. All alone. All with
heads cut up so bad you couldn't tell what in hell they'd
looked like. Oh, by the way, Wyatt Popling was from Con-
necticut. He was a missing person from New Haven and
much younger than the others. He was twenty-three. That
means shit, as far as our problem goes. Melvin Johnson,
the gyppo, lived in a motel in Saltese and was worried
about paying the rent."

I was impressed with Yellow Bear. That seemed a lot of information to have dug up in such a short time. He was always surprising me. I suppose because he was so absurd-looking and growled when he talked, I had a hard time thinking of him as efficient—though I found time and again that he was. I was too used to a slick, well-dressed chief of detectives in Seattle, with a polished desk and smooth manners, who had facts at his finger- and tongue-tips that he seemed to store up for use when he needed them to chew out one of his detectives for screwing up. Yellow Bear was nothing like that man in appearance, but he seemed to know an awful lot when it mattered.

"Ideas?" He puffed on his cigar and eyed us. No one said anything.

"OK, the first question is, did anyone see anything, like a gray-haired but pretty amazon carrying an axe and calling people Egyptian?"

All but Manny Sanderson laughed.

"The truth is, we have nothing but the story Al got from that guy named Bailey, and he was shitfaced. Al, what do you think? You're used to murder. It's not one of our most frequent felonies, and the ones we do get aren't anything like this."

I had been trying to sort out Bailey's story. "OK," I said. "My first impulse was to doubt Bailey's story. For several reasons. One is, he's short himself, and a woman maybe five ten might look like six eight to him. Bailey could very well be sensitive about height, and he might very well exaggerate the woman's height. Also, he was a little drunk already, partly from last night and partly from stops in Thompson Falls and Plains. Then that business about Egyptian. She might have said 'gyppo.' It's a word we hear a lot around here—Red just used it a few moments ago. Then, Bailey is hung up on nationality, when he drinks, at least. He mentioned Finns, English, German and Irish during our short talk. He might hear gyppo as Egyptian. I've gone all through it over and over. I don't want to believe him—I suppose one reason is, I'd feel like a fool if I did."

"Shit, who can believe that crap?" Manny said. "A fuck-ing drunk with a wild story like that?"

"Wait a minute, Manny," Yellow Bear said. "I see Al's

point. The big problem is, we don't want to believe it. It's too wild. That's right, isn't it, Al?"

"That's right. It's the kind of story where the weakest thing about it is the mind of the listener, my mind, yours." I deliberately avoided looking at Manny. "Certain things impressed me about Bailey. He's very funny, and funny people, while often given to exaggeration for humor, seldom exaggerate something when there's no laugh to be had. Also, he wasn't so far gone that early in the morning that he didn't stop and offer her a ride. The fact he did stop means he wasn't afraid. He had no idea what had just happened—you can't see where McCreedy was fishing from the road. So if there's a woman, and if she did it, for Bailey, it was just someone on foot who might need a ride. So he wasn't overly impressed at the time. Also, Bailey is a teacher—I suppose grammar school or maybe high school; great detective, I forgot to ask him what he teaches—and he's used to hearing people speak. Some teachers seem to have pretty sharp ears—it's a habit they get into—hearing others. Anyway, if you want my recommendation, I say, since we've got nothing else at all—either on this or the other killings, if they're connected, but we have the other killings and we assume they are connected—we ought to go ahead as if Bailey is telling us the gospel truth. He really saw a woman six eight, and she was carrying an axe, and she called him an Egyptian."

"Jesus Christ," Yellow Bear growled, "do you know what we are saying? We are saying that for at least three years a woman so damned tall anyone would remember her has been running around Idaho and Montana, butchering guys' heads and calling people Egyptians, and no one has seen her until now. Can that be? That no one has seen her but Bailey? Furthermore, she's a fucking banana. A cracker, for Christ sakes."

The deputies stirred a bit and fell silent. Cops, like most other people, are awed and frightened by the mentally deranged. I've seen cops, who aren't afraid to fight it out with the toughest crooks, tremble when they had to pick up a mental case and take him or her to a hospital.

"That's my thinking," I said. "I think we've got a deranged woman, very tall, who goes off now and then and axes complete strangers, always men. But she lives somewhere and she's passing for sane, or at least she's getting along, and if the others think anything about her, they probably just think she's odd—that would fit in, anyway, because she's so tall. I think we ought to notify every sheriff and police officer in Idaho and western Montana and see if we can turn up any abnormally tall women. We've got to be arbitrary, and we've got to think in terms of which town is a good or likely base of operations for the axe lady. We'd better make the memo confidential and— well, I'm not sure how much we should tell them."

"Tell them nothing," Yellow Bear said. "Just ask if they have any tall women—you said we'd better be arbitrary— say, any women over six two; that gives a six-inch margin of error for Bailey's story. If we tell them what we want her for, any woman over five eight is going to be rousted in some town or other where there's a cop who wants to make points. Any other ideas?"

"I think it's nuts," Sanderson said.

"What else have we got?" Pop Powell asked gently. Sanderson shut up.

So we sent out the alert for women over six two as far south as Boise and as near as Hot Springs. We assumed all we could do was wait.

Two days later, Lee and Lynn Hammer closed their house, left their car—one of their cars, I was sure—locked in the garage of the house, so they could use it next year when they returned, and rode to the airport with Robin Tingley, who saw them off on the plane to Portland.

The day after that, the first mill worker to arrive in the morning found Robin Tingley's body in between two stacks of logs. Tingley's head had been split open by something heavy and sharp, like an axe.

8

By ten the body had
been removed. Everyone we could think to question, we
did. We went over the grounds three times, at least. Nothing.

I got the Hammers' Portland number from the mill
office and called to give them the news. Their reaction was
much like the one setting in all over the town of Plains.
They were stunned. Lynn, on an extension, wept. Lee was
nearly speechless. I told them how sorry I was and asked
them to call me later at my home, or I'd call them when
we'd had a chance to absorb this latest jolt. I had the feeling
that it was one too many for them. Lee mumbled something about just having said good-bye to him yesterday
and something about bringing two good men all the way
from Portland, only to have them killed by some maniac.
Her voice choked, Lynn tried to comfort him, to assure
him he was not to blame.

The whole town was dead by now, as subdued as the
small group had been a few days before on the shore of
Rainbow Lake. It was as if to speak, even in a normal
voice, would have violated something sacred. McCreedy
had been a nice enough guy but quiet and not very well
known. As plant manager, Tingley's popularity put him
up there with Lee and Lynn Hammer in the town's affections. They had looked on Tingley just as they had looked
on the purchase of the mill itself by the Hammers at the
last minute. Tingley and the mill's new owners were all
one package of salvation in the eyes of the workers and
of the town itself. Even the bar crowd who imitated Mycroft at the gate knew that the Hammers could do no
wrong. They could have moved Red Square from Moscow
to Plains, and it would have had the approval of the majority. Now, with Tingley killed, much like McCreedy, the
town went cold and silent and thoughtful. I was afraid it

32

would ultimately get angry, but so far all I could hear was the silence, the suspension of anything animated.

When I drove to Orney's, dogs outnumbered people two to one. I saw one dog.

Arlene poured me some coffee. We forced grim smiles at each other. In our minds the same thing was going on, I was sure: we were both glad we were alive and had each other, and we were both feeling a bit guilty that we were feeling that, instead of grieving about Robin Tingley. It was a time when whatever you felt or thought or said seemed wrong, so you shut up. We stayed shut up for over ten minutes. I was the first to break the spell. I said something brilliant like, "Jesus Christ."

"How do you like the peace and quiet of Plains, Montana, Officer Barnes?" she said.

"That's what I came here to get away from. How many murders have they had in Sanders County before this?"

"Not many. A couple of bar killings, you know, guys too drunk and too angry. I remember a murder case in Thompson Falls years ago, when I was still married— before I was widowed."

"You know what? The whole business makes me want you more and more, like all the time, like right now."

"Me, too. It makes me feel exactly the same."

We went into the back where she kept a small single bed and gave the world our only answer to the horror that had struck the little town of Plains. No one came into the bar for a drink while we were in the back. Or someone came in and went away thirsty.

I hadn't been home ten minutes when the phone rang. It was the Hammers. They seemed much more composed, now that a few hours had passed.

"I'll have to call Marnie and tell her," Lynn said.

"Who's Marnie?"

"Marnie Tingley. They were separated. She's still a close friend. We were all friends in high school. She visited us for a few days in Plains a couple of weeks ago."

"I didn't know you went that far back together. It must be a dreadful damned business for you. Sorry I was the one who had to tell you."

"Someone had to. Can you give us some details?"

"It was like McCreedy, only not so messy," I said. "I

guess it was an axe. We found him in the log yard between a couple of log piles."

"Any idea at all who's doing this?" It was Lee's voice.

"We've got one lead. I'm going to follow it up some more."

"I want him caught," Lee said. "I want him taken out of circulation. Goddamn it, he's killed two close friends of mine, the rotten bastard."

"Honey," Lynn pleaded, "they're trying all they can."

"I'm sorry, Al," Lee said, "sorry I talked to you that way, but not sorry for my feelings, not a bit sorry for them."

"They're my feelings, too," I said.

"I know," Lynn said. "So does Lee."

"Sure," Lee said.

"I'll be in touch."

I hung up and sat staring out the window. I couldn't quite make out the Clark Fork River from this modest house I rented, but I could see the canyon cut away and the pines and tamaracks growing straight up out the steeply slanted hill, and I knew at the base of it a river was running beautifully because it was autumn. It was taking yellow cottonwood leaves home, and maybe nearby a fisherman was trying a few last casts with a fly before it got too cold to fish. Then I remembered that, for some fishermen, it was seldom too cold to fish, even in Montana. I remember my surprise on first learning of fishermen who kept maggots in their mouths to keep them warm so they'd go easier on the hook, standing in the ice-cold water of January and February trying to catch whitefish. Some people do what they love every chance they get. Fishermen. Lovers, even those approaching middle age, like Arlene and me. Murderers? Was there a very tall woman here in the West who loved to sink axes into the skulls of men again and again—the phone rang.

"Red here, Al. The more I think about this tall-woman idea, the more I like it. Even Manny is beginning to soften to it—if you can say anything he does is soft."

"It's a long shot but the best we got."

"Look, Al. I know I depend on you too much these days, but you're the guy with the experience with murder—"

"It's OK, Red. I'm here, and you're paying me. Not much, I know. But—"

"OK, OK, let's cut the shit. I think you ought to talk to Bailey again. See if you can catch him sober. See if he remembers anything else, or if his story is different now that he's not drunk—if he's not drunk. The way you made him sound, he may never be not drunk."

"I'll go see him."

"Oh, and Al."

"Yeah."

"Dont wear your uniform in case you have to go to the school where he teaches."

"I'd already thought of that."

9

The woman who answered the door at the stylish house in the Lower Rattlesnake area of Missoula was not much more than a girl. Her face was soft like a high school face, and she was dressed casually in jeans and a sweater that was too big but showed she wasn't too small at the same time. She was blonde, though not naturally. Her hair looked good. Her eyes were light blue, about the color of Sanderson's, but except for the color they weren't like Sanderson's at all. They were very alive with the still innocent wonder of someone recently married. They were alive with possibilities, eyes that said she and I and the world had every chance. She was a fresh, pretty girl, the kind every guy falls in love with once before he's had a chance to talk to her.

"I'm looking for Shelly Bailey," I said. "Does he live here?"

She smiled, and winter had no possibility of ever getting to Montana. "Yes, he does. I'm Johnnie Bailey, his wife. Shelly's over at school right now. He has a class today."

"A class?"

"Yes, at the university."

"The university? I thought—" I shut up just barely in
time.

"Yes. The University of Montana. He teaches there.
You can catch him after three in his office. That's when
his class is out."

"I wonder if I might ask something, Mrs. Bailey."

"Of course. Please."

"What does your husband teach?"

"Comparative literature. He's lecturing on Paul Valéry
today. Do you know Paul Valéry's work?"

"I'm sorry, I don't. He's twentieth-century French, I
believe. Very profound." I felt both stupid and a bit dizzy.

"Why don't you try to get him there? Liberal Arts 226.
He'll be there in a half hour or less."

"Thank you, Mrs. Bailey. I appreciate your help." And
I appreciate you and everything you are, even if all of it
is doomed to harden and crack.

I walked back to the car with silly ideas about starting
all over, getting a Ph.D. in comparative literature and
marrying a lovely young girl who believed in me and the
world, who every morning opened her fresh eyes and told
me she loved me and this would be a lovely day, and sure
enough it was. There wouldn't be any Ralph McCreedys
or Robin Tingleys getting their heads chopped up in that
world.

I found a parking place within a few hundred yards of
the university and walked across a big, wide playing field
and onto the campus. Mrs. Bailey had started me thinking
about essential things, like pretty girls. I saw quite a few
on my way to the LA building. I asked three of them
directions within two hundred yards of the building just
to get a closer look at them; each one pointed to the building and smiled just as innocently as Mrs. Bailey had. It's
a sure sign you're getting old when the girls look prettier
than they used to.

I found Bailey's office on the second floor in the west
wing of the Liberal Arts building. The door was slightly
open. A black nameplate with gold letters was on the
door—Shelly Bailey. I peeked in. He was dressed like the
governor. He had a white shirt and a dignified blue and
green tie. He wore a mustard sports jacket that couldn't

have been more than a week old. I couldn't see his trousers or shoes behind the desk. He looked up and saw me.

"Hello. Can I help you?" He was very polite, a little stiff.

"Yes. I wondered if I might see you for a minute."

"Surely," he said with some formality. "Please have a chair." He gestured toward a hard, dark-brown wooden chair. His bookcases were filled with volumes of Greek, German, French, Spanish and South American authors. I'd heard of about five of them. Other ponderous-looking books of criticism were on the shelves, as well as books about high cultural matters. One book I couldn't help but notice was a thick volume called *Western Civilization and Mankind.* I appreciate ambition, especially when it soars to heights like that.

"Yes, sir," he said a bit briskly, as if I were a student. "What's on your mind?"

"You don't remember me, do you, Mr. Bailey?"

He looked at me closely. "Hmm. I wonder." He appeared thoughtful. "Perhaps the MLA conference in New York? No. No. It couldn't have been. Wait. Could it have been the comp lit conference in Denver last year?" He was a bit stuffy and in a vague way slightly superior. It irritated me.

"Try the boilermaker conference in Dixon last week."

"Oh, shit." He jumped up and went to the door and closed it. He was shaking.

"Deputy Al Barnes of Sanders County."

"Yes. Yes, of course." He was almost blushing. "How did you—?"

"You gave me your address."

"I did?"

I nodded.

"Jesus, I'm only an assistant professor. If my chairman found out I go on those dumb forays—"

"How long have you been in Montana, Mr. Bailey?"

"It's my second year. I came here from L.S.U. I'm from Philadelphia originally. Well, just outside Philadelphia." He looked uncomfortable, as if I'd just discovered he was from a better-than-average background, and he was responsible for my knowing about it.

"Well," I said, "it's not for me to make speeches, Mr.

Bailey, but this is one of the few places left where fun is still in style. Anyway, if you're going to spin out on solo drunks, you won't keep it a secret very long here. There just aren't that many people to hide in. The last thing you ought to do in Montana is try to hide your quirky humanity. Besides, you're a good drunk. Actually, you're very funny."

"OK," he said. He seemed to feel better. "But I hope the chairman doesn't find out. If he does, good-bye tenure, hello MLA."

"Can we go over the story about the tall woman again, please? It's very important."

We went over it all again. Nothing had changed. The woman was still six seven or six eight. She still carried an axe, still had wild gray hair and green eyes, and still had called Bailey an Egyptian.

"Did the axe have blood on it?"

Bailey thought for a moment. "No. I don't think so." That figured. We believed she had wiped the axe on the towel McCreedy had used to wipe his hands after handling worms or fish. Both trout and human blood were on the towel, and the human was McCreedy's type. I went after refinements.

"Did she have a long neck, like a lot of tall people?"

"No. She was in good proportion. Have you ever read Baudelaire's poem, 'The Giantess,' by any chance?"

"No. Sorry, I haven't."

"You should. She made me think of it. You should read it in translation, unless you read French."

"I don't." I felt a little embarrassed. I was sure he was thinking, "Dumb cop, doesn't read French." I wish I did.

"Funny thing about tall women. They think men don't like them. They have no idea what mountain climbers we are, deep in our groins."

"This may turn out to get messy," I said, appreciating his wit but unable to add any of my own. "If we catch this woman and she's the killer, you may turn out to be the star witness."

"I know. When I read about the murder in the *Missoulian,* I knew what I'd stumbled into. Did you know it made the national news services? I mean the first one. A friend called me from San Francisco. He'd read about it down there. And some bright reporter dug out those other un-solved axe killings from the West. Needless to say, this latest killing makes us look like Detroit. It seems bigger when a lot of people are looking, doesn't it?"

"It sure does. But it isn't any bigger. Just better known."

"I agree," he said.

"I hope to be seeing you again," I said. I really did, too, with or without, but preferably by far with the killer on trial. We said good-bye. I walked down the hall and found the secretary and asked if I could see the chairman. She buzzed and said into the phone, "A man to see you." She hung up. "It's all right. Right across the hall," she pointed.

The chairman had a full mustache. He was a short, compact man, quite dapper, with friendly crinkle marks around his eyes. I shook hands and told him who I was. He seemed surprised.

"One of your staff, Shelly Bailey, may be a key witness to one of our two murders up there."

"Shelly?"

"He saw someone who may turn out to be the killer."

"Must be the first killing. McCreedy? Was that the name?"

"Right. Tingley was the second."

"School hadn't started yet when the first murder hap-pened. Bailey must have been on his final tour drunk before he had to get back to work."

"You know about his drunks?"

"Sure. It keeps him alive and human—he comes from a stuffy family, I gather—and it helps make him one of our best teachers."

"None of my business, but he thinks it's a secret. He thinks no one knows about it, and if someone did he'd be out of a job."

The chairman laughed and laughed.

10

"Butte. Boise. Kellogg and Orofino," Red Yellow Bear said. All the deputies were in his office. "We sent word to all sheriff's offices in the west of Montana and all through Idaho. I gave a six-inch margin of error and asked for any women over six two. By the way, the FBI is helping on this one—but they don't know about what we're up to. I had a call from the Missoula office, and an agent is coming up here tomorrow. Since state lines have been crossed, or anyway they seem to think so, they get to help. But I want to solve this baby ourselves. If we don't, the Republicans might wipe me out come next election." He paused and looked us over. "Any of you guys fixing to run against me?" No one said anything.

"Anyway, in Butte there's two women, one six two and one six three. There's a woman six four in Kellogg and a woman six six in Orofino, Idaho. The Butte cops have found out that both women were in town there when McCreedy got killed. I forgot to mention a woman six four in Boise. She's in the hospital with brain cancer and has been for some time. So she's out. That leaves us Kellogg and Orofino. Now, Kellogg is a good bet for the Saint Regis killing and for our two, but it's a hell of a drive to Riggins and Cottonwood. The way I see it, the killer, if there is only one killer, has some kind of fast car. She, if it is a she, gets the urge and drives like hell far away, finds a victim and bango. Then she drives back home. If she's real tall, like we are thinking she is, she probably doesn't stop anywhere because she'd be noticed and remembered. So she has got to appear like she's never far from home for very long—that's why I think she must be driving a fast car. If it's the one in Orofino, then it's likely to be a sports car, because you need one to make any time on the Lochsa River road. It's twisty as hell. The problem is, the one in

Orofino has blue eyes, and someone saw her in Orofino the day McCreedy was killed. But they don't remember the time of day. Then there's a problem—if she's six six, can she fit into a sports car? She's young, too, twenty-four. By the way, none of these women have wild gray hair. So where in hell are we?"

We kicked it around for the next half hour. We looked at a map of the western U.S., hoping it would tell us everything. We calculated the time it would take to drive from Kellogg to the scenes of the five murders. We did the same for Orofino. When he wasn't looking at the map, Red Yellow Bear looked out the window and puffed on his cigar. We finally figured that from Orofino to the farthest killing took at least a half hour less than from Kellogg to the farthest killing.

Red Yellow Bear finally decided. "Al," he said, "I want you to go to Orofino. I talked with the sheriff there, a guy named Fairman, nice guy. He says Mary Lou Calk—that's her name, by the way, Mary Lou Calk—is a real pretty girl and she sleeps around, but he says she's got a strange side to her sometimes. He didn't say so, but I think he's screwed her himself. I was honest with him, told him what we had in mind. He said she's a possibility. She drives a Sunbeam, and, according to Fairman, she drives faster than hell. I didn't ask him how she could fit in it. She works various shifts at a motel in Kamiah, that's this side several miles. But he couldn't find any records of when she worked what shift, so he doesn't know if she was free to kill on all those times or not. He'll meet you when you get there. I'll call him and say you're coming. No uniform. He's not picking her up. I told him not to. You'll have to go and meet her and see what you can find out, any way you can."

We went over the maps. I had never been down highway twelve through Idaho, but I could see my route clearly from the maps. I drove back to Plains. I knew just what Yellow Bear had been thinking. Mary Lou Calk was the closest to six eight of any of the women over six two, and we were still going on the theory that Bailey had been telling the straight goods. The town of Plains was still subdued. The two bars, Orney and The Wild Steer, were

grossing about eight dollars between them for a day and
a night.

Arlene was washing glasses behind the bar. I didn't
know why. No one had been using them. I told her I was
off to Orofino to see a tall, beautiful murder suspect, who
was young and liked to screw a lot.

"If you screw her and I find out about it, you're going
to be short, old, ugly *and* battered."

I looked at my well-set, handsome woman. How very
lucky I am. I went home and got into some civilian clothes,
put my gun holster on under my sports coat and took off.

11

When I wasn't think-
ing about the coming encounter with Mary Lou Calk and
wasn't awed by a glimpse of some magnificent landscape,
I was worrying about Tingley's murder. It was different.
What in hell did the pathology report say about the
McCreedy killing? Was it twenty-three to thirty-seven
blows of the axe? Thank you, oh, most learned pathologist.
Tingley had been hit no more than twice. It didn't fit the
pattern of the others.

Of course, if Mary Lou Calk had returned to do the
Tingley job—what was I saying? Christ, maybe Mary Lou
Calk was innocent. But if whoever killed McCreedy also
killed Tingley, then maybe the murderer hadn't had a
chance to butcher Tingley the way he/she (that's better,
Deputy Barnes) had McCreedy.

Another thing bothered me. If these murders over the
last few years had been done by one person, Tingley's
murder was the first one where the killer had struck twice
in the same place—more or less. Maybe the killer liked
the Plains area. Couldn't blame him/her. It is quite nice,
and up to a short while ago it had been very peaceful.

Soon after I crossed the border into Idaho at Lolo Pass,
I found myself twisting and turning down a heavily wooded

highway that was running along one of the loveliest rivers
I'd seen. The Lochsa's olive-green water made the stones
and huge boulders on the bottom yellow or black or dark,
dark green. The river danced gold in places. In other places
it pooled so deep, light was turned away two fathoms down
in the olive water. It was a playful river, a mysterious
river, a creepy river, a horrible river, and, for all of that,
a lovely river. I ached to fish it someday.

I couldn't make good time. The road turned often and
sharply, probably, I thought, to keep the river from getting
mad they'd ever put a road in there in the first place. I
could see Yellow Bear's point about the sports car. If she
was the one, she'd need that Sunbeam to make any time
on this road. It seemed weird if it was true. A woman that
tall, running around for three years committing axe murders, and, until Shelly Bailey had come along, no one had
seen her, no one had a clue? Well, I recalled a case over
twenty years before where a hitch-hiker killer, who had
killed five or six people, was five five, had a glass eye and
the words "hard luck" tattooed on his hands, one letter on
each knuckle, and no one reported seeing him for weeks
after his description went out. These axe murders were
like skid row knockovers. The motive was obscure, and
the murderer might have had no relation to the victim.
Just gratuitous killing.

What bothered me about the Tingley killing was that,
if someone was trying to hide his murder among a bunch
of others, it meant that some brains—I couldn't tell how
many or how much—were operating. That bothered me
plenty. Most criminals are dumb. I'd reluctantly come to
that conclusion after long years in police work. They just
weren't very bright. But if someone other than your
friendly neighborhood axe killer had planned the Tingley
job, it meant someone was at least doing some thinking.
But why did that someone fail to butcher Tingley like the
others? It might not have happened if that reporter with
a good memory somewhere hadn't dug out those other
killings and recognized the pattern.

Too many questions. If it was another killer, did revulsion at what he or she was doing stop him or her from
going ahead and butchering the head to pulp like the others? If it was the same killer, did something or someone

frighten him/her away before the mutilation could be completed? Did that leave a frustrated killer who felt the job wasn't really done and so would strike again soon to make up for it?

A few miles below the point where the Lochsa river picked up the Selway river and together they became the Clearwater, I passed the town of Kooskia. I didn't see it. It was hidden around behind a hill. The next town was Kamiah. I crossed a bridge over the Clearwater, by now a sizable flow, and drove along a street that seemed to border the bottom of the town. To my left I saw an interesting-looking old hotel and bar, stuck out here all alone on a bare corner. A few moments later, I passed the lower end of what looked like the main street of the town. A couple of eating joints and gas stations flowed by on my right. I was tired.

Kamiah seemed a town of light. It was in open area, not pressed too closely by the hills. A few miles later, Orofino, back over the Clearwater, and another bridge, seemed in contrast a town of darkness. It was tucked into the mouth of a canyon. The hills pressed on all sides, except where the town started to fan out near the river. By now the town was no longer contained, as, I was sure, it had been for years. Houses and trailer homes spread up and down the bank of the river, and across the river, from where I'd come, the town was spreading along the highway, with bars and stores and gas stations. But the old town, the town that had been the town for a long time, was pinched back into a canyon and came toward the river and fanned out a bit. It was dark. Even in daylight I felt it must be dark in there. Now it was getting near evening. It was an unpretentious little place. I liked it.

I found the deputy's office tucked away behind a drugstore that looked like they still sold ice cream sodas there. Well, more luck to them. The deputy's office was so small I wondered why they'd even bothered. It was like a doll's house, a one-room doll's house. For a small doll.

Fairman was a young deputy and eager to help. He'd just had a haircut and looked like a retouched photo of himself as a high school student.

After the introductions and preliminaries, he said, "I just can't believe Mary Lou could have done these killings.

I've known her ever since I came here from Lewiston. That's over two years ago."

"Does she originate from here? Have family here?"

"Oh, yes. Her father is deeply religious. Almost a nut on the subject. I can't stand him. Neither can anyone else. One brother, Ossie Calk, is six ten. He played basketball for Oregon State but couldn't make the pros. The other brother is only six two. He's the oldest. Dan Calk. He's a florist in Salt Lake. Mary Lou is the youngest. The mother died in the state asylum about four years ago."

"What makes you think she couldn't have done it, Chuck? It is Chuck?"

"Right, Chuck. Well, you know. You just can't believe anyone you know does those things."

"Her background makes her sound somewhat likely," I said.

"Yeah, I know it," he said reluctantly.

"Does she live with her father?"

"Christ, no. Mary Lou likes a good time. She likes to drink and dance—"

"And screw?"

"That, too. She likes the boys."

"Chuck, this is none of my business, except of course it is all our business now. Have you had relations with her?"

He hesitated. "Yeah, yeah, I have."

"Well?"

"Well, what?"

"Oh, come on. What is she like—I don't mean in bed; I mean, how does she strike you? Does she really like guys, or is it just some kind of triumph?"

"Well, it's almost a pattern, near as I can tell. She's a real good-looker. You'll see that. Blue eyes and great face bones. She usually starts drinking with a guy, then has something to eat, then goes to a little bar in Kooskia where they have a dance floor in the back—if the guy will go along. Since the guy wants to get into her pants, he does. This dance floor in the back is real dark. You can hardly see in there. She likes that because her date usually only comes up to her chest. She doesn't like dancing in a brightly lighted place, like the bowling alley dance floor in Kamiah, because people stare at her and her partner.

After a couple of hours there, she comes back to Kamiah and has a few more drinks with the guy, then shacks up with him in her room at the motel. They let her stay in one of their rooms as part of the payment for working there. She can cook in there. They're never full, or not often, anyway. They figure it's easier to let her have a room than to pay her full wages for working on the desk. So she lives at the motel in Kamiah, the River Shore Motel."

"Does she stay OK throughout the night, I mean her behavior?"

"Sometimes she gets a bit bitter, even sort of surly, after she's had a lot to drink. But by that time, you're so drunk and eager, you don't pay any attention."

"You?"

"I mean the guy with her. You know."

I didn't get much more from him, except a pretty good steak dinner he bought me back in Kamiah. We decided to try to get me booked at the River Shore Motel. He seemed a little depressed. I tried to reassure him that, after all, it was just speculation and pretty wild speculation at that. It was, after all, the best lead we had, but I tried to convince him and myself it might not turn out to be her at all. Inside, I was already convinced she looked awfully good for the killings.

"She's on duty tonight at the motel. Tomorrow she's off."

"Do you think I might date her?"

He looked puzzled.

"I mean, am I too old for her? Does she go out with forty-year-old guys?"

"I suppose she might. Christ, what a dirty business."

"It sure is," I said. "Specially those corpses with raw stew meat where their heads used to be."

He shuddered. "How did I get into this fucking business?" he asked himself aloud.

We drove the short distance to the River Shore Motel.

Mary Lou Calk smiled down on us like the sun shining down on two dirt farmers. She was really tall. I'm five eleven, and Chuck Fairman is six two. We both felt like pygmies. We must have looked like it, too.

Her hair was red-brown, and her eyes were blue and

wide set. She had high and lovely cheekbones, a long, full nose and a wide, full mouth. She looked right at me.

And I looked right at her and tried to imagine anyone this statuesquely lovely hitting a man in the head with an axe, over and over, until there was no head, until that head was something else that had no word for it.

"Mary Lou," Fairman said, "this is Al Barnes, a friend of mine from Montana. He needs a room."

"You came to the right place, Al," she said, flashing her big smile from the mountain. "We've got lots of rooms. Just the one night?"

I tried to make love with my eyes, hoping it would flatter her enough to accept an invitation to go out. I hoped I wasn't being too obvious. My tendency is often to overact, but I usually get away with it. "I thought I might stay a couple of days," I said, letting my eyes rest for a brief moment on her ample breasts, then averting my gaze as if I were embarrassed. I returned my eyes to her face. It was still radiant.

"You fix him up, Mary Lou. If you need anything, give me a ring. We used to fish together years ago," he said. I was grateful when he left. He was starting to make up too many stories. The more you do that, the better the chance of slipping up.

"I could use a guide tomorrow," I said. "Chuck's on duty, and I don't know the place at all, or anybody in it."

"You know me," she smiled.

"Would you mind, tomorrow? Should we tour in the morning or what? Do you work again tomorrow evening?"

"I'm off tomorrow afternoon," she said. "You look like a nice guy. Let's do the big cities, Kamiah and Kooskia," she laughed. Her laughter held a trace of bitterness. It made me uneasy, seeing a woman that big and that young who held resentment—at what, living in a place she had begun to find dull?

"Tomorrow it is, then. I'd appreciate it," I said. It was that easy to date her. It seemed that she'd dated me.

She handed me the key to my motel unit. "I live here, too, in twenty. Why not just meet at my cabin at three or so?"

"Thanks, Mary Lou. I'll be there."

I went to my cabin. It was a cozy little unit. There was

a kitchen with a range and a refrigerator and a decent shower. The bed was the usual motel double but quite comfortable. The TV worked OK, but I couldn't get interested. I kept trying to imagine that tall, lovely girl putting an axe in someone's skull. It seemed wrong. Despite the trace of bitterness, she seemed too nice. Then I remembered a nice old man in Seattle who'd put me in a hospital bed for months and forced my retirement. If I was going to do any good down here, this heart of mush would have to turn to stone for a few hours tomorrow. I slept about as soundly as a lookout in the Battle of the Bulge.

12

I picked her up at three. It had occurred to me when I was dressing that if we went dancing she'd be able to feel my gun if I kept it in a shoulder holster. So I put the holster on my belt in the small of my back where my coat would hide it and she wouldn't feel it. She invited me into unit twenty. It was just like mine, but lived in. She poured me a drink. Her drinks were as big as she was. She wore a white sweater that didn't disgrace her, tight jeans and white casual shoes. She didn't make the mistake of trying to dress herself to look shorter like a lot of tall women do. The smart ones seem to dress to accentuate their height. She didn't do that, either. The drink, which I had to gulp to keep up with her, left me reeling.

"We'll go to the hotel in Kamiah," she said. "The drinks are good there, and a lot of town characters come in. It will give you an idea of the place."

We drove to the hotel in her Sunbeam. It seemed remarkably easy the way she slipped into the driver's seat, as if the car had been designed for her. Even though we were already in town, she seemed to drive awfully fast. I assumed the cops all knew her and laid off. But then, there weren't many cops. She seemed confident as we screeched around a corner, and I found I was looking at the interesting old hotel I'd seen on the way in yesterday. We took a table in the bar. Everything was plain. The walls were bare and bright. The tables were just tables. Nothing was any more than it had to be. I liked it. I thought I might bring Arlene here someday and take a room, just for the hell of it.

"Does it bother you, my being so tall?" Her question brought me back.

"You can be as tall as you want, just so you're lovely. And you are."

She smiled her great wide smile. The sensuality spread across her mouth like whipped cream. "You're a nice man, Al."

"Does being tall bother you?" I was intent on her answer but tried to look as if I was only making conversation.

"It did a lot, in high school, especially. You know how mean boys are at that age. All the wisecracks. Some of them used to come and peer up real close and say, 'High, big Mummy, how's the weather on the mountain?'" She laughed, but the same bitterness was in her laugh that I'd heard the night before. "Anyway, that's all over. You'd be surprised how many propositions I get these days."

"The hell I would," I said, letting my eyes stroke her face and breasts. The bartender brought us bourbon and water. I hadn't seen her signal, but he seemed to know what we wanted. I could still feel that first slug from her cabin. We had two more, and I tried to nurse mine along. She was no light drinker; she guzzled recklessly. I hoped she wouldn't notice I was dragging my heels. If I didn't, someone was going to be dragging them for me in a couple of hours. Swell detective. I was out with the number-one suspect in five axe killings, and I was getting drunk. That, I said to myself, is not only dumb, it is dangerous. I wished Fairman had warned me about her capacity for booze. She seemed about as drunk as Billy Graham. I was grateful when we went to the restaurant next door, also part of the hotel, to get something to eat.

During dinner, which was very plain and usual—meat loaf and mashed potatoes and string beans, and, to my way of need, very good—she asked me what I did for a living. I said, real estate. I kept watching her closely without seeming to, but nothing happened that made me suspicious. She went on being beautiful and tall and pretty good company.

By nine we were in the bar in Kooskia, the one Fairman had told me about. It was a dark little bar, and the room just off it was even darker. I could vaguely make out a couple dancing as they passed near the door leading onto the dance floor. The music poured from a jukebox. All through the night guys came by and said hello to Mary Lou and tossed me that "who he" look. We both had some peppermint schnapps to help the dinner along, and now we were drinking beer to cure the thirst the schnapps had given us.

I enjoyed touching her when we danced. She was soft in the right places. The dance room was the darkest public room I've ever seen that was dark on purpose. I put my head on her bosom and felt like a little boy. Time on the dance floor seemed different than the time at the bar. She was clever with her body. She made you feel you could overpower her whenever you wanted to. It was some trick she had of relaxing at certain key moments during the dance. Being big, she made me feel powerful. I tried to keep my mind on my work.

By eleven we were back at a bar in Kamiah. To this day I don't know the name of it. It's an old bar, with a stuffed deer head and not many customers, at least not that night. The bartender is named Oscar, and he has two fingers missing on his right hand. It has some nice booths for couples to drink in and talk. The walls of the booths are high and give an illusion of privacy. I wasn't holding my liquor much better since we had eaten, and was still bleary.

"God," I said, "I'll bet you're something in pajamas."

"You better know it. Mine are fireproof," she laughed. Something had changed in her face, I realized. Some contortion that I'd not noticed before had been taking over for maybe an hour, and now it had arrived. Also, her last remark had been delivered in a crude, harsh tone of voice. She seemed suddenly less than civilized. The sensuality in her face had been replaced by a cruelty that I found exciting. I found it sexually exciting, and I found it exciting because I believed I was really with a killer. I was drunk

enough to be unable to sort out the two excitements. I was
sure I would not have found her sexually exciting were I
sober. But I wasn't sober. She went to the can, saying over
her shoulder, "Pee time, buster." All gentility had vanished.

I wanted to go through the purse she'd left on the table,
but Oscar could see me from the bar. When she came back,
something else had changed. I wasn't sure what it was at
first. I tried to shake my vision back to perfectly clear from
50 percent haze, but it was hard going.

"Want to see my pajamas?" she said. "Want to see a
beautiful big hunk of woman in pajamas?" There was
something nearly disgusting about her. Her eyes shone in
green meanness—green? Why were her eyes suddenly
green? What had Bailey said—something about green
eyes that glowed like a cat's? Then it came to me. Contacts.
Cosmetic contacts. She must have taken them into the
john with her because she'd left her purse at the table.
Had they been in the pocket of her jeans? Had she just
palmed them when she had left a few minutes ago?

I was scared. Really scared. I had no doubt she had
killed all those guys. I had to keep my head clear. It wasn't
easy. I was fighting the booze, my passion that wouldn't
let up and my fear that I was with someone who could kill
me without feeling anything but enjoyment.

Outside she said, as we slid into her car, "Wouldn't
think an amazon like me would fit in this fucking thing,
would you? Well, I fit in fine. And what's more, I drive
like hell. You ought to see me make time on the twelve
going east, all those big American cars that have to slow
down on those curves. Not me. Not my little Sunbeam.
Jesus wants me for a sunbeam. Know that one? You religious?" Her voice sounded like a steel mill in full operation.

"No. Not religious."

"Me neither, not no more," she snarled and pulled into
the motel lot. I was surprised we had been so close. I
wanted to sober up. I wished the motel had been a hundred-
mile drive from Oscar's bar, but now we were there at her
door. She swore, trying to fit the key in the dark. When
she got the door open she turned and said, "You got a real
woman tonight, buster." Her façade of manners had de-

teriorated like her face, from something attractive and
warm to something crude and low on the scale. Inside, she
took off her clothes so fast I barely had time to sit down
and open one of the beers we had brought from Oscar's.
She stood before me, completely nude, her big hands on
her well-contoured hips. Her smile was about as warm as
Fu Manchu's. Her breasts were high and even bigger than
they'd seemed when she had been dressed. It was the first
time I'd seen her legs. They were her best feature. I could
have run wind sprints on them, but some other time. Keep
your head, Mush Heart Barnes. You are alone in a motel
room in a strange town with a woman you know—you are
by now absolutely certain—is dangerous and vicious. I
tried to keep my eyes off her. What an erotic macrocosm.
I must be drunk. I never use the word macrocosm.

"You're so lovely, can't we sit down for a moment and
have a beer? I want to feast on you for a while."

She flopped on the edge of the bed. "Sure. Like what
you see? It's really something, isn't it? Best body this
damned valley ever saw."

"I can believe it," I said. If I was sober, I thought, I
could direct this scene better. I tipped the beer. Sometimes
beer can sober you up—when?

"Best fucking body anywhere," she said.

"How fast can you make it to, say, Missoula in that
Sunbeam?" I asked. Was that too obvious? I must be careful.

She looked at me sullenly. "Plenty fast, buster."

"I'll bet you can't make it in three hours."

"The hell I can't." Her eyes were narrowing, just
slightly.

"I really like looking at you. You're beautiful. Just un-
believably beautiful."

"You better know it, Jack."

"I could look at you all night."

"You better do more than that, buster."

"I will. I want to look first, though."

"Just like the Japanese."

"The Japanese?" I alerted myself through the haze. She
moved from the bed to the small table and sat down and
crossed her legs.

"Sure. The Japs. They like to arrange their food in

designs and look at it before they eat it." Her face looked ready to explode.

"What does your father do?" Was I doing right? I wasn't sure.

"That prick. He reads the Bible and gets mean."

"Was he mean to your brothers?"

"Shit, and to me, too. Hey, we didn't talk about my family before this. How do you know I got brothers?"

"Sure we did." I said, hoping I wasn't talking too fast and trying to cover my mistake. "In Kooskia, at that bar. Remember?"

She was very tense, and her eyes didn't like me anymore. "I don't remember," she said.

Then I really blundered. "Maybe Chuck mentioned it, your family." The moment I said it, I was cursing myself and the booze.

Her eyes were thin, and no sparkle came from them. I let the silence go on too long.

"You talked to Chuck about me?"

I tried to think of something to say. I couldn't find it. She stood up.

"What are you, mister?" Her voice went off like a shotgun in a phone booth. Now her eyes were two slits in a cloudy sky, and a mean sun was coming through both. Hours went by, and I couldn't find anything to say. I'd blown it all.

Then, for no reason, I remembered something she'd said earlier about the boys calling her "Mummy." I took a big blind chance.

"Well, for sure I'm not a goddam Egyptian."

She started to cackle. It came from some other throat, some other world. It crawled my spine. Then she sprang at me.

"You son of a bitch," she said and hit me in the mouth with her fist. It was a hell of a blow. I slammed back against the wall. I managed to duck her next swing and lashed out my right in a drunken hope. It collided with her somewhere, and I heard her gasp. She bloodied my nose with a long, looping overhand right. I saw it coming but couldn't move fast enough.

I backhanded her across the face with my left. She cackled like an insane hen. I hit her hard in the mouth with my right. She staggered back.

It came to me I was drunk and in a fight for my life with a giant woman who was naked, and it struck me as absurd. I started to laugh. I couldn't stop.

"You prick. I'll kill you, you fucking Egyptian," she whined.

We looked at each other for a moment. She came at me again, swinging wild fists. I bent down and got my arms around her legs and lifted. She fell over backwards on the bed. She started to raise up. All the socially complicated feelings about fighting a woman had disappeared. I caught her with a right on the jaw as her head was on the way forward. Her head snapped back. I was still laughing when I hit her again. It was the most ridiculous situation I could ever remember in my life. She lay stunned on the bed, moaning. Then I remembered I had a gun. I got it and pointed it at her. She saw it as soon as she raised up the next time.

13

We found the axe in the trunk of the Sunbeam. We found the gray wig in the glove compartment, where I'd never thought to steal a look.

Extradition was a cinch. We had the only witness, Assistant Professor Shelly P. Bailey of the University of Montana, so we had the case. Idaho couldn't prove a thing against her. In a matter of days she was in the jail at Thompson Falls.

I couldn't believe how easy it had been, how our guesses proved right, every one of them. The reaction was wide and loud. Red Yellow Bear had his picture in both *Time* and *Newsweek*. The *Missoulian* editorial writer had a field day. "Our hats are off to Sheriff Yellow Bear of Sanders County. Let them stay off for a long time. All of Montana salutes this outstanding law enforcement officer. Well done, Sheriff Yellow Bear, and the same to the people of Sanders County who had the wisdom to elect him."

Arlene threw a party for the sheriff's department, and a lot of people I'd never seen, as well as some I had, showed up and got very drunk. Red Yellow Bear puffed his cigar and sipped his bourbon and couldn't hide the smug way he felt. Even Manny Sanderson came close to smiling.

Red and I went over the case several times alone in his office. We replayed it like Seattle TV had replayed a Rose Bowl game years ago when the University of Washington finally got the bowl bid and surprisingly wiped out Wisconsin. We just couldn't get enough of our good fortune. We went over Red's decision to send me to Orofino instead of Kellogg. We replayed his hunch about the fast sports car. We prided ourselves that we had taken Shelly P. Bailey at his word and so had decided to try the woman closest to six eight.

But something was nagging both of us, the same thing that had nagged at me when I was driving to Orofino. Neither one of us believed Mary Lou Calk had killed Robin Tingley. For one thing, she eagerly admitted killing four men. In fact, she bragged about it in her weird cackle. But she denied killing Tingley.

"Why would I hit twice in the same place," she said, "when the world is filled with you fucking Egyptians? Sooner or later, I'd have killed you all. Every fucking one of you bastards."

The psychiatrist's preliminary report had phrases about the psycho-dynamics of repeated anger and humiliation, and the deflected Oedipus impulse, and the psychic compounding of excessive verbal coercion. As near as I could piece it together, it had to do with her father who was mean and repressive, and with the teasing she got from the boys because of her height. Somehow she'd parlayed the nickname "mummy" into a fantasy where all men were Egyptians, and she had to kill them to keep from being mummified. It didn't sound real. Those things never do. The murders were real enough.

"Fat chance of convicting her, for Christ sakes. She's flakier than overcooked halibut," Red Yellow Bear growled and threw the psychiatrist's report on his desk.

There was a dreadful scene in the jail when her father came, a red-faced man named Joseph Calk (not Joe, not *ever* Joe) with angry, righteous eyes. Right in front of Yellow Bear and me, this tall man stood outside his daughter's cell and called her a sinner and a disgrace to the family and the embodiment of evil, a repeat of her mother who had sinned against God. He finished in a rising voice, raving about the blaze of crimson shame that would be stamped on her heart forever. I couldn't believe the lousy rhetoric that rolled out of his mouth and bounced off the walls of the jail.

And Mary Lou wept. I thought she'd lash back at him. In fact, I was hoping she would. But all she did was cry and say to him, in the tiny voice of a frail, small child, "Daddy, can't you love me, ever?"

As we were showing Joseph Calk out, Yellow Bear said, "How could she have murdered all those people, Mr. Calk, when she comes from such a nice Christian home?"

"Is that intended as sarcasm, Sheriff?" Mr. Calk said, turning his angry eyes on Yellow Bear.

Calk was six four, and Yellow Bear was nearly eight inches shorter. But when Yellow Bear walked to him and stood close, something in his face said he was the taller of the two. Deliberately he blew a cloud of cigar smoke in Calk's face and said, "You fucking tooting, asshole."

Calk turned white, then red from embarrassment at having turned white, then redder with anger at having been embarrassed. But he judged Yellow Bear's eyes wisely. I think if he had said a word, Yellow Bear would have cleaned his clock right there. Calk said nothing. He turned quietly and left. He stopped outside and stared at the door for a moment. We watched him through the window. He thought better of it and turned away.

Yellow Bear and I sat in mutual depression and silence for a half hour. We said a lot to each other in that half hour, and we didn't break the silence once.

14

Within twenty-four hours, Yellow Bear had established that Mary Lou Calk had been in bed with a young game warden named Frederson in Kamiah the early morning when Tingley had been killed. I wasn't surprised. Fairman hadn't had too much trouble finding out for us. Frederson was sure about the date. He didn't get all that many women, it turned out, and who would forget the night he spent with a big hunk of woman like Mary Lou Calk? That was the right date, all right.

A kid named Pete Mitter, who was called Peter Meter by his friends, worked in the gas station on the edge of Plains. He had mentioned to someone that he'd seen a green car with Oregon plates the day Tingley had been killed. The car had stopped for gas at about eleven A.M. He'd remembered that day, all right. Jesus, he said, who wouldn't remember the day Robin Tingley got axed?

Then someone he'd mentioned it to had mentioned it to someone else, and that someone else had stopped into Orney's for a beer and had mentioned it to Arlene, who had mentioned it to me one night in bed during a lull.

Pete Mitter was a nice kid. Slender, light complected, a bit shy but eager to help. "I remember it, OK. For sure, Sheriff Barnes. I don't remember the kind of car, but I remember the plates. Oregon. And I remember the car was green."

"Can you remember any of the plate numbers or letters?" I asked.

"No, not now. I guess I never noticed that."

"Well, how about the driver?"

"A woman. Blonde. Might have been good-looking once, but too old now."

"How old?"

"Past thirty, at least," he said.

"Fading," I said.

"Oh, yeah, Sheriff Barnes. You know. On the down slope."

I was glad I wasn't young anymore. What a nice world it is when you get old enough to see how attractive women are at all ages.

That night I called the Hammers. Only Lynn was home.

"I've been reading about you," she said. "You're looking good up there in Montana."

"Class will tell," I said with good-natured sarcasm. "Listen, Lynn. This is very confidential, but we know the Calk girl didn't kill Robin Tingley."

She was silent for a minute. Then she said, "But she must have."

"She didn't. We know for sure she didn't. I never thought so, anyway. The killing was too different in too many ways."

"I guess I'm disappointed," she said. "I wanted Robin's killer caught, and I thought you'd caught her. Now I don't know what to think."

"Listen, Lynn. I wondered if you knew of anyone who might want to kill Tingley."

She hesitated. "I suppose I can think of two people, but one is a close friend. That's his wife, Marnie. Oh, God, I don't think I could stand it if she did it."

"And the other?"

"A guy named Vic Medici. Oh, God this all goes back years ago."

"Tell me."

"About twenty, no, I guess nineteen years ago, when we were all kids, some of us just out of high school, we had a big bust at a place my father owned at Cannon Beach. A girl named Candy Koski was murdered. This is weird, believe me. Candy had come there with Medici. She was only sixteen and a flirt. She was a real doll, a turn-on for all the guys. We'd sort of let her into our gang because she was in demand—you know how silly kids are about those social things. Anyway, she was killed. Really beaten up, and Robin Tingley found Vic Medici—oh, God, you won't believe this—Robin found Medici trying to make love to her, and she was already dead. Robin had to testify to that in court."

"Was Medici convicted?"

"No, he got off."

"That's a doubtful motive then for Medici to kill Tingley, especially after nineteen years."

"I know it, but you asked for possibilities. I admit it seems remote. But sometimes things fester."

"Do you think Medici murdered the Koski girl?"

"I don't know. He was a hot-tempered guy when he was eighteen, or however old he was then. And Koski flirted with everybody. He could have done it. He was tried for it, but he got off. To tell the truth, Al, it was a hell of a wild party. Everyone was running around, stoned on marijuana or drunk with booze or both. We had dope in those days, too, you know. We were just more secretive about it. Anybody might have killed Candy that night. God, I think half the people there could have killed her and not known about it, I mean not realized they'd done it. It was late, maybe after two in the morning. Anyway, the cops found some bruises on Medici's knuckles, and with Tingley's story, they took him in. It was a long time ago."

"What about Marnie Tingley?"

"She's a good friend. I love her. I guess you didn't meet her when she was in Montana this summer. Oh, Jesus, what a messy business."

"But how about her for her husband's murder?"

"I don't know. She's an alcoholic, and she sees a psychiatrist. She's very wealthy in her own right. She could have built up something about losing him, but they've been separated for a couple of years at least, maybe longer. I just can't believe she did it."

"What kind of car does she drive?"

"A Buick, I think it is."

"What color?"

"A sort of green, but not real green, you know what I mean."

"You want her caught if she's the one who did it, don't you?"

"I suppose so. Oh, God. This is awful. Why couldn't it have been that girl who did the others? Why not her?"

It seemed futile to go on. She was too upset. I said good-bye and hung up. Then I called Yellow Bear and told him what I had found out. We kicked it around for a couple of days. Manny Sanderson said we were nuts; we had the killer already. Who would believe her story? She was crazy. And what was the worth of the word of some guy who claimed he was laying her that night when it was that long ago?

"Goddamn it, Manny," Yellow Bear said, "we've proved she was in Idaho when Tingley was killed."

So I ended up going to Portland, but not without a warning from Yellow Bear that if the Republicans found out I was doing police work in Oregon, my time there became my vacation, and I had no expense account since Sanders County couldn't afford one. I called Lynn back, and she offered me a room at their place. I took it. Then I called my old friend John Mrvich, on the Portland police force, and told him everything. We kicked old times around briefly on the phone, those days we had both been rookies on the Seattle force, with a promise to do more of the same when we saw each other in Portland tomorrow. He said he'd try to dig up what he could from years back on the Koski killing. He said he couldn't remember ever hearing about it.

Arlene and I made love that night as many times as I could, but the fifth time was a struggle.

"This should hold you until you get back," she said. "And if it doesn't, don't tell me about it."

I could have slept all day, but somehow Arlene got me to the Missoula airport and on the plane. I was sure I was the most relaxed passenger on board.

TWO

15

It would be good to
see Mrvich again and the Hammers, too. Mrvich had kept
writing poems all these years. Every so often, he'd send
me a copy of some little magazine with a poem of his in
it. Then, about a year before I got shot up in Seattle, he'd
sent a book he'd published with a small press in California.
He'd inscribed it to me, "For Al Barnes, best poet on the
Seattle force. John." It made me feel good for him and a
bit lousy that I hadn't kept writing myself. It was a good
book and got good reviews in the Seattle and Portland
papers and even a very favorable one in the *Los Angeles
Times.*

John was right about one thing. I was the best poet on
the Seattle police force, and I hadn't written a line in years
when his book arrived. Mrvich had no doubt taken some
ribbing from his fellow cops, but John was a dignified guy
and had a good sense of humor. He could handle it. Now
he was a captain of detectives. No one kids captains.

The trip was splendid. We flew near Mt. Rainier, Mt.
Adams, Mt. St. Helens, and the day was clear, a bright,
open, hard October day. All three mountains shone blue
and early-fall white and looked appropriately pompous.
Well, if I were a mountain I'd be pompous, too. I winked
at Rainier as we crawled past and told it to hang in there.
It said it would and stop winking at me, you dumb bastard,
I'm a mountain.

John Mrvich grabbed my hand and then my bag at the
head of the exit ramp. "Lord, you are putting it on," he
said, looking at my waistline. "Home cooking?"

"Home something," I said, thinking of Arlene. "How
the hell are you, Murv? You look great." He did, too, his
face having gotten more handsome and interesting with
the years. He was as big as I remembered him, and he still
moved easily, as if he had lots of energy in reserve.

We picked up my other case at the baggage pickup. "You got a gun in there?" Mrvich asked.

"Yeah, I got a gun. I couldn't very well carry it on the plane without showing a bunch of stuff. Seemed easier this way."

"Keep it, but if anything comes up, I didn't know about it, OK?"

"Right you are."

We drove along in his car for a while, catching up on who had died or retired or remarried or divorced. "By the way," Mrvich said, "where are we headed?"

I gave him the address.

"Jesus. That's Portland Heights in the West Hills. Who do you know there?"

"The Hammers, brother and sister. They bought the mill in Plains and saved the town from getting wiped out. They live there four months a year. Nice people. They're putting me up."

"The lumber people? Hammer-Index Plywood. Hammer Pine Products. Hammer Lumber Supply. Those Hammers?"

I nodded. "That's them."

"You've improved the company you keep."

We talked about some of the lower orders of citizens we'd known in Seattle, the junkies and pimps and stoolies.

From a high bridge over the Willamette River, the city of Portland was beautifully ablaze in the October sun which seemed just about two inches off on my right. From that perspective it appeared beautiful, the aggregate of tall, sparkling buildings. It was good to be in a city again, and, as cities go, you can do much worse than Portland. But I knew if I got into it for long and began to see the life inside that glittering wall, I'd long for Plains again. For right now, Portland looked good. I decided I must not be too old if I still found a city exciting.

"You sure made the papers here, Al. That must have been some bust in Kamiah."

I told him all about it, including how drunk I'd gotten. He took it in quietly.

"It was a lucky shot, first time. A lot of good guesswork. Have you ever been in a motel room alone in a night with a beautiful naked girl six six who was trying to kill you and so drunk and bewildered you forgot you had a gun?"

"Sure," Mrvich said. "Lots of times." We both laughed all over the car. Mrvich's dark, Slavic face and big body shook with laughter.

"I'm looking into that killing years ago for you. Your friend, Medici, by the way, controls the distribution of porno in Portland,. and he makes a hell of a lot of money doing it."

"If it's the right porno, he *is* my friend," I said. We'd passed the metropolitan business area and were going up some tricky roads that switched back and made sudden 180-degree turns. I was lost in the maze of roads and huge hedges that restricted my view. I could glimpse big private homes in back of the hedges, with enormous trees in the yards. Mrvich drove with absolute assurance. I felt I couldn't find the Hammer house if I lived in Portland one hundred years and drove there once a week. West Hills is a bewildering network of well-paved roads winding in no appreciable pattern through thick woods and high hedges. Many of the homes seemed from another time, but they were huge and still very expensive.

"Listen, Al. If you can, have dinner with me tomorrow night at Jake's; it's a seafood place in Portland. I should have something for you on that old killing. A defense lawyer named Petrov will join us. He's a pal of mine who writes poems, too. We'll give you what help we can. The food is real good, Al. And Petrov is a great guy."

"I'll be there. I sure appreciate your help."

"Do you think it will help you with the killing of—?" he trailed off uncertainly.

"Tingley. Robin Tingley. I don't know. It's just a hunch. There're a couple of people might have wanted him dead, and they're in Portland, and both were at the Koski killing years ago—I mean at the party where the Koski girl was killed. But it seems remote. We know the Calk girl didn't kill Tingley, and we can't decide who might have. They're working on the possibility that someone in Montana might have wanted him dead, but he wasn't up there all that long, and besides, everyone liked him there."

We took more turns and twists than a pinball and finally stopped at a big hedge with a huge brown house far in back of it. Roses and ivy were crawling the walls of the house, obscuring much of the brown board. When we passed through the gate, I spotted Mycroft trimming the hedge from the inside, eying it with the same imperious look. He turned and looked at me, no recognition in his rigid face.

I gave him as phony an informal American wave and a "Hi" as I could, hoping it would annoy him. He said, "Good afternoon, sir."

"What's he doing here?" Mrvich whispered. "Did Louis the Fourteenth die?"

Lynn threw open the door. "Al. Good to see you. Come on in." She looked very classy in a white dress and black pumps. Her dark features, hair and skin were set off by the dress.

"Al," she said again and gave me a hug. I introduced John.

"Pleased to meet you, Miss Hammer," he said a bit uncertainly.

"Lynn, please. No one calls me Miss Hammer, or Mrs. Ponce," she said, and I could see John succumb immediately to her charm and relax.

He mumbled something about lots of paperwork, reminded me of our dinner tomorrow night and took off. I walked in, feeling good.

16

The Hammer house was what I might have guessed—big and beyond the reach of most, and tasteful, cheery and comfortable. Like the Hammers themselves, I thought, especially Lynn. Lee, too, usually.

The carpeting wasn't so deep you felt you were in quicksand. The walls were a kindly off-yellow and the ceiling a warm tone of gray. The furniture looked like you could use it without feeling you were violating civilization. But the house was big. You could have played basketball in the living room, if the ceiling had been a bit higher.

The paintings on the wall were good ones and, I assumed, by local artists. Portland enjoyed a reputation for good painters and also for being a town that supported them. I imagined Lynn and Lee Hammer would be among those who accounted for that reputation, the kind who would spend generous amounts on local art.

Lynn led me to my room, a light-blue walled room with a big bed and a connecting bath. There were a couple of chairs and a writing desk. Lamps. Out of the windows I could see some rose bushes and beyond them a short stretch of lawn and the hedge.

"Let me lie down a minute," I said to Lynn. "I feel sluggish all of a sudden."

"It's the altitude. From over four thousand feet to sea level. You'll sleep like a baby here. It's got something to do with reduced red-blood corpuscle count."

I flopped down. Lynn sat on the side of the bed. "Anything you need?"

I looked hard at her.

"Don't get ideas," she laughed. "I meant a drink or a sandwich."

"Nothing, thanks. I thought for a minute I was lucky."

"Not a bad idea, but there's Arlene who would kill me if she found out, plus some other complicated factors."

"There usually are," I said. I felt myself getting drowsy.

"We got a car for you to use while you're here. Take a snooze. Dinner around seven. I'll see you later," she said and walked out.

I lay there glad I came but wondering why. It seemed such a long shot. What was I looking for? Oh, sure, the murderer of Robin Tingley. But I was worrying that our hunch that had paid off with Mary Lou Calk resulted from luck that had probably run out. When I fell asleep, I was wondering if there really was any connection between the Tingley killing and the murder of a sixteen-year-old girl that had happened nearly nineteen years ago.

Lynn cooked a wonderful steak dinner that night. She served the steaks sizzling, along with some mashed potatoes with cheese mixed in and asparagus and tomatoes. She did it all so easily with the grace of someone who had always known money—none of that nervous hostess flutter. It was a fine meal. They didn't let Mycroft serve, either. He was out of sight.

Lee seemed a bit remote. "Sorry," he said, "to be so out of it this evening. We're thinking of buying a mill in Eureka, California, and I can't get the thing out of my head. It's a risky proposition, and I've been in conference on it all afternoon."

"Do you ever involve yourself in the business?" I asked Lynn.

"I spend the profits," she said and laughed her bright laugh.

"Does she ever," Lee grinned. I realized they were joking for my benefit. It was like them to be aware most of us don't have all that much money. It didn't make any difference how much she spent, and I knew it.

Her son entered the room after dinner. I assumed he'd eaten earlier. "Mike? Come in," Lynn said, "meet Al Barnes."

He was as relaxed and confident as his mother and uncle, and bigger than his uncle already at fifteen. He was one tall, handsome boy. I thought of the crushes of a lot of young girls, the passes by older, unfulfilled women.

"Mike. This is Al Barnes. Al, my son, Mike Ponce." The boy shook hands like he liked doing it. He chatted now and then as we were eating. He was a bright boy.

After he'd left for better things, we exchanged a few observations about him.

"Can we talk a bit about that murder years ago?" I asked. "I really have to know."

"Sure. Sure," Lee said. We walked to the living room and sat in comfortable, dark-green chairs. Lynn started it.

"It was in 1959," Lynn said. "Around Easter. Lee and I were going to Eugene in Oregon. We were very social in those days, and all our friends were going there. Father didn't like it. He wanted us swish swish in the East, Lee in Harvard or Yale and me in Sarah Lawrence or Bryn Mawr. But we held firm. I don't think we were good enough students to get into those places, anyway. Besides, we had our friends and wanted to stick with them. So UO it was."

"We sort of ran in a pack," Lee said. "A bunch of us

partied together all the time. We had started in high
school."

"Most of us were seniors together in high school.
Candy—Candice Koski, her name was—was a sophomore.
God, was she cute. A doll. The boys fell out of the trees
when she walked by. Lee had spasms every time he saw
her," she laughed and added playfully, "the jerk."

"Jealous bitch," Lee said in equally good humor.

"Anyway, Father owned this place at Cannon Beach.
It was a nice big house. Lots of room. We decided to throw
a spring bash there, partly because in those days most of
the kids went to Seaside. To raise hell," she added. "A few
years later, that got out of hand—you remember the Seaside riots, early sixties? Well, we were dreadful little snobs
and thought we were different. So while everyone else
went to Seaside, we went to Cannon Beach for the Easter
holiday season. Candy was old for a sophomore. Looking
back, I guess she wasn't too bright and was a little behind
in school but not much. Lee and I were college freshmen
by then. So was Robin Tingley. Let's see. Marnie was still
a senior in high school, and Vic Medici—was he with us
at Oregon?"

"No, he was still in high school. Remember, he was
unanimous all-city halfback, and we tried to talk him into
attending Oregon. But another thing, Lynn. Candy was
a first-half junior that year. Remember, she was a midyear
student."

"That's right," Lynn said. "God, it really is hard to
remember. Betty Huff?"

"Still in high school," Lee said. "All the others were
with us at UO."

"Yes. Dale. Marge. Cud. How about Stinky?"

"He didn't go to college, remember?"

"I guess that's it. We were pretty close for that age. I
mean, most kids that age part company when some leave
high school and others stay. We planned this bash months
in advance. Booze. Marijuana. A three-day blast at Cannon
Beach. Candy was young to be in the gang, but she was
so damned good-looking that every gang wanted her. You
know how looks bring prestige at that age. We got her
because we were older, seemed to her smoother, maybe,
and I think because some of us had money. Lee and I.

Marnie, too, Robin not so much, but his family had some. They weren't loaded like we were and Marnie's family. We impressed Candy, and we felt superior because she became one of us."

"It happened the second night we were there," Lee said. "But even now we don't know what really happened. It was about two in the morning, and we were high as hell."

Lynn broke in. "I was down on the beach with Dale and Cud—Dale always liked two girls with him, and he usually managed to work things so he had two girls. Lee came running down and said Candy was dead."

"Robin had told me up by the house. He'd come out shaking," Lee said. "He told me Candy had been beaten something awful, and then he told me—I was high, but this really shook me, I remember—he told me he'd found Vic Medici on top of her body, trying to screw her. Oh, Jesus. I ran down and told Lynn and Dale and Cud, who were living it up by a beach fire."

"In those days booze was serious trouble if you were under twenty-one, and dope was a real secret, not out in the open like now. We got rid of everything. We collected the gang, rounded up everybody and sort of huddled around in the kitchen. Candy's body was out in the front room. We waited until we'd sobered up a bit; some of us tried to sleep, and around dawn we called the cops. Robin wouldn't talk to Vic, he was so shaken. Vic seemed angry. He got angry a lot in those days. He was a tough guy, and other boys stayed out of his way and made sure they kept on his good side." Lynn trailed off.

"We were too young, and the cops broke us down fast. They got the story about Medici from Robin in no time. I guess because of the murder they didn't push on the booze and drug thing, though some of us admitted it. Besides, they had no evidence. They arrested Vic, and he stood trial. He'd just turned eighteen, so they could try him. Robin had to testify. He felt rotten doing it. We were all friends. Anyway, Medici got off. He had Art Matthew for a lawyer. In those days he was the best. We were relieved. All of us. None of us were really sure what had happened, and I suppose we all felt responsible. We took her down there. The booze and dope and all. God, she was lovely and sixteen." He looked at the floor. Lynn looked at him, then at me.

"What a damned mess," she said.

I got out a notepad and a pen. "I suppose I'd better take the names of all the people involved," I said. I felt what I was doing was futile. If Medici had been angry, why wait nineteen years to kill Tingley? I said it aloud.

"Sure," Lynn said, "I agree. But you wanted possibilities, and that's what I thought of. I know. It's remote."

In a few minutes I had a list.

Lee Hammer
Lynn Hammer
Candy Koski
Vic Medici
Robin Tingley
Marnie Ross (Tingley)
Betty Huff
Dale Robbins
Marge Appleton
Joyce "Cuddles" Bebar
Robert "Stinky" Rasmussen

I handed it to Lynn. "Anyone else?"

She looked at the list and handed it to Lee. He stared at the names. "No. No one else," he said. He looked at Lynn.

"I think that's it, but it was a long time ago," she said.

"Do you know where these people are now?" I asked either of them.

Lee said, "Vic's in town. He owns something called Stallion Enterprises. I don't know what Vic's business is." I didn't say anything. "Marnie's here. She married Robin, and she's a good friend of ours. We see her quite often. She lives a mile or so from here. They were separated a couple of years ago. She drinks a lot. Sad business. Cuddles Bebar got married a long time ago. I don't know where she lives now. Betty Huff. Not sure. Marge Appleton is dead. Dale Robbins lives in the southeast section somewhere, near Reed College, I think. Stinky has been in Buffalo, New York, for a long time. I think he's in the steel business."

I took notes as fast as I could. I stood up. "Can I make a call?"

"Sure. Sure. Phone's right there," Lee waved at the phone.

I dialed John Mrvich's home. He answered.

"John, can you have your lawyer friend...what's his name, Petrov?"

"Rick Petrov, right."

"Do you think he could look up a trial record for us? It would really help."

"Sure, he would. He's a great guy. Very helpful."

"It was in 1959. Vic—I suppose Victor or Vittorio— Medici was tried for killing a girl named Candice Koski—" I looked up at Lee. "Where did the trial take place?"

"Here in town."

"Here, John. Portland."

"I'll have Rick look for us. He knows his way around those records."

I thanked him and hung up.

"Well?" Lynn asked.

"I guess I'll start with Medici," I said.

17

Stallion Enterprises was paying more for decor than for rent. I'd driven down in the car generously provided by my hosts. It turned out to be just an average two-year-old Mercedes, soft blue, and I'd parked within a block of the Ironfast Building on Second. That was where, according to the phone book, Stallion Enterprises were housed.

The Ironfast Building had been made a loner by that old favorite force of yours and mine, progress. All other buildings had been torn down on that side of the street except one, a little coffee shop on the corner a couple of lots from the Ironfast Building. The rest of the block was

graded dirt, and I imagined it would soon be parking lots.
In a hundred years there will be two kinds of people, those
working for the International Grand Conglomerate and
those starving. Those who are starving will hang around
the IGC parking lots for handouts when the employees of
IGC get off. If you work for IGC, you'll think the system
is benevolent.

The Ironfast Building is one of those old office buildings
that were ugly when erected and grew beautiful with age,
especially when compared with the new office buildings
that look like breakfast-food packages with windows. It
ran up eight stories, a tan brick structure with some gin-
gerbread cement stripping above the first floor and a roof
that tried not too hard to look like the roof of a castle in
Europe. Fake minarets adorned the corners, and a cren-
ellated wall cut into the sky with square jabs.

The doors were revolving. I hadn't seen a revolving door
in years. Inside, the address board was almost empty. A
firm called Brody's Donuts occupied a small office on the
third floor, and another called Allen's Knitwear was on
the fourth, according to the board. But the board didn't
look like anyone had touched it in years. Stallion Enterprises was listed as being on the seventh floor.

I got into a creaky old elevator that looked like it might
make seven floors if it felt like it and pushed the right
buttons and shot up about as fast as smoke rises on a hot,
windless day. The elevator shuddered and groaned. Once
in a while it gave a little lurch. I hoped I was aging that
slowly.

Finally, it being my lucky day, we made seven, and the
doors opened about as fast as the elevator climbed. I
stepped out, and I was already in Stallion Enterprises. I
suppose I'd expected a small office, possibly a secretary
and an overworked Mr. Medici taking phone calls from
irate operators of massage parlors because the police protection had broken down. That's not what I found.

The entire floor was white shag right up to a black wall
that ran the length of the building. Painted on the wall
was a young woman with not much on, but with stars
meant to signify glamour seeming to shoot from her body.
She was about thirty-five feet long lying down, blonde, of
course, to contrast with the black wall and smiling with

teeth about four inches long and three inches wide. She wore a flimsy, revealing nightgown. Off her right hip, the one she wasn't resting on, were shiny gold letters: Stallion Enterprises. Right in front of the wall, in the dead center, was a lone receptionist. Behind her was a door that opened, if it ever did, through the crotch of the thirty-five-foot woman resting on her left hip and smiling. I looked for the artist's signature but found none.

The receptionist was brunette and from a distance— and there was quite a bit of distance before I got to her— seemed attractive. But distance reduces most women to basics, and most women are basically attractive. She stared at me, and as I got closer she smiled. She was dressed in a short sequined gown, and her desk was glass so anyone could see her legs, which were not bad.

As I got close, I could see that distance was what this woman needed. There was some terrible vacancy in her eyes, as if feeling had run away years before. Her smile was as empty as it was flashy. She looked like she'd fall apart if you asked her anything more complicated than the way to the rest room.

"Smell her breath," she said.

"I beg your pardon?" I fumbled.

"Her breath. Smell her breath."

"Whose breath?"

"Her. Her." She waved at the giant head of the woman painted on the wall.

I hesitated a minute, then walked to the figure's head and put my nose close to her mouth. The mouth was about a foot and a half wide. A giant whiff of cheap perfume hit me in the face. I looked around at the brunette just in time to see her take her hand from a button on her desk. She was laughing wildly.

"Isn't that something?" she laughed some more.

"I've never seen anything like it," I said.

"It's Mr. Lamarr's idea. He's very intelligent. Has all kinds of ideas, Mr. Lamarr."

"I wonder if I might see Mr. Medici," I cut in, hoping I wasn't ruining her good time. For someone so young, she'd probably had a lot of bad times. She became automatic.

"Whom may I say is calling?" she said.

"Mr. Barnes," I said, wondering why I'd called myself Mr. and realizing it was because it didn't take much more than that to impress her.

"Mr. Medici is very busy. He's the president, you know. Is he expecting you?"

"I should have called ahead," I said. "Frankly, I didn't know you had this large an operation. I'm investigating a murder and could use his help."

"Mr. Medici is always willing to cooperate with the police," she said. She said it before, many times, or she couldn't have said it so easily. "Cooperate" was a big word for her. "You are the police, aren't you?"

"Yes, I am, but in Montana."

That was too fast a curve for her. She was flustered. Something tried to happen behind her eyes and didn't. In a weak voice she said, "Perhaps you should see Mr. Lamarr. He's Mr. Medici's assistant." She dialed a couple of digits on the phone. "Mr. Lamarr, there's a gentleman from the police here to see Mr. Medici. From the Montana police. Yes, sir. Right away." She hung up. "Mr. Lamarr will see you. Through the door, straight down, last office on the left." She pushed another button. No perfume this time, just a door that opened Miss Wall Adornment's vital parts. I stepped through.

Beyond the black wall, the white shag went on down a wide, long hall. On either side were doors with names and titles on them. Mr. C. Johanson, Accounts. Mr. L. G. Zimmerman, Contracts. One door said, Typing Pool, and true to good old American standards that room was glassed so the men could look in and make sure the girls were working. All the other offices were blank, closed doors and blank walls. As long as we can keep the working classes under surveillance, we will survive. I imagined the men behind the doors weren't doing a thing. Behind the glass, four typists were working like hell.

The sign on the last office on the left side said: T. Curtoise Lamarr, Vice-President. I knocked. The door opened again by some remote control. Lamarr's desk was in the dead center of the room. It was at least as big as a Ping-Pong table.

Lamarr came around the desk and offered his hand. He was dressed in red. Everything was red. His tie was a brighter red than his shirt which was a brighter red than his suit. I looked down briefly. Even his shoes were red. His clothes didn't look cheap, as far as price went.

"I'm Curt Lamarr, officer," he said. I took his offered hand. He was a soft-looking man. His flesh was unusually white, his hair an unimpressive shade of mousy brown. His face was the one of someone who had been picked on a lot years ago in a schoolyard. He counteracted the softness of his face with a slight sneer that at first I thought was the result of some muscular defect because no one would sneer that obviously. Then I realized he was really trying to look tough.

Lamarr reminded me of a boy named Sammy Klein who had been in my class in grammar school. He had that same soft, white flesh, perhaps from some glandular condition. I remember Sammy, big for his age, used as a punching bag by the bullies. I'd been ashamed of myself that I never did anything but watch Sammy take his lumps and whimper. He retreated into books. He was a physicist now, maybe MIT. Very bright fellow. Lamarr was big, too, and just as uncoordinated, I suspected. I found some sympathy for him, but less than for Sammy Klein, and none of the admiration I felt for Klein.

"I understand," Lamarr said, after he'd sat down and offered me one of the two leather chairs, "that you are a policeman from Montana. Or is it Wyoming?" His contempt was obvious.

"Montana," I said. "I'm a sheriff's deputy from Sanders County. Plains, Montana, is where I work." I tried to sound as innocent as possible.

T. Curtoise Lamarr smiled. His smile was about as sincere as that of W. C. Fields smiling at children. I could see the chicken shit oozing out between his teeth. "So what's a small-town sheriff doing here? This must be a bit big for you, isn't it?"

He was so dumb, I decided to play along. It might get me to Medici faster, and I might even pick up some information that could help. "Well, shucks, Mr. Lamarr," I said, "I know I ain't up to your ways here—" was I pouring it on too thick? That "shucks" wouldn't fool many people these days—"but we've got a little kiling on our hands up there, and we could sure use Mr. Medici's help, if you don't mind."

Lamarr's smile became almost benign, if your standards aren't too high. "I see, Sheriff Barnes. A little killing on your hands." He was mocking me. God, he'd fallen for it.

"We're right fresh out of clues," I said, hoping I wasn't being taped. If Mrvich or Yellow Bear heard this, I'd never hold my head up again.

"You amuse me," he actually said. "I think maybe we can arrange for a meeting with Mr. Medici." He filled out the act by absently playing with a gold letter opener. I wished he watched more recent movies, except that if he did, I couldn't have put him on so easily. A dumb guy like that who needs to feel superior to somebody is always easy to manipulate. I had no doubt the reason I was getting to Medici so fast was that I made Lamarr feel good. "Excuse me a moment," he said.

While he was out I took note of the pithy sayings of nobody in particular that were in gold script on blue paper and framed under glass.

VIRTUE IS ELUSIVE BUT FOUND IN UNLIKELY
PLACES.
THE FOOLISH JUDGE. THE WISE UNDERSTAND.
SIN IS FOUND ONLY IN THE HEART.

That's what you think, T. Curtoise Lamarr. In a moment Lamarr was back, and he beckoned me to follow him. I walked out and turned left, and at the end of the hall was a door with Victor Medici, President, on it. Lamarr opened the door, and we went in. He introduced me to Vic Medici.

Medici was not a large man, but he was compact, and his body suggested power and coordination. He was as different from Lamarr as he could be. His eyes were bright with intelligence. His skin was a sort of fig-brown, and that made his white teeth even whiter. His hair was black and wavy. He wore a no-nonsense black suit, and his blue tie wasn't kidding, either. I had the immediate impression of a man with whom one should not kid at all.

He waved Lamarr out of the room and bade me to sit

down. His desk wasn't as big as Lamarr's. He sat down behind it and studied me.

"Lamarr says you're a hick sheriff. Are you?" His voice cracked.

"I'm a sheriff, yes. A deputy in Montana. I used to be in the Seattle police but had to retire early. I put on an act for your VP, and he bought it." I decided right away that the only way to approach Medici was to be direct. If I wanted to hide anything, I'd better not even talk near it.

"He's dumb," Medici said. "Not smart at all. But what the hell. You don't get people from the Harvard School of Business applying here." He shook his head. "I pay him thirteen thousand a year and let him call himself Vice-President, and he's impressed with himself. He could only make ten thousand anywhere else. But he does a few things right. What about this murder?"

"You know Robin Tingley?"

"Sure. Knew him years ago in high school. He was a year ahead of me. Haven't seen him in years."

"He got killed in Montana."

Medici didn't respond.

"Somebody killed him with an axe."

He still didn't respond. His bright eyes fixed on me. Suddenly he said, "What's this about? The Koski case?"

He threw me with his frankness. "Well, you might tell me where you were on the day of October sixth. Were you by any chance in Montana?"

"I've never been in Montana. Is that when he was killed?"

"Yes. I know he testified against you in the Koski case and that might be a motive, but it happened so long ago."

"Motive? Christ, that was what, eighteen years ago, the trial was, no, by God, nineteen. Fall of 1958. No. Fifty-nine. That was it, 1959. Besides, Tingley didn't testify against me. His testimony helped me."

That surprised me even more than his candor.

"Mr. Medici, my information is that he found you on top of Candy Koski's dead body trying to—"

"Oh, hell. By the time we got to court, we had that looking like artificial respiration. Tingley said as much, and, besides, he said he didn't think I'd killed her. He helped me."

"I noticed you said, 'looking like artificial respiration.' In fact, it wasn't?"

Then he threw me the biggest surprise of all. "No," he said. "I was trying to screw her."

"Knowing she was dead?"

"Yes."

"Can I ask why?"

"Sure. I was doped up, and I'd had some booze, too. When I found her like that, dead on the floor, I thought that sex might bring her back to life."

"Isn't that a bit primitive?" I wasn't sure "primitive" was the right word.

"Look. I was eighteeen and high and, like any kid that age, dumb. I wasn't Cary Grant trying to seduce Sophia Loren. In that dumb kid way, I loved Candy Koski, and there she was, dead, and I was desperate. Maybe you haven't read all of Tingley's testimony."

"None of it, yet. A guy is taking care of it right now for me."

"Well, you should know I was bawling, too, like a damned baby, and I couldn't get it up at all. I was trying the only thing that occurred to me in some dumb idea it would save her."

I stared at him for a minute. I really liked him. He was tough and honest. "And you didn't kill her?"

"Christ, no."

"Do you have any idea who might have."

I got another surprise. "Yes."

I waited.

"I won't tell you," he said. "I don't know, so why put someone in jeopardy who may be innocent, too?"

"A hint, maybe?"

"No."

It was very final. I rose to leave. "You don't have any idea who might have killed Tingley?"

"I lost track of him years ago. I don't know who, if anyone, was mad at him."

"Thanks very much for being so candid," I said. I

stopped at the door. "Can I ask you something, Medici? Do you still think sex can bring the dead back to life? Is that why you deal in porno?"

"No," he said. "I make a hell of a lot of money."

18

Big John Mrvich looked very much at home in his office. Captain of detectives, John Mrvich, had come along nicely, and why not? Intelligent, tough, humane, a very good cop, probably the best I'd known. His office suited him, spare, simple, good usual office furniture, the office of a man who comes to work.

"I didn't expect to see you until tonight," he said.

"I need a little help, Murv. I got a list of people here who were at the party nineteen years ago when Candy Koski was killed. I know where some of them are, and I've talked to Vic Medici already."

"Vic? How's Vic?"

"You know him?"

"What kind of detective would I be if I didn't know the chief of porno distribution for western Oregon?"

"That big? I thought just Portland."

"Oh, no. Lots more than just Portland and lots more than just porno, too."

"What more than just porno?"

"He's got some legitimate movie distribution, and he even has a finger into some construction, but porno is the big and consistent money-maker."

"Know a guy named T. Curtoise Lamarr who works for him?"

"Guy who dresses in one color at a time?"

"That's him."

"He was picked up, once, on a morals charge. A kid was involved, eleven or so. We didn't make it stick. He's a sad guy, really, a soft oyster trying to make it in a hard world.

One of those guys who never won a fight when he was a kid and couldn't understand it because he was bigger than some of the others."

I told him about the conversation with Medici. John took it all in and mused about it over a cigarette. He stood up and looked out the window. I could see some sky that was blue and some sky that was white over his shoulder. A gull poured by the window.

"I think your instincts are right. Near as I know, Medici is an OK guy and real honest. But he may have killed the Koski girl. He was violent in the old days. He beat up a few guys in his time. He's faster than hell with his fists. Never heard of him hitting a woman. Still, when he was a kid and if he got jealous he—say, what in hell is this to do with Tingley's murder?"

"I'm beginning to think nothing," I said sadly. "I'd heard Tingley had testified against Medici, and someone had suggested Medici might want him dead—but after all this time? Medici says Tingley didn't testify against him but for him. He also said he knows someone who might have wanted Koski dead, but he wouldn't spill. Not a hint."

"No sense trying to shake him down. Too tough, and he's got a whiz for a lawyer. Besides, if he wanted anyone dead, he wouldn't do his own dirty work these days. Besides that besides, he wouldn't hold a grudge over ten minutes. I know him. If he's mad, he takes care of things right now."

"You can help me if you will, John. Jesus, I know how busy you are, but if you could run down a few names." I handed him the list. "That's all who were at that party at Cannon Beach. Candy and Tingley are dead, of course. I know where the Hammers and Marnie Ross Tingley and probably Dale Robbins are. I think the Bebar woman married and is in the area. The Hammers think Rasmussen is in Buffalo."

"I'll check them all and get back to you. Shouldn't take long. That's Huff, Robbins, Appleton, Bebar and Rasmussen. Right?"

"That's it. I understand Appelton's dead."

"My pleasure. Now get the hell out of here and let me solve a few major crimes before I go home."

"Appreciate your help, John."

"Don't forget tonight. Jake's. Terrific seafood. Don't eat until then."

"Promise."

19

I didn't make over a dozen wrong turns finding my way back up the West Hills to the Hammer place. By now I had a better sense of their house. It really stood on two streets instead of one. The front of the house stood on an upper street and the back on another street lower down the hill that curved into the upper street where their property ended in a blaze of rich grass and high trees. You parked the cars, all three of them, off the lower street into a huge carport that dug into the back of the house. As I was getting out of the blue Mercedes, it occurred to me that no one had questioned my authority or my right to ask questions, even though my authority here was nil. I decided if I needed backing, Mrvich would provide it. He disliked murder, too, no matter what state it happened in.

Lynn greeted me when I walked in. "Hi, Sheriff Barnes. Caught any killers today?"

"Not even close."

"See any of the old gang?"

"Medici."

"How is Vic? Haven't seen him in ages."

"Tough and hard and pretty damned honest."

"That would be Vic, all right. Did you find out anything?"

"Nothing. Says he knows something but won't tell."

"Well, you'll never beat it out of him."

"With him, I wouldn't want to try. Can I phone Montana?"

"Sure, there's a phone in the bedroom, your room."

I remembered seeing it. I excused myself and went to

my room and dialed Arlene. For the first two minutes we groaned about how much we missed each other already.

"Seen anybody yet?"

"A guy named Medici. I'm going to learn some things tonight. Tomorrow I'm going to try to see Tingley's widow. What goes in Plains?"

"The place has come to life again. Quite a few customers, specially when the mill lets out. Red put Manny Sanderson down here in your place. He gives me the creeps, those eyes. He's a slob, too. Had a couple of drinks yesterday and started yapping about how crummy it is to work for an Indian."

I told her I loved her and called Red.

"How's it going, oh great detective?" he growled.

"Nothing. Talked to one guy so far who might have had a motive if you stretch a point. Tonight I'm going to get some help. But I think following this nineteen-year-old murder is just taking us away from Tingley's killing. I can't believe they're connected. Things have been lying around too long collecting dust. Maybe we should be concentrating our work there, finding some more immediate motive, somebody right there in Plains who wanted Tingley dead."

"Yeah, but I've been going at that for two days and can't turn up a thing. Jesus, the mill workers to a soul thought Tingley was the Albert Schweitzer of mill superintendents. It bothers me a little that we can't seem to find any sex life for him here. No girls. No boys. No sheep or cattle. The guy lived here for a year, and it looks like he went celibate."

"I think he may have had some interest in Lynn Hammer," I said. "But that's complicated. Tingley had been separated for some time but he wasn't divorced, and what's more, the Hammers are on good terms with Marnie Tingley. I think they were all too much friends too long for anything like that to develop. I'll talk to Lynn about it. If Mrs. Tingley is as big a lush as people say she is, she could have let the idea of losing him forever play on her until she got the urge to axe him. But if she's that lushy, could she face driving all the way to Montana, sinking the axe, then driving all the way back? And could she do it without being seen?"

"Find out if she's got a green car," Yellow Bear said. "Meanwhile, don't worry about Plains. Manny's got those teenagers so scared, the town is quiet. It's nice to have a real cop down there for a change."

"Thanks for the confidence, chief. By the way, Marnie Ross Tingley does have a green car."

"Noted. And you note this. We found the axe. At least an axe, brand-new. It was in the river. Some fisherman spotted it. We can't prove anything. It's new and clean. We assume it's the axe used on Tingley because it seems stupid to be throwing a new axe in an old river."

"Where in the old river?"

"Six miles downstream or so, toward Thompson Falls."

After I hung up, I went back and found Lynn in the kitchen. "Can we talk," I asked, "about Robin Tingley for a minute?"

"Sure. Can I fix you a drink?"

I looked at my watch. An hour and a half before dinner at Jake's. "Sure. Scotch with some water." I sat down on a stool while she started to pour. "Lynn, can you level with me about a few things? Not that you haven't always, but in this case it involves your friends of long standing."

"I'll try," she said and gave me a smile. She handed me a drink and sat down on another stool with hers. It was a cheery kitchen, bright orange walls and a pale blue ceiling, gleaming range and refrigerator, a big chopping block in the center of the room, a counter with four stools, including the two we were occupying, where you could eat breakfast and drink coffee and feel good about it being morning. I decided to have breakfast here tomorrow if it was OK with Lee and Lynn.

"It's about Tingley. Lee put him in charge of the mill last year, or maybe earlier. And he's been living in Plains ever since, so he's been separated from his wife at least that long."

"Oh, yes. They've been apart some time now."

"Can you tell me why they've not divorced?"

She looked at me for a moment, then at the floor. "I suppose you'll find out," she said with a quiet regret in her voice. "Robin was afraid of divorcing Marnie. He was afraid it would upset her. Marnie's not too stable. I hate to say that about her. She's an old, old friend, and I still enjoy seeing her. We see her quite a bit. But she's been seeing a psychiatrist for years, and it's a little more serious than just the rich, neurotic woman who wants some attention. Robin couldn't live with her, but he was a kind man, and he couldn't hurt her. He really cared about her. He was sort of—you know—noble. God, what an old-fashioned word. But he was an old-fashioned guy."

"If she thought he would divorce her, could she have been mad enough to kill him?"

Lynn looked out the window at the huge lawn below. "Oh, Jesus," she said. "Oh, Jesus. My oldest friends."

"Well, could she?"

"I want to say no, but in all honesty I don't know."

"OK, sorry to press you on it. I know it's painful."

We sat silently for a minute and sipped.

"Let me ask you something. We can't find any trace of a sex life for Robin in Plains. He didn't know any women intimately, even though he'd been there for some time. Do you have any idea if he had any sex life up there? I know that's a shitty question, but we're out of leads, and we're groping right now."

"I don't know," she said. "I honestly don't know. But Robin was the sort of man who could go without. He might have felt loyalty to Marnie even if they were separated. He was really old-fashioned in a lot of ways."

"How about Marnie? Was she loyal, too?"

She answered with a laugh that was as close to being nasty as anything I'd heard from her.

"Well, if she was getting laid, it might eliminate the chance she could have killed him."

"I suppose so. I hope so."

"Who's laying her?"

"I don't know, but I think several are. You can tell when a woman's getting laid and when she's not, especially if you know her very well."

I puffed on my cigarette. Evening was creeping up the lawn outside. I looked at the classy woman who sat next to me. She was really attractive. Something fresh was left over from her youth, like some wind in her black hair that wouldn't quit blowing, the way it did for most women in their late thirties. That was a good age for women, I

thought—still very attractive and a minimum of seduc-
tion needed.

"Can I ask if Robin was interested in you?" I said. "I
mean seriously. Was he thinking of divorcing Marnie and
marrying you?"

"I think so, but I wouldn't have let it happen."

"Why not?"

"With Marnie my close friend? I liked him a lot. But
that was out. If I remarry, it will be someone I haven't
known that long and who doesn't have a wife who happens
to be one of my closest friends."

"Do you want to remarry?"

"Not especially, no."

We had another drink and switched to lighter conversation. I still had nothing, but at least a possibility was
showing its ugly head. Tingley's wife? Some psychological
problems?

Before I left for Jake's, I got the address of Marnie Ross
Tingley, to make sure I had it for tomorrow in case I didn't
see anyone at breakfast.

20

The crab had been
superb. I was digging into some dessert that was green
and black and tasted wonderful. Rick Petrov, across from
me, had already finished his and was sipping a brandy.
He had sad Russian eyes and a face that looked just a bit
put-upon and more than just a little aware of how funny
the world was, including faces that look put-upon. He was
a slight man, maybe one fifty at the most, and about ten
pounds of that looked recent, the result of food his good
fees could buy.

Like Mrvich, he wrote poems and had had a book published, and he enjoyed a certain local reputation as a poet.
Mrvich told me Petrov was good, and I'd already decided
to buy his book. But I didn't have to. He handed me a copy

right after we finished dinner, inscribed to "Al Barnes, friend of John Mrvich, and therefore my friend. Rick Petrov."

"Thanks very much. I'll read this shortly. Appreciate it very much."

He nodded and grinned. He had an attractive grin that showed a flash of silver filling in the front. There was something just a bit charmingly shady about him, a sort of con man on the right side of things. I trusted him completely.

And I reflected on how much I liked Mrvich. A lot of cops fall into a good guy-bad guy way of thinking that I suppose is normal after years of police work. For them, defense attorneys are bad guys because they get criminals off after the cops have worked like hell to get the criminals in. A lot of cops wouldn't have anything to do with a defense attorney. John Mrvich had lived in a big world ever since I'd known him.

I spent about fifteen minutes filling them in. I told them everything I could think of about the case, what I'd been doing and how discouraged I was starting to get.

"I've gone over the trial record," Rick Petrov said, "and what Medici told you is right. The prosecution tried to make out that Medici killed the girl after she resisted him, just so he could have her. Frustrated blind lust, the D.A. called it. They got Tingley on the stand, and he testified that he'd found Medici mounting the girl's dead body. She was naked, by the way. Not a stitch.

"Art Matthew, who was a real hotshot in those days, made hash of the prosecution. He got Tingley to admit on cross that Medici could have been trying artificial respiration, and he even got Tingley to say that he didn't think Medici had killed her. The judge told the jury to ignore it. But they'd heard it.

"Where they really cracked the prosecution's case was on the testimony of the Clatsop County coroner. He wasn't a pathologist, just a GP. He claimed he came down from Astoria and inspected the body and found evidence of intercourse. This guy, his name was Whitlow, said on the stand that in his opinion the intercourse had taken place after death. Matthew put two pathologists from UO medical school on the stand. Both said that there was no way Whitlow could have determined intercourse had even taken place unless Koski's flesh had been torn in the vaginal region. It hadn't. And clearly no way to tell if anything had happened before or after death. Ten hours had gone by before Whitlow looked at the body. It was a clear case of a doctor testifying to what the authorities wanted him to. Happens all the time. They might have gotten away with it in those days in Clatsop County if Medici had had a lousy defense attorney. But against Art Matthew? Forget it.

"Another big part of the prosecution's case rested on some bruises on Medici's knuckles the cops had noticed when they had first questioned him in Cannon Beach. Matthew dug up a guy named Desk, Clarence Desk, who admitted that he had gotten in a fight with Medici outside a tavern in Cannon Beach earlier that day, about six that evening, when Medici had gone into town for some cigarettes. Medici won."

"I'm not surprised. If he had lost, Desk would be someone to stay clear of," I said.

"I can get you a runoff of the transcript if you want," Rick put in.

"I don't think it would help. None of the others even got on the stand, then?"

"No. They couldn't help the prosecution, and Matthew, for some reason, didn't call any of them. I can't understand that exactly. I suppose he thought he'd nail it down with no more help. So he saved the other youngsters the trouble. He wasn't a bad guy, Art Matthew."

"Did you know him?"

"Slightly. He was winding up his career when I started."

"Is he still alive?"

"Gone to the great appeals court in the sky."

"Well, that remains a mystery," I said, "but not the one I'm investigating." But I wasn't fooling Mrvich. I could tell by the way he looked at me he knew damned well I wanted to solve that one, too, after nineteen years.

"One thing, they weren't even sure she'd been beaten by someone's fists. They were only sure she was beaten. Matthew scored on that one, too, with his two pathologists from UO. She died from strangulation, actually, probably

with a towel around her neck, something like that. The
beating may have come after death. Any questions?"

I said I couldn't think of any.

"You should have one, at least," Petrov said.

Mrvich and I both looked at him and waited.

"Medici came from an average family. His father was
a garbage collector. Where did Medici get the money to
pay Matthew?"

"Jesus," Mrvich said, "that's right. Matthew didn't
work for free."

"In fact, even in those days, he charged twenty thousand
dollars for a murder defense," Petrov said.

"And with major felonies, you got to put the money in
the attorney's hand before he makes a move."

"He's an honest guy," I said. "He might just tell me.
He's really very candid for someone in the rackets, if they
are the rackets. He's not your closed-mouth syndicate artist."

"I doubt if he would," Petrov said cryptically but with
some wisdom of experience behind it.

"Let's hear some jazz," Mrvich said. And we rode in
Petrov's car to a club where we drank beer and listened
to dixieland jazz and talked between sets. It was a fun
evening, and I regretted a couple of times that I didn't still
live in a city. During one break I asked Petrov who had
been the judge on the case.

"Willow. John Willow. Not a bad judge. Retired a few
years ago. I tried a couple of cases in front of him."

"Did you win?" I asked.

"Got one guy off with forty years," he said.

"Good work, counselor," Mrvich put in. "Remind me not
to hire you when I murder my mother-in-law."

"The bastard murdered three people with a sword, one
in front of seven witnesses," Petrov said, looking a little
sadder than he had at dinner. I didn't miss the city quite
so much, I decided. There's something about living with
that violence around you all the time that leads you to
accept it as a norm. You find yourself joking about it to
make sure you're still human.

Full of beer and good feelings, we drove back to where
I'd parked my car. Dixieland was such a warm music. It
always made me feel good. We were saying our bleary good

nights, and I was thanking them in slurred speech for a great evening, when Petrov said, "Jesus, you should have had another question. Why in hell didn't I think of it, for Christ sakes? How could I have missed it?"

"Why, what have it been?" Mrvich said, his English suffering from too much Michelob.

"Why was Medici tried in Portland? Why not in Clatsop County where the crime took place?"

Even relaxed with beer and music, I felt myself tighten a bit.

"Can you find out?"

"I sure can. I'll get back to you."

I drove home very carefully. Half drunk, I didn't make any wrong turns. I felt good. Now we had a couple of big questions.

I sat on the edge of my bed, trying to think and staring at a picture of Lee and Lynn Hammer, all dressed up. She was holding flowers, and it looked like a wedding photo. I hadn't noticed it before in the room. I stared at it and wondered where an Italian kid from an average family had found enough money to pay a big-time lawyer and why a trial that should have taken place in Astoria had taken place in Portland.

21

Marnie Ross Tingley lived in one of those apartment houses where everyone looks young and single and rich, and where in your gloomier moments you know they are living out all your sexual fantasies and feeling no guilt or remorse. It was called Ming Arms, and everything was stone, plastic, vegetation or tile. The swimming pool, which I got a glimpse of through an entrance in the sandstone wall, was tile. No one was swimming, but the water was there, clean and blue. The Ming Arms had a doorman who kept out the undesirable, like cancer and crude manners.

"Can I help you, sir?" He didn't have that old-fashioned pomposity of Mycroft. There was something sharp about him. I thought he might be an ex-cop from L.A. or some big city, a very good ex-cop who had been a very good cop. He wasn't anyone to spit on. I fell into formality naturally with him.

"Mr. Barnes to see Mrs. Tingley," I said, hoping to match his seriousness.

"Yes, sir. Mrs. Tingley is expecting you. Fifth floor, room five-o-seven. The elevator is straight ahead and to your left, sir."

I passed a couple on my way to the elevator who only confirmed my suspicions that there were people who were free and happy. They were young and beautiful and unmarried, and both reeked of that smug independence of wealth.

In the elevator I remembered what Lynn had said when she had put down the phone after calling Marnie Tingley for me. "I feel like a rat. Marnie's such an old friend. If she killed Robin, I want her caught, of course, but I feel like I'm setting her up. Anyway, I don't think she killed Robin, or I might not have called her. I suppose she's a possibility—but God, I've been like a mother to her. I've helped control her over the years, even put her to bed sometimes when she was real drunk. I feel like a rat. Anyway, I told her who you are, so I guess I can't blame myself."

I could appreciate her position. One good friend dead. Another who might have killed him. Lynn could think pretty straight. But who wouldn't be confused under these circumstances? I had tried to comfort her, pointed out that if Marnie Ross Tingley had killed her husband, then she could be dangerous to Lynn and Lee Hammer, too, if she thought they might help convict her. What worried me was not just the people who stood to be hurt, good people like the Hammers, but that I was getting involved more and more with the wrong case. The Koski killing was beginning to obsess me. I kept telling myself that I was only pursuing it because it might lead me to Tingley's killer. But I had to admit to myself that I wanted to solve that nineteen-year-old murder just as badly as I wanted to solve Tingley's. I'd failed to solve a lot of murders. Any homicide dick has. And I'd never been able to take it lightly. I worked on eighteen murder cases that remained unsolved, and I could tell you every one of them, who the victim was, how far we got in the investigation, who I suspected, if anyone.

One thing I never understood was the attention the police agencies paid to bank robbery as opposed to the attention they paid to murder. You rob a bank, every police agency from federal to local gets on your ass. You kill someone, and unless that someone was important, only a couple of local detectives pursue the case. I thought of the skid-row knockovers, someone planting a rock into someone's head just to grab a bottle of cheap wine. It must be the final feeling of unimportance to know that even if you are murdered, chances are the cops won't follow the matter long enough to find your killer. And, of course, we couldn't do much with those. No clues. No connection of killer to victim. Any one of a thousand derelicts could have done it. If no one came forward with some information, you finally wrote it off. And if you were me, you resented it.

The elevator doors opened so quietly, preoccupied as I was with my thoughts, I would not have noticed them had I not been looking at them. I found five-o-seven and pushed the bell. I couldn't hear it ring inside. The rooms seemed soundproofed. A maid opened the door. She was black and very pretty. She wore a black maid's uniform that looked great on her. Anything would have looked great on her. I trailed her to an expensive couch and sat down. "Mrs. Tingley will be with you in a moment, sir," she said tonelessly. I watched her legs flash away in silk under her short skirt, her black high-heeled pumps almost dancing out of the room. Her bottom danced, too.

The furniture was quite high-class. The room was somewhat sparely furnished with just two large chairs; the couch I was sitting on and a neat coffee table. There was a fireplace that wasn't being used. Prints of Monet and a painter I've seen a lot of in reproduction, whose name I can never remember, hung on the walls. Also one original painting by someone local, a big painting, maybe five feet by four feet. I was trying to make out the artist's name when Marnie Ross Tingley walked in. She wasn't anything like I'd pictured her.

For one thing, she was neat and her color was good. She didn't look like an alcoholic at all. I'd expected someone run-down, bleary-eyed, not too well kept. She was almost tiny, maybe five feet one or so, and her proportions were as close to perfection as I'd seen. She was dressed in a green print dress and wore gold pumps. Her feet were tiny, the dainty size three or maybe even two that women used to envy twenty years ago. Her blonde hair was carefully set with subtle curls and waves that came down the sides of her impish little face. Her nose was turned up slightly, suggesting that naughty, pert, saucy kind of girl we loved secretly in high school. She looked just a bit like a blonde miniature Lynn Hammer, but she seemed much younger, though I knew they were about the same age. With her small dimensions and her excellent proportions, she looked like a plaything—but an expensive plaything.

We exchanged greetings and a few words about the Hammers. The first thing she asked me was unexpected. She said, "Do you have any authority in Oregon, Sheriff Barnes?"

"Actually, I don't. But if I need it, I can get Captain Mrvich of the Portland police to back me up. I'm sure he'll even send over a detective if I ask him."

"That's all right," she said and sat down in one of the big chairs and crossed her ideal little legs. "The question was just academic," and she wrinkled her nose and giggled, both just slightly. I wondered if she were drunk. It was eleven A.M. I decided not. She didn't look drunk.

"I'm sorry about your husband," I said. "I knew him slightly and liked him very much, the little I saw of him."

"Thank you, Sheriff Barnes. It was a surprise. Robin was a nice man. We'd been separated for a while, so I suppose the blow wasn't as bad as it would have been." She looked right at me as if I were entertaining her. She crossed her legs the other way. One of her tiny gold pumps loosened as she flexed her foot. It seemed about ready to slip off.

"Still, I'm sorry for your loss."

"Thank you. I'd really lost him, anyway. I guess that's what I'm trying to say. But that makes it sound like my loss is what matters, doesn't it? And, of course, Robin's loss was the real loss, wasn't it?"

I didn't like what was happening. What was happening was I was being turned on and hard. At my age, and after a great night with Arlene only a couple of nights ago? What in hell was happening?

Her foot flexed again, and a faint ripple went up the calf. She was smiling. I sensed she sensed my discomfort.

"Mrs. Tingley, I—"

"Marnie, please."

"Yes. Marnie, I hope you realize I must ask some questions that I don't want to. But I'm trying to find your husband's murderer, and it's essential I ask you these things. I hope you understand."

"I certainly do, Sheriff Barnes." She crossed her legs the other way. Same flex of the other foot, same ripple up the calf. It was all done so easily and subtly.

"Would you like a drink?"

"Thank you, no. I had too much last night," I said, hoping to convince her that as a fellow drunk she ought to level with me. I thought, one drink, lady, and I'm going to turn into Dracula and suck your blood. I was really getting sexed up. And I wasn't sure how she was doing it. I could see her slight gestures and what they were intended to do, but they shouldn't be working this well.

"Whatever you say," she said. It wasn't supposed to mean more, but it did.

"I wonder," I said, trying to concentrate on business, "if you can think of anyone who would want to kill your husband?"

"No, I can't, Sheriff Barnes," she said. She recrossed her legs, and I wanted to shout "stop." She smiled at me again and wrinkled her nose ever so slightly.

"Can I ask, Marnie, if you own a car?"

"Oh, yes. I own a new Buick LeSabre."

"Can you tell me what color it is, if you don't mind?"

"Surely. It's green."

"Can you tell me if you were in Montana when your husband was killed? That was October sixth."

"No, I was there earlier in late August, visiting Lee and Lynn. Were you there?"

"Yes." I wasn't quieting down. If I didn't get out of here pretty soon, I was going to be a very bad cop.

She wrinkled her nose faintly once more. Her small,

sensuous mouth pouted slightly. All old tricks, I thought. Why are they working so well?

"Can you tell me where you were on October sixth?"

"I'm sure I don't know," she said, "but I must have been here. I want a drink," she said. It was a sudden announcement, like a little girl who suddenly wants milk. "Lila," she called.

The black maid swished into the room. With the two of them there, the place was electric with sexuality. While the maid was pouring a drink over in the corner of the room where a cabinet stored some bottles of booze, Marnie Tingley yawned and stretched her arms high, and the green print dress tightened over her round breasts. I looked at the floor. I looked at the paintings. I looked at the fireplace. I looked at the legs on Lila. That last look didn't help things a bit.

"I suppose I must be going," I said. "But I wondered if you remember the party nineteen years ago when Candy Koski was killed?"

"Oh, yes. I'd never forget that. I was with Robin, only he had left me outside when he went in. We were walking on the beach near the house, and he said he had to go in for a minute. So I waited outside. That's when he found Candy and—do you know about Vic Medici and—"

"Yes."

"Well, then, you know. It was all so confusing, and we got everybody together and waited in the kitchen with Candy's body out there in the front room, and finally the cops came." She shuddered just slightly. All her responses were slight but somehow magnified because of it. The maid handed her a drink. She tilted it toward me and said, "Salute," and sipped. She smiled at the drink, then at me.

"By the way, Marnie, do you have a picture of yourself I might take? I'll return it in a few days."

You can be sure she had plenty of pictures of herself, all seductive. I picked one that wouldn't oversex a kid who worked in a gas station in Plains, and that looked very much like her. I planned to send it to Red so he could check with Peter Mitter. When she handed it to me she let her hand rest ever so softly on mine.

I was steaming. I decided to get the hell out of there. Marnie Ross Tingley was some kind of witch, I thought.

Outside, I cooled down slowly by walking fast to my car and by thinking about anything I could find that wasn't Marnie Ross Tingley and wasn't the butt or legs on her maid, Lila.

As I passed the doorman, he said, "Nice day, sir."

"If this place ever starts losing money, convert it to a massage parlor," I said and left him tight lipped, wondering what I was talking about.

When I got back to the Hammer mansion, Lynn had a sandwich all ready. I asked her how she knew I'd be there, and she said Marnie had called and told her I'd just left. "And how did you find Marnie?"

"She's not what I expected," I said, hoping that was vague enough.

Lynn laughed. "She turned you on, didn't she?" Her voice was teasing.

"How did you know?"

"She has the knack. I've seen her do it to Lee. That perfect little body of hers and those little movements and gestures." She laughed again. "You want to hear something funny? She went to a gynecologist once, and he tried to make her. Lost all professional restraint. Now that's what I call a sexy woman."

I couldn't help laughing. I had to admit, that was the true test of a woman's sex appeal.

"By the way, that cop, Mrvich, called. He wants you to call him back."

After I had a cup of coffee, I called John. The girl who answered the phone asked who was calling and, when I told her, put me right through.

"Al. Are you solving any murders?"

"I feel like I couldn't solve anything. I'm not sure I'm not wasting my time down here."

"Well, I've got that information for you, about the people."

"Jesus, that's fast, Murv."

"I have pull," he said with mock pomposity. "Got a pencil and your list?"

"Just a minute, let me catch this in my room here." I moved down the hall to my room, got out a pen and the list and picked up the phone. "Murv? OK."

"All right. Here's the dope. Rasmussen is still in Buffalo. The Buffalo police checked him out, and he hasn't left town in months. So he's out for the Tingley job. The Koski case? Well, any of them are possibles, aren't they? Betty Huff lives in Dallas. She's married to a guy named Stang. She's also crippled with arthritis and pretty bad, I gather. So she's pretty much out. Marge Appleton was married twice. She died in a car wreck outside Merced two years ago. Dale Robbins lives in town. That was a tough one. I found him in the phone book. Joyce Bebar is now Joyce Clueridge. She's married to a stockbroker and lives in Lake Oswego." He gave me the address. I jotted it down, along with the other notes.

"Thanks much for all this, Murv. I can't believe you got it all so fast."

"Wasn't hard. Good luck."

I took the address of Dale Robbins out to Lynn. She looked him up in the phone book and called him for me. "How are you? Been ages. How are things going? Got a friend from Montana who's investigating the murder of Robin Tingley. You remember Robin? He got killed in Montana. With an axe. Oh, awful, Dale. Let's get together one of these days and talk old times. My friend is on his way over. Please help him if you can. He's a good guy. Not your typical cop at all."

So within twenty minutes, by following Lynn's directions, I found myself going up the walkway of a large frame home with a laurel hedge and huge maple shade trees. The house was white frame and pretty expensive. The neighborhood was not as expensive as the West Hills area, but it didn't exactly need government support. I put the homes in the eighty to hundred thousand class.

It was barely one-thirty, and Robbins was home. I wondered what he did for a living. It was a question I never liked to ask, no matter if the person was rich or poor. But, of course, I'd often had to in this business.

The girl who opened the door was bare to the waist. I managed to keep my composure enough to notice she was about twenty and blonde and blue-eyed. I couldn't judge her height very well because bare tits make a woman seem bigger than she is. I tried to respond with sophistication and dignity.

"Ma'am, I'm here to see Dale Robbins." She was stacked like a candy rack. "A friend called for me."

"Please come in," she said. She didn't smile or seem to feel much of anything. I glanced over my shoulder at the street and realized the hedge and trees pretty much restricted the view of anyone passing by. The girl walked in front of me. She had on tight leotards made out of some shiny material. She wore high heels that made her bottom pinch up into a compact package, not small, but not big, either. She led me into a room where a man was sitting on the floor in a kimono, sipping a tall drink that looked like a mint julep. Another girl was on the floor beside him. She also was bare to the waist and also in tight leotards and high heels. She was brunette, and her face showed a bit more expression than the blonde's.

I managed by great will power to get around to noticing Robbins. He was a handsome man, who looked, if your standards were crude enough, a little like Peter Lawford.

"Barnes," he said pleasantly. "Lynn's friend. Please sit down. Join us on the floor here, or take a chair. Whichever you wish."

I took a chair. The blonde sat on the floor and spread her legs and rested on her hands and looked at me. The brunette played with Robbins' hair. He smiled that "I've got it made smile" at me and even winked. Neither of the girls seemed too bright. No one offered me a drink.

I told Dale Robbins what had happened to Robin Tingley and asked him if he knew of anyone who might want Tingley dead.

Robbins tried to look thoughtful. I didn't think he'd ever had a thought in his life. Now that I'd got a longer look at him, I amended my description to a demented Peter Lawford.

"Please understand, Mr. Robbins," I said, hoping some

civility was in my voice, "I'm wondering if the Koski killing nineteen years ago had anything to do with Tingley's
death. That's why I'm questioning the people who were
there at that party when Candy Koski was killed. I'm just
looking for a lead."

"I can't think of any reason the Koski killing would
have something to do with the murder up there in Montana," Robbins said. He pushed the brunette away. "Let
me alone a minute, Collins." Collins stopped playing with
his hair and pouted. The blonde finally smiled, somewhat
sadistically, at the brunette's put-down. Robbins slipped
back into his pose of deep thought. He stood up, and I could
see he was about five eleven, maybe a hundred seventy
pounds. He didn't look like he engaged in anything but
orgies. He sat down in a huge easy chair. The blonde stood
up and went to his chair and sat on the arm. The brunette,
Collins, pouted from the floor.

"Mr. Robbins, do you have any idea who might have
killed Candy Koski?"

"Oh, sure. Vic Medici killed her."

I was surprised at how easily that came out of him.

"See, Vic was a real wild ass in those days." He patted
the blonde's rump. The blonde started to play with his ear.
The brunette glared at the blonde. Robbins made no effort
to introduce us. I doubted he knew their last names.

"Of course, I didn't see it. I was down on the beach with
Cuddles Bebar and Lynn Hammer. A sweet twosome, yes,
sir."

He narrowed his eyes and sipped his drink. Narrowing
his eyes didn't put a bit more behind them. "I think Lee
Hammer was off necking with Marge Appleton, and Stinky
had Betty Huff off somewhere. Robin and Marnie were
together. They got married later. I guess you know that,
don't you?"

I nodded. By now the room had stopped being exciting.
I'm slightly square, and that may be part of the reason.
I didn't like the obvious way Robbins was using the two
girls, but, of course, he didn't have a gun to their heads.
It all seemed suddenly like a sex show put on for the
audience, in this case, me. I almost expected to be asked
for my ticket.

"We were all high as hell, and none of us were sure

what really happened, but Robin found her—Koski, I mean. I think he was looking for her. We were all looking for her, at one time or another. What a sweet piece to have missed. Candy, dead, for Christ sakes."

He was really disgusting.

"Candy had an eye for all of us, too. She loved her power, knowing she was beautiful and all that. She played to every guy sooner or later. She was poor, too—I mean her family—so both Robin and Lee got their share of attention from her, you can bet. And you can also bet it was Medici killed her. He was a hot-tempered little wop in those days and hair-trigger. Got off, too, the lucky bastard. Killed her and beat the rap. Want a little?"

His question took me by surprise.

"What?"

"Want a little?" He nodded at the brunette on the floor. The girl looked at me with a matter-of-fact expression on her face.

"You can have her if you want. She's good screwing. She really is."

"No offense, miss," I said directly into her tits. "You're a delightful young woman and lovely. Any man would want you, I know. It's just that I'm happily married and deeply religious. Please understand, it's a private thing, my religion, but I live it every day." I could think of at least six people I was glad weren't there to hear that. It was all I could come up with in the awkward situation.

"Mr. Robbins, I notice that the party had one more girl than boy. Didn't people pair up in those days?"

He had to think that over. "Yeah, I suppose so."

"Well, for example, who did you go with?"

"Cuddles Bebar, I suppose."

"Who was the odd girl? Was it Candy?"

"No. No. She was Medici's date. Let's see. Lee took Marge. Stinky took Betty Huff. Hey, I guess Lynn was the odd one. Only we didn't think much about that. I mean we were just a bunch of kids having a party."

"Yes, but Lynn is awfully good-looking. Wasn't she good-looking then? And didn't she have a boyfriend, maybe someone who couldn't make the party that time?"

"Oh, sure, Lynn was a doll, right enough. I suppose she was with me, too. I mean I always liked two girls, you know. I think I took both her and Cud. Jesus, I don't know. That was a long time back." The blonde took his glass out to fill it again.

"Can you think of anyone who would want Robin Tingley killed?"

"Only Medici," he said. "Robin testified against him at the trial."

I didn't bother to correct him. When I left, the blonde was back playing with his ear. He was sipping the fresh drink. No one bothered to show me to the door. I didn't remember to ask him what he did for a living. Whatever it was, and disgusting as I found him to be, I had to admit he was doing very well.

23

Outside, I looked at my watch. It wasn't even two-thirty. I checked the address of Joyce Clueridge. At a gas station I got directions to Lake Oswego and set out. I crossed a high bridge called the Selwood Bridge over the Willamette, then headed south on a beautiful wooded street that ran high above the river. I could glimpse the water now and then out to my left through the thick trees and bushes that bordered the road. For several miles there were no houses visible, just that dark, thick, green, near-tropical growth of the Pacific Northwest, ivy, grass, bushes and trees.

It would be worth knowing where all these people were the night Tingley was killed. Mrvich had a couple of detectives working on that. What bothered me were the connections between most of the old gang and Tingley. They'd been broken years ago. Only Medici and Marnie seemed possible suspects and, as far as the present was concerned, only Marnie seemed possible. It bothered me because I'd gotten interested in the Koski killing, and the facts staring at me told me there was no connection between the two cases. That meant my excuse for pursuing this—that it *might* lead to something vital in the Tingley case—was just a damned lie, and I knew it.

At Lake Oswego, I stopped at another gas station and got directions to the Clueridge place. Lake Oswego is one of Portland's better bedrooms. Hopelessly respectable homes and yards sit block after block. Huge, towering pines and firs rise up out of the yards, and well-kept flower gardens ring many of the houses. The leaves had started to fall from the maples and alders, and they lay sodden and mealy on the roads. A threat of rain was in the air. That didn't mean it would rain. It meant you think it's going to rain, and if it doesn't, you'll think it did. I remembered that from my Seattle days.

The Clueridge house was one of the those red-brick homes built in the thirties and, because it was brick, still in good shape. A big place. The driveway swept in under a brick archway that had had to be widened as cars got bigger. There was no porch, and I parked almost in front of the door. I found the house cold-looking. No friend could live there.

In front of the house, just beyond the archway, stood my least favorite natural thing: a monkey tree. A lot of people would, had they the opportunity to eliminate one creature or piece of vegetation from the face of the earth, choose the mosquito, or the coral snake, or poison ivy, nettles, skunks—oh, you name it. But me, I'd not hesitate to choose the monkey tree. It must be the most loathsome-looking tree in all the world.

This maid was black, too, and definitely not like Lila. She was about forty, and her face was twisted by what could have been a stroke, though to me it appeared to be bitterness. Her hostility was so evident I had the urge to tell her I was not wealthy, I had many black friends, the Mercedes wasn't mine, and I worked for an Indian I liked very much. That would have melted her heart about as fast as the polar ice cap.

She showed me to a seat in a room that was very clean and neat and terribly uncomfortable. Little china dogs, about a hundred of them, were arranged on doilies on glass shelving about the room. The walls were a loathsome shade of pink, and the fireplace was a bright red brick that didn't belong with the pink or with any other color I could think of. The carpet was blue and expensive and so soft I wanted to peek under it to make sure there was flooring before I took another step. The furniture, including the chair I sat in, had a precious look about it, as if it belonged on display in an antique show. When I sat down, I was sure the chair would break.

"Mrs. Clueridge asked me to offer you whatever you wish to drink," the maid said in a voice cold enough to pour a triple slug of gin over. "A drink, sir? Coffee?"

"Coffee will be fine, thank you." The coffee came before Mrs. Clueridge. Quite a bit before. I was beginning to think I'd been tricked when Mrs. Clueridge swept in.

There are women who get better-looking as they get older, like Lynn Hammer. There are women who manage to preserve that pert girlish quality of their youth for years, like Marnie Ross Tingley. Then there are the Joyce Clueridges.

She looked at least fifteen years older than Lynn or Marnie. Her hair would have been gray if she left it alone, and she should have left it alone. She was two pounds short of being fat and many contour lines beyond being simply shapeless. She wore a pink gown that was almost as insufferable as the wall. Ruffles of white jiggled on the cuffs and collar. Faintly it reminded me of some costume I'd seen in a movie, only then it was in black and white, and someone like Billie Burke was wearing it and simpering.

OK. Don't get on me. I don't want all people to be beautiful, women or men. A lot of ugly people are fascinating, and a lot of pretty people are dull. But Joyce Clueridge looked like she thought she was beautiful, and to me she had as much character as the monkey tree outside, which had about as much character as all other monkey trees. She looked as interesting as a can of cleaning fluid.

"Mr. Barnes," she said in a high voice that was trying for elegance. "Sheriff Barnes isn't it? Lynn Hammer called. Such a surprise. Such a lovely woman. It's a shame how we drift apart over the years, isn't it? Many good friends, scattered." She sat down, and I, who'd risen to greet her, sat down, too. She was so respectable, I slipped into my diplomatic voice. I started out in a low tone of confidentiality.

"Mrs. Clueridge, I'm here on a somewhat delicate matter, and I really would appreciate your help. I realize how painful the past can be, for all of us. I've things in my past I'd just as soon forget, but under the circumstances I'm going to ask—with your permission, of course—I'm going to ask you to try to recall some things you'd probably just as soon not think about anymore." I was afraid my voice was getting too unctuous, but she seemed to think I was speaking normally. I wondered why all people couldn't talk like the Hammers, or Medici, or Mrvich or Petrov. Her reply told me why she thought my speech had been normal.

"I understand, Sheriff Barnes. I'm sure your work takes you into some forbidden corners of people's lives, where you'd just as soon not go. But it has to be that way, doesn't it? I mean, if we are to live in a world of order, we must allow those who are charged with maintaining that order to proceed with their work."

It seemed impossible she'd once been called Cuddles. Her grave white face that makeup couldn't do much for was earnestly waiting for my questions. It struck me that I knew that hairdo: Shirley Temple curls. She looked as absurd as she was.

"You're quite right, Mrs. Clueridge. That was very well put. Our work would be much easier if all citizens were as understanding and intelligent as you are." I really couldn't stand myself. "Perhaps you recall a party nineteen years ago at Cannon Beach at a home owned by Lee and Lynn Hammer's father. A girl was killed that night, Candy Koski."

She flustered a bit. "Oh, yes. My goodness. Lynn said you were investigating the death of Robin Tingley."

"I am, Mrs. Clueridge. But certain matters have led me to the Koski murder. I fear there may be a connection." I fear there is no connection at all, Mrs. Clueridge, and I'm just kidding myself. "One of the participants at that party," I went on, wondering if I'd ever used the word "participants" before, "was Robin Tingley, as I'm sure you recall. He was recently murdered in Montana."

"Goodness, what a terrible world. Murders. Rapes. Holdups. It's enough to make you think, isn't it?"

"It is indeed, Mrs. Clueridge. Mrs. Clueridge, I'm going

to ask you something I don't want to ask. But as you yourself so elegantly put it a few moments ago, I have the responsibility to ask you this question."

"I understand, Sheriff Barnes. Please proceed."

"I understand you were on the beach with Dale Robbins and Lynn Hammer when the murder happened?"

"Yes, I believe so. We were roasting wieners over an open fire, I recall. A sort of late snack, so to speak."

No, you weren't, you lying, hypocritical broad. You were doped on marijuana and drunk with booze and you were screwing Dale Robbins. I said, "Are you certain, Mrs. Clueridge? It's very important."

"Well, of course, none of us were certain exactly when the murder happened, but I'm sure when poor Candy died, we were down there on the beach roasting wieners."

"Mrs. Clueridge," I tried to make my voice soft and intimate, "do you think Vic Medici killed her?"

"This is in confidence, isn't it, Sheriff Barnes?"

"Yes, Mrs. Clueridge, it is." My voice was so earnest, I wondered how I might do in politics.

"Well, then, Sheriff Barnes, in the strictest confidence, I'll tell you that Vic Medici is certainly the one who killed Candy Koski. I have no doubt of it. He was vile-tempered and a violent man. But then, most of those people are, aren't they?"

"Those people?"

"Italians. They're not like white people, I don't care what anyone says. Haven't you known many violent Italians, Sheriff Barnes?"

"There certainly are some violent Italians in this world," I said.

"They really aren't white people, you know, but they pass for white."

"I wasn't aware of that, Mrs. Clueridge."

"Oh, yes. Look how dark they are. Think of all the violent Italians you've known in your line of work."

"Yes. I remember a lot of them over the years." I was trying to think of some, and the only one I could remember was a guy named Canvas Jaw Garricci, a welterweight who had a twelve and forty-six record before he finally called it quits. He sold newspapers at a big stand in downtown Seattle and outside the ring was just a sweet, slightly punchy slob.

"Vic Medici was a terribly violent young man. He beat up several nice boys in high school. I'm sure he murdered Candy Koski."

"Were you surprised he wasn't convicted?"

"Yes, but you know what our courts have become. They let criminals go every day. And especially those who aren't white, like the Negroes and Indians and Italians."

I hoped my feelings weren't showing. I felt like using a little violence on her, like punching her in the mouth.

"We were a strange group, about to break up. Some of us were in high school and some in college. We'd sort of banded together in high school, and the gang stayed together the first year some of us were in college. It seems odd who you are friends with, doesn't it, Sheriff Barnes? The only ones of that group I'd ever care to see again are the Hammers and the Tingleys. Sorry. Of course, only Marnie is left, isn't she? I talk to her on the phone once in a while."

I thought, yes, just those with money and respectability, right, Joyce Cuddles Bebar Clueridge? Well, people as classy as the Hammers wouldn't give you first base if they were fifteen runs ahead in the ninth. And they are.

"Mrs. Clueridge, do you think Vic Medici is capable of holding a grudge for nineteen years?"

"Oh, yes. He's capable of carrying a grudge forever."

"Do you think he could have murdered Robin Tingley after nineteen years because Robin testified against him at the trial?" I asked, already feeling a bit hopeless and remembering Tingley's testimony had helped Medici.

"Oh, yes. I'm sure of it."

"Did you testify?"

"No. None of us except Robin. We gave our statements to the police at Cannon Beach, but we weren't called on later, except for Robin."

We sat in silence for a moment.

"Can you think of anyone else who might want to murder Robin Tingley?"

"No. Of course, I haven't seen the Tingleys in ages. What was Robin doing in Montana?"

I told her. We sat in silence again.

Suddenly she said something that was almost touching. "I was pretty then. Would you like to see how I looked?"

"Of course I would, Mrs. Clueridge," I lied.

"Excuse me a moment." She pushed out of the room and in a moment was back with an old high school annual. She opened it and thumbed a couple of times. "Here," she said.

The book was opened to a page that had in large block letters the word "seniors" printed on the wide outside margin. She pointed to a photo of herself taken nearly twenty years ago. I never would have recognized her. The face was one of those meringue-pussed darlings that are in every high school.

"There I am. Joyce Bebar," she said a bit wistfully.

"Most recognizable," I said. "You haven't changed all that much."

She turned back to the juniors. "And here is Vic Medicj," she said, pointing at his photo. He was recognizable. Even then he looked tough.

She turned back to the seniors. "Lee and Lynn," she said. I looked at their two Eskimolike faces side by side. They looked fresh and alive. I found Rasmussen and Marge Appleton, who had been a doll, and Betty Huff. I had the book now, and she released her grip on it. I found Marnie and Dale Robbins. I found Candy Koski in a group picture of sophomores. Her face was so small it meant nothing. It might have been the face of Calvin Coolidge. I kept staring at the book, wondering if it held some secret. Then I realized how ridiculous I was being and put the book aside.

"Well, you've been most helpful, Mrs. Clueridge," I said. Like hell. "Thank you for your cooperation. I wish all our citizens were as helpful as you are."

"And thank you, Sheriff Barnes. I've certainly enjoyed our talk. Mary," she called. "Mary."

The hostile-looking black woman came in.

"Mary, would you show Sheriff Barnes to the door, please? Thank you again, Sheriff Barnes," she said, offering me her hand. I took it as much as I could without touching her for over a second.

"My pleasure," I said. And so help me, I bowed.

I was almost through the door of the room when something struck me as odd.

"Oh, Mrs. Clueridge. One other matter. Who of the Hammers was behind?"

"I beg your pardon?"

"Which one of the Hammers was behind in school? I mean, they were both seniors at the same time. One of them must have been behind. Which one is older?"

"Why, neither, Sheriff Barnes. Lee and Lynn Hammer are twins."

"Twins?"

"Why, yes. They were very close, the way twins are, you know."

"Thank you, Mrs. Clueridge."

At the door, just because I felt like it, I whispered to Mary, "You must really need the money."

It was the right thing to say. She burst out laughing. It made me feel good. I imagined she didn't get many laughs.

24

"Why didn't you tell me you were twins? That's the one thing I learned today, and what a hell of a piece of useless information."

Lynn laughed at my grumpy speech. "I never think of it anymore. It's no secret. All our friends know, at least our old friends. We certainly are twins, and what a couple of conspiratorial brats we were. Like all twins. We gave daddy a terrible time. Mommy, too, but not so much. We used to turn off the water when they were watering the lawn. We had a system worked out where one of us would sneak through the house and turn off the water sprinklers on the back lawn, while the other was getting scolded for turning off the sprinklers on the front lawn."

"You must have been terrific," I said. "Lots of fun."

"Two regular little gangsters."

"I've talked to all of the survivors except Betty Huff, who's in Dallas and crippled with arthritis, and Rasmussen, who's in Buffalo. I can't connect the two killings up at all." I hesitated. Lynn had her full, open face directed right at me. She was a woman a man could talk to.

I opened up with her. I told her all about Mush Heart Barnes, my career in Seattle, the stupid way I let myself get wounded, my obsessive reaction to murder. Then I told her I'd been kidding myself about the Koski and Tingley murders. I had no reason to think they were connected. I'd just gotten interested in the Koski case because it was a murder and it hadn't been solved. And I'd kidded myself into thinking it had something to do with the Tingley case.

When I finished, she looked at me with obvious admiration. "You're a right guy, Sheriff Barnes," she said. And she leaned over and kissed me. It was a nice kiss, full of affection and kindness and just a hint of sexuality in it, enough to make it a real kiss. .

"You're pretty much all right yourself," I said. The kiss reminded me again I was getting a bit hard up already after a few days away from Arlene. I looked at Lynn, hoping my expression was void of carnality, because my mind wasn't. God, but she was a good-looking woman, and a good woman. Kind, understanding, with real warmth, a fine sense of humor. For just a moment I thought about how it would be to have her for a wife. Then I thought how good it would be to have her. Then, with some effort, I focused on the problems at hand.

"I suppose I'll have to look to the recent past about Tingley. Can you tell me anything? You knew him for a long time. What was he like? Did he have a lot of friends? Any enemies?"

"No enemies I know of. Robin was a sort of aristocrat, in the best sense. He really cared for other people. He had a dignity about him. Even in high school. He was the sort of boy other boys respected. Not because he was tough, you know, like Vic Medici. That kind of guy gets all sorts of admirers in high school. Robin had a sort of quiet depth, I guess you'd say, something others noticed and respected. He was a serious and kindly boy. Not weak, mind you. He was brave. He even stood up to Vic Medici once, and Vic backed down."

I picked up on that. "Were you there? Can you tell me about it?"

"I was there, yes. It was at a dance, and some girl was involved. Oh, hell, of course. It was Candy."

I sat forward. Maybe. Just maybe. "What happened?"

"I'm trying to remember. I think Vic got mad because Robin cut in on him a couple of times. Vic started to give Robin a bad time. A bunch of us crowded around. Vic invited Robin outside. Then Robin said something like, 'OK, Vic, I'll go outside with you, and I'll fight you and I'll probably get beaten, but that won't make it right. This is a dance, and cutting in is one of the rules. All it really means is you can't live within the rules like others'—or something like that. He said it with such poise and dignity that Vic told him to forget it. I think Vic was sensitive; his father was a garbage collector, and Vic felt some kind of deep—oh, shame, maybe, about it.

"Robin wasn't from real big money like Lee and I, and Marnie, too, but his folks did all right. Oh, I'm making it sound awful. It wasn't like that. He didn't hold himself above anybody. It was Vic who felt himself from some lower order. Robin hit him where he hurt. Vic was embarrassed in front of the other kids. Robin had called attention to his inability to handle anything except with his fists. I don't think anybody else could have brought it off, none of the other boys. Vic would have beaten them up good. But Robin had that special quality. He could make a speech like that stick."

"Was he insightful? I mean, he sounds like a first-rate psychologist. Was he?"

"In a way, I suppose. He had a brother who's a psychiatrist, you know."

I thought I had remembered a brother being mentioned, but I wasn't sure. "What's his name?"

"Ralph Tingley. He practices here in town. He was in Los Angeles for several years. He moved back here about four years ago. He's older than Robin by a couple of years. By the way, in case you're wondering, he isn't the doctor who treats Marnie."

"I hope not," I said. "He must be home now. Can I call him, do you think?"

"Sure. He's a nice guy. I don't know him real well, but he was here a couple of times with Robin before we put Robin in charge of the plant at Plains—I mean the mill."

She went and got me a phone number. Before I could call, Mrvich called and invited me to lunch the next day at Rose's. He said Petrov had found out some more stuff and would meet us there.

Then I got hold of Ralph Tingley. He had a nice voice over the phone. I told him what I wanted, to talk about his brother, that it might help me to solve his murder. He agreed to see me in his office the following morning.

We ate when Lee got home from the office, which was after eight. A violent rainstorm was pelting the windows, and Mycroft had a fire ready after dinner in the large study at the far end of the wing opposite the one where my room was.

The three of us sipped brandy until after eleven, and we chatted about anything that occurred to us, except for the murders of Koski and Tingley. Those seemed off limits that night. It was a night to relax around a fire and forget about the awful things we do to each other.

The brandy did its work. I went to bed thinking that Vic Medici, all-city halfback, tough guy, had been put down by Robin Tingley in front of a lot of others. Do people harbor something like that for nearly twenty years and then one day murder because of it? You're damn right they do.

25

I was ushered into Dr. Ralph Tingley's office at ten-thirty. A patient had just run out past me, a young girl who was blushing with embarrassment, tears of shame running down her contorted face. I suppose psychiatrists see that all the time. Someone who tells them something he or she has never told anyone before. Choking it up through a throat that tried to strangle it back and wouldn't. Then the awful knowledge that the rotten person he or she was, was out now, and the reaction.

"Come in, Mr. Barnes. I'm Dr. Tingley." He held out his hand and gave me a firm shake. He was taller than I remember Robin being, but he looked a bit like Robin, same quiet, confident face. He was less expressive, though. His face seemed more like a mask. "Please sit down."

He went back behind his desk and sat down and studied me. I felt a bit like a patient. His office was almost spare. It wasn't very big, and the closest thing to display was his degrees under glass that hung on an otherwise blank wall. I saw he had graduated from medical school at the University of Michigan and had studied psychiatry at the University of Illinois. He was a psychoanalyst, not just a psychiatrist. A lot of schooling.

"It's kind of you to give me the time," I said. "I know you're busy."

He didn't gesture or say anything. I felt a bit awkward.

"I wondered if you could tell me something about your brother. I've been investigating the possibility that the Koski killing nineteen years ago might be tied in. Now I'm starting to think it may be the work of someone with a more recent motive. Can you help me at all? What was he like? Did he have enemies? That sort of thing."

"I hadn't seen Robin for nearly a year," he said, "but I'm sure he had no enemies."

"What about his wife?"

"Marnie?" He sat there. "Marnie? Are you asking if she could have killed him?"

"In a way. I'm asking you to tell me anything you think of that can help me."

"Have you met Marnie?"

"Yes." I found myself resenting some superiority he seemed to feel.

"What was your reaction?" He smiled at me. It was meant as a friendly smile, but I didn't take it that way. I thought I'd better impress him with honesty, hoping it would loosen him up.

"She had me so steamed up I damned near raped her," I said. "What's more, I wasn't quite sure how she was doing it, though I saw a couple of tricks she was pulling."

He studied me a bit longer. Something close to human had come into his eyes.

"I'll tell you something about the study of psychiatry,"

he said. "Any man who studies psychiatry is warned to be on the lookout for undue sexual excitement when a woman patient comes to see him the first time. If a woman comes to see a doctor and the doctor finds himself unaccountably turned on, there's a very good chance the woman is an hysteric. She has developed special ways to direct attention and energy toward herself."

"Are you saying Marnie Tingley is hysterical?"

"I'm only telling you about the study of psychiatry and one of the things we are cautioned about. The males, that is."

He sat back for a moment. We looked at each other.

"Is an hysteric capable of murder?"

"Almost anyone is."

"I know. But would an hysteric be more likely to kill?" He shrugged. "Impossible to say."

"Is there anything else you can tell me about Robin?"

"Only that our profession lost a good man when he didn't go into medicine. He would have been an excellent psychiatrist. He had sharp insights into people. He was very bright."

I sensed the interview was over when his buzzer buzzed and a voice said a Mr. Something-or-other was here now. "Thank you, Rhonda," he said.

I said, "Thank you, doctor," and went out to find Rose's Delicatessen.

26

Rick Petrov turned out to be as fast as Mrvich. I'd just put away a pastrami sandwich that should have been given an award, chasing it with a worthy beer. Mrvich was licking up the last of some chopped liver, and Petrov had polished off some lox and cream cheese on rye.

Petrov threw a photo reproduction of an old editorial at me. It looked a little ghostly sitting there.

"This is what did it," he said. "A hell of an inflammatory editorial that appeared in the *Seaside Beacon*. That's a newspaper they used to have down there. It died about twelve years ago. Medici had been arraigned, but when this appeared, Art Matthew had no trouble getting a change of venue. He argued in front of the judge in Astoria that a fair trial in Clatsop County was impossible. The judge agreed. So they got the trial moved to Portland.

"The editor of the paper was a guy named Leo Colobrite. He's sort of retired now, runs a motel in Seaside called the Sea Bass Motel. Funny thing is that the damned thing is so blatant. Jesus, you'd think anyone would know better. Once Matthew got the prosecution off their home field, he destroyed them. They might have made it stick in Clatsop County. Feeling was already running high against the kids from Portland who came down to raise hell. A couple of years later, the Seaside riots erupted. But they had been coming for a long time."

I remembered reading about the Seaside riots—were they in the early sixties? Now, like most trouble, a meaningless piece of history. I remembered reading some article about their deep significance. Everything that makes headlines has some deep significance these days. The interpretation of that significance usually appears about ten seconds after the event. I read the editorial:

MUST WE PUT UP WITH THIS?

The people of Clatsop County have put up with a lot the last few years. Wild parties. Destruction of property. Unwanted interruptions of our basically peaceful existence. The young people of Portland seem once a year to devote themselves to wreaking havoc with our lives.

Now the most bizarre insult of all to decent citizens: a necrophiliac murder. A young man so driven and twisted by lust that he found himself capable and willing to murder a sixteen-year-old girl simply to have relations with her. If he couldn't have her alive, he'd have her dead. This is too much for any God-fearing community to tolerate.

The *Seaside Beacon* calls for swift and unremitting justice, the conviction and sentencing of the guilty party. No people should be called on to endure a crime of such heinous proportions that it sickens the very soul of the community.

Must we put up with this? The one possible answer, the only possible answer, cries out in righteous indignation.

So much for the passions of editorial writing in 1959. I was really surprised the paper had printed it.

"Jesus," I said. "That's pouring it on. They must have been bananas, putting a thing like that in the paper."

"It could have been just dumb small-town stuff," Mrvich said. "One of those cases where some punk editorial writer gets a sense of power and cuts loose, not thinking about the law or the consequences."

"It happens," Rick said. His sad Russian eyes held on the editorial for a moment. "What bothers me is that it looks almost put up."

"How do you mean?" I asked.

"Well, it almost looks like Art Matthew wrote it himself and got them to print it. Like it's a plant put there just to get the trial switched to Portland. It really is too obvious in its effect. I can't believe someone didn't know what the upshot would be." He clicked his tongue against the silver fillings in his front teeth.

"Maybe I ought to go down and talk to this Colobrite," I said.

"I can't offer you any help down there," Mrvich said. "But I can call an ex-Portland cop who works for the sheriff and tell him you're coming. He's in Astoria. A nice guy named Sam Boose. He might come down and give you a hand if anyone gives you a bad time."

"I'd appreciate it, Murv," I said. Then I told them about the way Tingley had humiliated Medici years before at a dance. "I've known that kind of thing to fester that long and then cause trouble," I added. "Medici seems too bright for that to have happened, but you can't tell. I'm off this afternoon to ask him who paid his lawyer's fees in 1959."

"Think he'll tell you?"

I shrugged. "He was awfully candid on first meeting."

"Don't mess with him," Mrvich said. "He's tough. I can send over some hard muscle in plain clothes if you want."

"No. I'll be all right. I only get tough with weak old ladies."

"Smart," Rick Petrov said. "Very smart."

27

I'd found a parking spot near the Ironfast Building and was just getting out of the car when T. Curtoise Lamarr came out onto the street carrying a briefcase. He looked around as if he thought he was being trailed by an international spy. He was dressed in green today. His suit, shirt, tie and shoes were various complementary shades of green. He wore a green porkpie hat that seemed out of date. I watched him walk in a phony way that was suppose to accentuate his masculinity. His shoulders moved a little too much. He walked away from me about a hundred feet and got into a yellow Porsche. For no reason I could think of, I followed him.

The Porsche pulled out like a car trying to get a good start in a race. I had to speed up to keep him in sight. He went a couple of blocks south, then swung onto the freeway system that took us over the Willamette River. After his initial melodramatic takeoff, he held the speed within ten miles of the limit. Keeping up with the Porsche took no effort on the part of the blue Mercedes. I was glad I had the Mercedes. Even if he spotted the car, he'd never guess it was me, an expensive car like that with Oregon plates. But I didn't expect him even to spot the car. People like T. Curtoise Lamarr were too interested in being tailed in their fantasies ever to notice it happening in real life. Right now he probably thought he was Humphrey Bogart and that Peter Lorre was behind him in a Rolls Royce.

He stayed at ten miles over the limit, no doubt to make himself feel more daring and manly. We headed north on the freeway after crossing the Willamette. Could we be headed for Seattle? For all the progress I was making on the Tingley killing, I might as well go to Seattle and say hello to some old friends.

We crossed the Columbia into Washington. Was T. Curtoise Lamarr really his name? It seemed as phony as everything else about him. We took the Vancouver exit and drove straight west through the business district. In about ten minutes the houses started to string out between vacant lots. Houses became scarcer and scarcer. A gray sky swept west, and there was in it, and in the huge trees a mile or so in front of us, a suggestion that in a few miles the world would end.

I worried a bit that he'd spot me, now that the congestion was behind us. Once I whipped around the block and came back one street further west, confident I wouldn't lose the yellow Porsche in this sparsely populated area. I didn't. It was about two blocks ahead. Parked.

I stopped a block back and got out. The wind was unexpectedly strong. I hadn't felt it in the solidly built Mercedes. I buttoned my coat. A smell of threatening rain was in the air. I walked toward the Porsche. Lamarr wasn't in it.

At the end of the street, a field of bending high grass and no buildings extended about a half mile to where the giant trees started. The trees were mostly alders. As I got closer to the Porsche, I could see the house he'd parked beside. It seemed to be the last house in Vancouver, the last house west in the nation. It was a faded house. The paint had once been yellow, but now the color was nameless. I guessed it had been built in the late twenties. The closest house to it was across the street and back toward town, at least five hundred feet away, and it appeared empty.

A cat who looked like a superb survivor ran across the street. He looked tough enough to eat people and smile while he did it. With the gray sky and the wind and the empty field, I got one of those lonely chills you get when you think you've found a sad, sad place, a place where loneliness goes when it leaves the cities. There was something so damned forlorn about it all. If the temperature had been eighty, I still would have felt cold.

The lawn of the once-yellow house had stopped being a lawn a long time ago. It was covered with tall grass and weeds that jittered in the wind. The mailbox had no name on it. I peeked in. No letters. I had the feeling there were never any letters. I had the feeling even the IRS didn't know about this place. I wondered if anyone inside could see me. The shades were drawn on all the windows. They were old-fashioned, green pull-down blinds. No curtains.

I walked across the tall grass to a garage that had been built when cars were a lot smaller. I looked into the garage. The door was missing. A chicken scratched inside. A Plymouth, 1938 or '39, black, was sitting on blocks. The engine was torn down. From the rust on the parts, someone had given up decades ago trying to repair the old car.

I walked to the house. I tried to peek in a window, but the green pull-down shade didn't give me a chance. I stepped to the next window. This blind had a couple of holes in it, and I looked through one. I could see Lamarr, his back to me, talking to someone. By shifting my eye left, I saw a man, maybe in his forties, with a simple, innocent grin on his face. He was dressed in old-fashioned overalls. He was about five eleven, a little shorter than Lamarr, and he hadn't shaved in a couple of days. He was overweight, as if he didn't eat anything but fried foods.

He offered a bottle of wine to Lamarr. Lamarr gestured it away. It was a cheap Washington State wine and looked like apple or muscatel. Even with Lamarr's back to me, I thought I sensed some superiority in his refusal of the wine. The man with the wine looked hurt. His dark face clouded like a child's, and I thought he was going to cry. Then he started to grin again. He looked very easy to hurt, the perfect target for someone like Lamarr who had to feel better than somebody.

The man with the wine started to dance. It was a clumsy dance but honestly joyful. A third party seemed to be in the room, someone the other two turned toward slightly and whom I couldn't see. Lamarr waved good-bye to the third party and walked out, carrying his briefcase.

I slipped around to the back of the house. I heard the Porsche start and then squeal away. I walked to the front of the house and knocked. No one came. The door was slightly open. I pushed it and stepped in.

I was in a parlor. An old piano stood against the wall, and piled on it were stacks of sheet music. On top of one of the piles was "Silver Threads Among the Gold." On top of another pile was "My Wild Irish Rose." The sheet music had turned a sickly cream color with age. No one had dusted the piano in some time. I heard singing.

I went into the next room. Empty. The living room. No rugs or carpeting. Just bare floor and one shabby green couch and one equally shabby plush-red chair. The singing was coming from the next room. I walked in quietly. It was the kitchen. The dark-faced man with the wine was singing "We're in the Money." A woman with snagged brown teeth was sitting in a high wooden chair clapping her hands. Neither of them had any sense of rhythm. The floor was covered by ancient linoleum with tears in it. A single light bulb hung down from the ceiling. It was burning with a harsh white glow. All the windows were closed off by green blinds so no daylight could get in. I had the feeling daylight never got in.

The woman was well beyond sixty. She was overweight, too, and had stockings rolled down to her ankles. Her legs were blotched with dark patches that looked like bruises. She was grinning the same innocent grin I'd seen on the face of the man with the wine, who was dancing and throwing twenty-dollar bills high in the air and watching them fall to the floor. He had no socks on under his shoes and no laces in his shoes. When he ran out of money, he scooped some more up from the floor and started raining it over the room again. The old woman cackled. Then they saw me in the doorway.

"Come in, sir," the man said. "Come in. Mother, someone's come to see us." They both seemed terribly pleased.

"Good. Good," the old woman said. "Robert, give our guest a glass of wine." Her left eye had a tic. Involuntarily she winked at me. Robert poured some wine in a cup and handed it to me.

I took it and thanked him.

"Mother, isn't this nice? First, Mr. Lamarr and now—"

"Barnes," I said with a tenderness that came naturally.

I took a sip of the wine and smiled at them. The wine didn't make smiling that easy.

"You're always welcome here, Mr. Barnes. Plenty of wine and every so often plenty of money." A week's dishes were piled in the sink. A steady drip of cold water on the top plate was causing a steady, slow runoff down the stack that disappeared somewhere under some cups and a frying pan. The old woman cackled, "Lots of money."

"Lots of money. Lots of wine. We're going to have a hell of a time," Robert recited in verse.

"That's a good one, Robert," Mother said. "How does that go again?" She winked.

"Lots of money. Lots of wine. What's so funny out of tune?" Robert said. He slapped his thigh. "I keep the chicken guessing. Yes, sir. No, ma'am."

"He's crazy, Robert is. He just came home to me a few days ago. He was in the hospital again, weren't you, Robert?" She winked at Robert.

"Lots of money. Lots of fun. Lots of where the hell's the wine," he said and howled with laughter. He started to pick up the money. There was quite a bit to pick up. I counted about five hundred dollars as best I could without looking like I was counting.

"No one ever comes to see us anymore," Mother said. "Except Mr. Lamarr. Mr. Lamarr comes every month with money, doesn't he, Robert?"

"Sweet Sally O'Brien," Robert said.

"Mr. Lamarr is very nice," Mother said.

Robert began to cry. I had the feeling anyone who dropped by would seem nice.

"Now. Now. Robert. Stop your crying or we won't have our dance," Mother said.

Robert broke into his grin again. "Dance. Dance," he said.

"Does Mr. Lamarr always bring money?" I asked.

"Oh, yes. My goodness, Mr. Lamarr brings us five hundred dollars every month. But he doesn't stay long, does he, Robert?"

"I wonder if he likes us?" Robert said.

"I'm sure he does," I put in.

"Do you think so? Really?" Robert grinned even more. "Mother, Mr. Barnes thinks Mr. Lamarr likes us."

"I'm sure of it, Robert. If he didn't like us, he wouldn't give us all that money, would he?"

Robert threw the money up in the air and started to jig.

"He keeps going to the hospital and coming home," Mother said. "I think those places do something to your mind."

I gulped the wine down as fast as I could, hoping to avoid the taste that way. I didn't.

"Dance. Dance," Robert cried.

"Let's all dance," Mother said. "Come on, Mr. Barnes. No one ever comes to dance with us anymore."

We locked arms in a three-person circle and started to dance. Mother hummed a few bars of "Margie." Robert started to weep. We put our heads together and kept slowly turning to our right.

"Don't cry, Robert." I was surprised I was the one who said it.

"Life's very sad," Robert said. "That's why I cry a lot. I'm crazy, and we don't have any friends. Only Mr. Lamarr comes. I'll go back to the hospital. The doctor doesn't like me to cry."

"What's your last name, Robert?" I didn't have to ask.

"Koski. Robert Koski, and this is my mother, Madeline. You'll come and see us a lot and dance with us, won't you, Mr. Barnes? You don't have to bring any money, long as Mr. Lamarr brings it. All you have to do is come see us and dance."

We kept turning, the three of us, under the harsh white light bulb.

"He's crazy, Robert is," Madeline Koski said and winked.

Maybe it was the wine or the sad color of the sky. I got the car started, and I thought of my father who came home one night, having lost his job, sitting there crying and my mother trying to comfort him. I thought of a black man in Seattle who didn't want to be a child molester and couldn't stop being one and who told me he was going to take his own life and did, by setting himself afire. I thought of a drowned little girl in a lake in Seattle and the mother screaming as we pulled her child's body from the water.

I thought of a world where life is always too hard, where we are asked to endure more than we can ever really bear. I bawled like a baby for no one in particular and for all of us.

28

         I stopped in Portland to get some gas and called Stallion Enterprises from a pay phone. I was told that Mr. Medici was in Los Angeles on business and would return in two days. I had several questions now. Who paid his legal fees nineteen years ago? Did he still feel anything about the put-down he'd suffered from Robin Tingley at a dance nearly twenty years ago? Why was he paying the Koski family five hundred dollars a month? Was that guilt? Had he killed Candy in a fit of rage and was he trying to make up for it? He wasn't looking as good as he once had.

Lynn Hammer cooked two ducks. They were excellent, but the meal itself was an odd one. Marnie Ross Tingley had been invited. Lee was absorbed in some business deals and sat silent most of the evening. Mike Ponce wasn't there.

Marnie Tingley wasn't the least bit sexy that night. She was subdued and even a bit sullen. She sent out no signals that I picked up.

Lynn easily dominated the evening with her bright talk. Mostly she directed her chatter at me. That was fine with me. I liked her best of the people there. Once in a while she would turn her gaze on Marnie, as if she was checking on her. Once she said to Marnie, "Marnie. Eat your meat," and Marnie sullenly picked at her duck.

I was glad when the dinner was over. It was uncomfortable with Lee abstracted, Marnie repressed and just Lynn and me to carry on. It was like eating with someone you like very much and having two strangers at the table with you. As soon as I could, I excused myself to make some calls.

I called Mrvich first. I told him about the day in Vancouver—or outside Vancouver in nowhere. He listened hard. I could tell that without seeing him. He usually listens hard.

"Could it be guilt? That's a possibilty, isn't it?"

"Sure could," he said. "He may have felt bad he got away with something long ago, and now he wants to make up for it. Well, it's happened before. I had a case like that a couple of years ago. Only the guy didn't do it. I mean the murder. He just felt bad about it and kept paying the victim's family money. Some people absorb guilt that isn't theirs, especially people with strong religious backgrounds. Medici was Catholic, I suppose. He could be putting himself on the cross. I'll have my best man look into it. We may question him a bit."

"I'm headed down to interview Colobrite tomorrow in Seaside. I'd sure as hell like to know more about that editorial, who wrote it, how it came to be printed. And I've got another question for Rick. Do you have a home phone for him?"

Mrvich gave a number from memory. "I'll call Sam Boose in Astoria and let him know you're coming. Just a minute, Al." I waited a moment. "Here's an Astoria number for Boose, just in case." He gave me the number. I jotted it down next to Petrov's.

We said our good-byes, and I called Petrov.

"Rick? Al Barnes. A question. Was Art Matthew capable of paying a witness to lie?"

Rick Petrov whistled. "What are you thinking?"

"Look, a guy named Desk turned up at the trial and said he'd gotten into a fight with Medici outside a tavern in Cannon Beach, and that's what accounted for Medici's skinned knuckles. OK. Today I found out Medici is paying the Koski family five hundred a month on the side. I don't even think they know it's coming from Medici. A creep named Lamarr brings it out to them. He works for Medici."

"I get it. And if it's blood money, then maybe Medici was guilty, and maybe Desk was a plant. Any bruises from a fight would have healed by the time they went to trial. Jesus. I suppose we'd better find out if Medici said anything about the fight to the police when he was being questioned."

"What about Matthew? Was he capable of pulling that?"

"I doubt it. He wanted to win in the worst way, but winning by breaking the game rules isn't winning, at least not in some books. I tell you one thing I'm sure of. If Matthew used a paid witness, the witness wasn't paid with Matthew's money. Not only is that too risky, Matthew wouldn't have shit in a masochist's face. Generosity was not his strong suit. If Desk was paid, someone else put up the money."

"So now we got another question. Who paid Desk to lie on the stand?"

"Don't forget the first question. Did Desk lie on the stand?"

I waited for him to think. Finally he said. "Let me study the transcript again. I can't remember everything in it. The question now is, when Desk testified, did the prosecution raise the point that no fight with Desk had been mentioned by Medici during police questioning? If not, then it could mean one of two things. One is that Medici did mention the fight to the cops. The other is that the prosecutor should have been raising chinchillas. I'll get back to you."

I looked for the number of a Clarence Desk in the Portland phone book. I couldn't find a listing. I called Montana. Arlene first.

We traded some sexual repartee. I swore I'd been faithful to her. She said I'd say that no matter what, just to save my life. I said you're damn right I would.

"Some odd news here, lover," she said. "Manny Sanderson is missing. No one has seen him in two days. Red's pissed when he isn't worried."

After a little more discussion and some vicarious sex that got so intense I thought I could taste her tongue in the mouthpiece, I hung up and dialed Yellow Bear.

I told him everything I could think of.

"Jesus Christ," he growled, "sounds like you're on the wrong case. Isn't it Tingley who got killed here, and isn't it his killer we're after? What's all this shit about Candy Koski?"

"It may fit," I said, trying to sound as if I believed it.

"The problem I'm having is finding some more recent connections of Tingley to Medici. It looks like they parted company years ago and hadn't given each other a second thought in a long time. But if Medici really did kill the Koski girl, and he looks better for that one every minute, then it's just possible that he feared Tingley knew it, and for some reason that had nothing to do with anything in Montana, the thing came up again. Let's say Desk lied on the stand and came back years later to blackmail Medici. Medici refused to pay but got worried and realized that Tingley could be a cooperative witness—that together Tingley and Desk could nail him for it."

"Wait. Wait. What in hell are you talking about? If Medici has been tried already, he must know he can't be tried again."

I felt awfully stupid. I went silent for a minute, then managed to salvage something. "I've sent Marnie Tingley's photo to you, to show to Mitter, that kid in the gas station. Maybe he can I.D. her as the driver of that green car with Oregon plates. It should be there tomorrow."

"OK. That fucking Sanderson's missing."

"Arlene told me."

"Two days now. I don't think the teenagers know yet. When they find out, Plains will be lots of fun—for them. At least that creep kept the kids shitting their pants, and maybe fear isn't the best keeper of order, but there are days you welcome it."

"Sooner or later, you get worse problems, though."

"I know it. But peace is something you got to enjoy while you got it."

"With a guy like Sanderson, that peace is about as durable as the Czar's in 1917."

"OK. I admit he's a shit. I inherited him. And I don't like having a cop like that on the staff. But he knows the county and, damn it all, he's done some good police work up here. Give him the credit he's got coming. Right now I'd like to know where the fuck he is."

When I hung up he was still grumbling. It sounded like a cigar was in his mouth. I went back to the table where they'd been having coffee when I left. No one was there. I found Lynn in the kitchen, stacking the dishwasher.

"Lee had to go back to the office. Marnie went home early. What's with you these days, Sheriff Barnes?"

"I got to go to Seaside tomorrow," I said, pouring myself a cup of coffee. "I've got to talk to a man named Colobrite. He used to edit a newspaper called the *Seaside Beacon*. It's out of business."

"Oh, God. Let me go with you. I'm getting rummy here. I never could stand those damned social affairs wealthy women keep themselves occupied with. They bore the hell out of me."

"I'd love it if you came." I had to admit I was thinking about that kiss. Let's face it. Possibilities are seductive in their own right.

"All I've got to do is go to movies, read, watch TV and keep Marnie in line."

"Keep her in line?"

"I sort of mother her, her drinking and all."

"She hides her drinking very well," I said. "She doesn't seem like an alcoholic."

"She is, though. Through and through. Has been for years. Part of it is her background. She grew up with money, and she keeps up her appearance."

"She sure does."

"Keep your mind on your detective work, Sheriff Barnes."

"Does she have money?"

"Loaded. Probably has more than we have."

"Then she wouldn't gain by Robin Tingley's death?"

"My God, no. She has scads."

"Cannon Beach is near Seaside, isn't it?"

"Few miles."

"Can you show me the house where the Koski killing happened?"

"Sure. But I doubt we can go in. Someone lives there now. Daddy sold it a couple of years after the murder. We never used it again. But I'll sure show you where it happened." She laughed. "I don't think you'll find any clues."

"I just like to visualize things," I said.

29

Seaside turned out to be a quiet town that looked like it could get noisy. We were lucky. A bright October sun had stuck with us all the way. We entered Seaside, and it was like a lot of other American towns—junky. The usual monuments of something that may, given the peculiarity of history, come to be called civilization. Motels with neon signs already lit up, saying "vacancy" and "yes." Seafood restaurants, most of them shut down. Souvenir shops. Hamburger and hot dog joints. A Kentucky-fried-chicken place. Pizza stands. I glimpsed a carnival ground with dead rides standing very still in the early afternoon sun. Why does a Ferris wheel seem more still when it's stopped than a car does?

We drove into a gas station and asked direction to the Sea Bass Motel. The attendant looked like he didn't want to be working there. I realized that his obvious resentment of me was because I looked privileged. It struck me I was driving a Mercedes and had a lovely, classy-looking brunette by my side. I must have seemed like a king to that poor kid.

I got a glimpse now and then of the ocean off to our left. I loved it. Later I'd stand on the beach and stare a long time into the void and pretend I was thinking deep thoughts about life and death. The ocean does that to me. It gives me license for all sorts of poses.

We turned according to the surly instructions we'd gotten from the gas station attendant and turned again. Now the ocean was on our right but hidden behind a low hill with modest houses and driftwood carvings in the yards. Lynn pointed ahead. "There it is."

The Sea Bass Motel was a dark-brown, stained, wooden structure that looked fairly recent. The units were connected in a long, dark, L-shaped row. The first unit on the right as we pulled in had a sign above the door in red neon,

126

"Office." A big neon sign high over that blinked on and off: Sea Bass Motel. And below the name in small, steady letters, also red neon: "Vacancy." The name was worked in blue and green letters, I suppose to suggest the sea, and swimming about behind the words Sea Bass Motel was a red neon fish that looked like a salmon.

It crossed my mind that Lynn was there, and this was a motel and—well, I could do worse than make love to and ultimately marry a charming, wealthy woman. I put those thoughts away as being bad. I had a good woman. Don't hurt her, you crumb.

"Is it OK if I'm with you when you question him?"

"Technically, you're a suspect. You might have killed Candy Koski, you know."

"But you don't think so or you wouldn't have invited me along."

"You're right. What makes you so smart?" Something else crossed my mind. "Listen, before we go in, I want to ask you something about that night. There was one more woman than man, I mean girl than boy. Someone said you were the odd one. Is that right? Was there a pairing, and were you the odd one?"

"God, I can't think. Let's see. I suppose the only real pairings were Robin and Marnie, and Candy and Vic. I think we weren't all that organized, really. I often went out with Dale Robbins. But he liked two girls, and, what the hell, when you're partying, it doesn't make all that much difference. Cud and I often ended up with Dale. We didn't think that much about it."

"He still likes two girls," I said. I told her about the two half-naked young things I had found with him at his house.

"Good old Dale. Never let the traditions die."

We walked into the office. When no one came, I rang a bell. Slowly a man in his early sixties or late fifties came into the room, parts of a nap still in his eyes. His hair, what little he had, was white. His eyes were a heavy brown color, and not very big as eyes went. He had a long nose and a small mouth. He looked like he hadn't trusted anyone in years. He was about five ten and a hundred sixty. I doubt he ever lost or gained weight.

"Hello, folks," he said with a professional cheerfulness. "Want a room?"

"Are you Mr. Leo Colobrite?"

Though he said, "That's right," as if candor came naturally to him, his small eyes got just a bit smaller.

"Mr. Colobrite, my name is Barnes, and this is my friend, Lynn Hammer. I'm investigating a murder that took place in Montana a couple of weeks ago, and I'd appreciate your help."

He stopped all movement. "How can I help you? I've never been in Montana."

I put down the photocopy of the old editorial on the desk. He barely glanced at it. "You used to be editor of a paper here, the *Seaside Beacon*. This editorial appeared in it, and as a result, a murder trial was switched from Astoria to Portland." He regarded me with no trust at all.

"Do you have any authority here?"

"No, but I can get it with one phone call."

The scene was getting heavy. Outside, a gull gave that two-note call they have. It seemed far away.

"This was a murder a long time ago," he said. "What in hell has that to do with a murder thousands of miles away today?"

"It's only five hundred miles if you're in Portland, maybe not even that. And the victim in Montana was a witness in this case, nineteen years ago."

"Fuck them," he said with unexpected venom. "I wish they was all dead."

"I wonder if you mean her, too," I said, pointing at Lynn. "She was a member of that party."

He looked at Lynn without comment. He was beyond embarrassment.

"Did you write this, Mr. Colobrite?"

"Hell, no, I didn't write it. Why would I? It helped get the bastard off. What was his name?"

"Medici."

"Yeah, Medici. Wop bastard. If we'd have tried him in Astoria, we'd have had his ass. Instead, this goddam editorial, and the trial gets switched to Portland and the murdering son of a bitch gets off scot-free with a little legal hocus-pocus."

I thought, yes, those sinful city people, but you, sweetheart, you are so damned righteous.

"Well, why did you publish it, then? You were editor."

"I didn't print that. I was out of town on a special assignment for the boss. Harry Bird wrote it and printed it."

"Who's Harry Bird?"

"He was assistant editor. We only had five people. Harry wrote most of the editorials. He wrote this and printed it, the dumb bastard. It's a wonder we didn't get sued for our shorts. What a fathead that Harry was."

"Where is he now, Mr. Colobrite?"

"Who knows? Who cares? The drunk bastard. He was drunk all the time, even when he wrote the editorials. Thought he was hot shit as a writer. I had to edit everything he wrote, the prick. Last I heard, he was on skid row in Portland, bumming quarters for lousy wine. I should have stayed and watched him. What an idiot. Those fucking kids ruined this town. This was a nice town once. Peaceful. Quiet. Then every spring these kids came down from Portland—"

"Excuse me, but this really didn't happen here, the murder, I mean. It happened in Cannon Beach."

"Sure, because that was a richer crowd and could afford to be exclusive, but it was the same thing. A bunch of punks raising hell. We should have nailed that wop for that killing."

We left him with his bitterness. His face was petulant through the glass as we drove off.

"I'll bet you didn't know you had fans like that," I said to Lynn.

She wasn't saying anything. She seemed to be thinking about how much hate their little party that had started out as only some teenage fun had ignited and how it was still burning in an aging little man who ran a motel.

30

I drove back a few miles toward Portland, then swung right down a heavily wooded road for about four miles. Just where we first glimpsed the ocean again, a road cut away down a hill for Cannon Beach. We took a couple of turns and came out at the bottom, past a couple of motels and a few private homes. We crossed a bridge over a slow-moving river that looked dark, fishless and uninteresting. We passed a school, a restaurant, some homes. We took a couple of sharp turns and found ourselves on the main street of Cannon Beach.

Cannon Beach was trying hard not to be Seaside and seemed to be making it. Many of the shops and bars were painted a uniform gray and blue. The place looked planned and orderly. It looked a bit like a town deliberately built for the privileged, but over the years, through carlessness, some commoners had managed to move in. I wondered if I disliked the junky American style of Seaside more than I disliked the pretentious attempt to avoid it.

Lynn directed me through the town, and as we left it we climbed a short hill going south and soon started passing homes that lined short roads going east and west off the main highway. We drove only about five blocks in that area before Lynn told me to take the next right and to drive to the end and park.

Every lot on the road seemed to have a house. The houses were big frame structures, several of them unpainted, and the lawns and flower beds were not kept up very well. I imagined people used the houses only during some of the summer months. The rest of the time they just sat empty. Few had a car in the yard, and most looked shut down. I imagined them very cold and damp inside.

I parked at the end of the street. A big sand dune was in front of us, but to the sides of it I could see out to the ocean rolling relentlessly in. Small waves, maybe three feet high at the most, crashed white onto the sand and crawled east, spreading out thinner and thinner until the supply ran out and the water eased back to collect itself for another try to take over the world.

A big stand of Scotch broom went several yards north up the shore. We stepped out. The house on our left turned out to be the one.

"We felt so damned exclusive coming here when everyone else was headed for Seaside. God, what dreadful little snobs we were. There it is."

We stood and looked at the big frame house. It had an old-fashioned porch and looked like it had been built in the early thirties, or even before. It wasn't painted. The outside was cedar shake, like a lot of houses near the ocean. Two old-fashioned, large bay windows stood on either side of the dark-brown door. The roofed porch made the rest of the house look like it was sitting far back in a cave.

"Daddy sold it a little after the trial was over. It's probably had a dozen owners since then. It was the only house on this street. The rest was woods. We had real privacy. Now look at it. The woods gone. All houses from here to the highway."

"Do you think we might go in?"

"I doubt it. The place looks empty. Probably someone's summer house. It must still be considered a good buy with nothing between it and the water except the beach."

We walked up on the porch and knocked. No one answered. After a few minutes Lynn walked to the left bay window and peered in. "There's where Candy's body was found. It's the living room, still."

I looked in and put up a hand to screen off the light that glared off the window. I saw a couch and a couple of chairs, a lamp and some magazines on a table. Nothing said anything to me.

Lynn shuddered at my side. "God, that was awful. Al, it was a terrible night. We were so scared and bewildered. No one knew what to do."

I nodded. We walked to the edge of the porch. We sat and looked at the ocean spilling all its secrets to a world that didn't care. Finally, I said, "I suppose Robin came in through this door and found Medici there on top of her."

"I think so. A lot of us were strung out in the dark along the beach. Dale and Cud and I were just down there." She pointed almost straight west. "I never did see the body. I couldn't stand to look. Word came down that she was dead, and we couldn't believe it. I can see, looking back, that it was more possible than we'd thought. Of course, we were just kids and having fun. You don't expect anyone to get killed."

"What do you mean, more possible than you thought?"

"Oh, you know. All the guys were turned on by Candy because she was so damned lovely and sexy; even at sixteen she was a real turn-on. And, of course, all the girls were jealous as hell."

"Were you?"

"Was I? Jesus, I hated that little bitch. So did all the other girls."

"How about Marnie?"

"Specially Marnie. Why do you think Robin was going into the house? He probably was hoping to find Candy alone. It was opportunity time, everyone high. You can see why she might get killed. A lot of frustrated boys, a lot of jealous girls. I didn't have a steady at the time, but if I had, you can bet I'd have kept a sharp eye out for Candy getting close to him. Looking back, of course, I can see she was only enjoying her power, not old enough to know what it was causing to happen in others."

"Let's walk."

We went around to the back of the house. "That's the door to the kitchen," Lynn said, pointing to the back door. "We got everyone in there and tried to sober up before we called the cops. God, what a night that was."

I could imagine it. A bunch of scared kids huddled in the kitchen all night, knowing what they had to face. We took a hard-packed trail over the dunes and started along the sand. At first the sand was soft, and we slipped a bit as we moved west toward the water. As we neared the surf, the sand got hard and wet. I found a few stones and tried skipping them. I'd been better at it as a kid. The sun had lowered itself behind some deep gray clouds that hung far out over the water. A freighter crawled the horizon.

This was the second lovely spot where murder was out of place. I thought of Ralph McCreedy's body and the sickening pulp that had been his head on the shore of Rainbow Lake. I realized it had been only a month ago. Not even that. It seemed a millennium. I looked at my watch. It was three-thirty.

We walked maybe a half-mile south on the hard sand, saying little. Thinking about McCreedy and Candy Koski and about death had led me to thinking about life, the way it should. I glanced at Lynn Hammer who stood with her hands on her well-formed hips, looking out at the foreverness of water. She really was lovely. The right thoughts passed my mind. Or were they wrong thoughts? Oh, Arlene, you'd understand, I'll bet.

We walked back slowly. There was still lots of daylight left.

"Why don't we go to the Tolovana Inn and have a drink?" Lynn said.

"Sounds real good," I nodded. We speeded up. The gray front was closer now, and a chill was in the air, suggesting rain. We angled the last five hundred yards toward the house with the car in front. Sand fleas seemed to be working hard. Twice the sand jumped to my left a few feet. I thought I heard a snapping sound. I heard it again. It was a crack really, like a rifle. Rifle? I heard it again. The sand jumped about two feet from my foot. Jesus, someone was shooting at us.

I grabbed Lynn and threw her down on the sand. "Al, what is it?"

"Someone's shooting at us with a rifle."

"Oh, no. Who would do that?"

"I don't know. Wait a minute." Had it stopped? I started to stand. Another crack. This time the bullet hit a stone or something hard and went whining off out over the water. I ducked back down. We had no cover. I told myself not to panic. No self-lecture was ever more necessary.

I calculated the distance to the water. We could run for it and submerge and let the water deflect the bullets. Oh, Christ, what a stupid notion. We'd be trapped. If the guy wanted us dead, all he had to do was come down to the shore and wait for us to pop up for air. I thought of my gun, but I couldn't be sure where to shoot.

It was a good hundred yards to the cover of the dunes. Some grass behind the dunes would give us some cover, but no protection. The rifle cracked again. I didn't see the impact or hear the bullet ricochet. I decided with no more hesitation.

My arm was around Lynn's head. "Look. We've got to run for it. Head for those dunes and get over them. I think it's me they're after. So you run south at an angle, and zigzag. I'll head directly toward the dunes. The guy with the gun is up there, I think, in the Scotch broom. That patch near the house across the street from your old place. He's in there somewhere, I'm sure of it. When you reach the dunes, get over them and come back toward me, but not until I wave to you. OK?"

She nodded. We were both breathing hard from fear. I crawled in front of her. "OK. Go."

She started running back at an angle toward the dunes. I jumped up and headed straight away from the ocean. It's not easy to try to run a hundred yards and look too small to shoot at the same time. I thought I heard another shot, but I wasn't sure. I could hear my blood in my ears. I wished I hadn't put on those twenty smug pounds in the last year or so. Change the diet, Arlene. Not so much pasta. More greens.

Fifty yards from the dunes I glanced south. Lynn was still zigzagging and I hoped was out of range. My breath was coming harder and harder. Somehow I was putting the next foot forward. Twenty yards, and my lungs were crying for help. In the humid ocean air I started to sweat, despite the coolness. I was only a few steps out. Lynn was nearing the dunes, I saw with a quick look. I dove over the dunes and rolled into the tall grass. Someone had left a tin can in the grass long ago, and I cut my hand on it. I didn't mind.

I lay back and sucked my bleeding left hand and let a lot of air collect in my lungs and a lot of boiling blood simmer down. I couldn't hear any more shots. I couldn't hear anything but the surf and a faint wind through the grass over my head.

I pulled out my revolver and stood up. The house that had once belonged to the Hammer family blocked off my vision of the Scotch broom. So if that's where he was, he couldn't see me anymore. I was surprised I'd run that deep out of the line of fire. Something stirred behind me. I swung quickly. It was Lynn.

"Jesus, I told you not to come until I signaled."

She giggled. "This is almost fun," she said.

"A basket of smiles," I said. "Nothing beats getting shot at for kicks."

"I'm sorry. I was so damned frightened. It was just a reaction."

"Now look. He may still be there. I think the house across the street from yours is empty, too. I doubt there's anyone who saw him, so he's taking no risk hanging around to see if he can kill us, or at least me. Now, damn it, you stay here. And this time, do it. I mean it." I sounded very masterful. I liked sounding masterful to her.

"I'll go up there and see if he's there. He doesn't know I've got a gun, so he may get over-confident. But damn you, you stay here until I signal you."

She said, "Yes, Al." She looked at me in a way I liked very much. I felt like King Kong, until I started toward the back of her old house. Then I felt less like King Kong and more like a scared guy with a gun in his hand, hoping he wouldn't have to use it. Or if he did have to use it, that he'd use it well.

I hugged the wall of the house and slipped around the east side. When I got to the front, I could see the car still there and beyond it, about twenty yards, the Scotch broom. It was quiet. The surf sounded dreamy and far off. The slight wind moved some sporadic grass faintly. The gray front was nearly overhead.

I crouched down and moved as fast as I could in that position straight for the car. I got the car between me and the Scotch broom. I waited behind the car. Then I ran for the house across from the old Hammer place. I ran around the east side of the house and circled back toward the Scotch broom. I didn't think the guy would wait all that time and let me circle around behind him. He hadn't.

I found five shell casings, 30.06, and some blurred footprints that, in the soft sand, no one would be able to tell anything about. He had stood in a sort of cup formed by the broom. I imagined kids thought of that place as a clubhouse, a natural one formed by the vegetation. I imagined someone had lost his or her virginity there once and had rested happy and sky-eyed on the sand afterward. I didn't touch the casings.

I could see a block north down the sand and grass and broom to where the next street closer to Cannon Beach also ended. I imagined that was where he'd parked, and while I was making my way here, he had slipped back down the beach to his car and had taken off. I went back and waved to Lynn.

I waited while she drove to a phone and called the cops. The deputy sheriff who came looked about fourteen. He took our story. Picked up the shells without bothering to see if they had fingerprints on them and stuffed them in his pocket. We went over the area and then over the grounds at the end of the next street north. We found as many clues as we would have if we hadn't looked.

The deputy muttered something about nuts in the area who think it's fun shooting at people to scare them. "Goes on all the fucking time," he muttered. It sounded like the first time he'd ever uttered a naughty word.

31

Lynn was lovely. She had been lovely in Plains when I'd run into her after spending all night with Arlene. Now that I was on my fourth scotch and hadn't seen Arlene in several days and was getting horny, Lynn was very lovely.

By now we'd rehashed the day. Colobrite. The shooting. Like anyone who's survived something and feels like a survivor, we made a lot of jokes along the way. Good jokes. Mediocre jokes. We laughed at them all.

Lynn was very lovely, guzzling vodka martinis at the Tolovana Inn. The bar at the Tolovana Inn was lovely. No one was shooting at us. The bartender looked like he wouldn't let anyone shoot at us. The bartender was lovely. He looked like he'd been in the ring.

It was six-thirty. Rain was beating against the windows, and the night was black outside. I couldn't see Haystock rock any longer, sticking up majestically out of the ocean. I was sure a million gulls were on it, waiting for the rain to stop. Lynn was lovely.

"I don't feel like going back," I said. "Too far. And too dark and rainy."

"Me, neither. We'll get a couple of rooms."

"Why two? Is someone joining us?" The scotch was telling.

She put her finger lightly against my face. It was one of those light touches a woman gives that weighs tender tons. I felt my groin tighten pleasantly. It had taken her one trip to the ladies' room to look dazzling after our sandy escape. I watched her smooth, dark face, and she watched out the window at the ocean she couldn't see that was pulsing somewhere out in the night not far away. I was pulsing, too.

We ate a very good dinner in the restaurant and took one room. I registered as Mr. and Mrs. Al Barnes, just in case the staff was prudish. The registration clerk looked as prudish as Mae West.

The rooms at the Tolovana Inn were elongated, bedroom, bath, kitchen, strung out in a line. Pleasant orange and blue furnishings. And a black table in the kitchen. The phone in the bedroom had an extension in the kitchen. Lynn suggested we call Lee, and I picked up the kitchen extension when she got him.

Lynn told him about our adventures.

"Jesus, who—?"

"We don't know," I said. "Somebody took five shots at us with a thirty-ought-six from some Scotch broom."

"You know, honey," Lynn said. "Those bushes across the street where the beach rises up and stops."

"I can't remember," he said. "It's been years."

"That's where he shot from. But who could it have been?"

"It probably wasn't Colobrite," I put in. "I would have seen him if he'd trailed us from the motel. Besides, I doubt he's got the guts or the reason. Medici? Too much coincidence. He had no way of knowing we were coming. Did anyone know we were coming you know of?"

"Oh, my God," Lynn said. "I told Marnie."

No one said anything over the phone for a moment.

"I told her last night over the phone to tease her. You know, Lee, how we always playfully compete for men—it's just a game—who's most attractive, who can get the guy's attention. We've been doing it since high school. I told her I was coming down here with Al, that's you, Sheriff Barnes. She thinks you're attractive, and I knew it would get to her. But—"

"Jesus," Lee said. "I don't like it. Are you coming home?"

"We got a couple of rooms here," Lynn said. "We'll be back tomorrow."

"Take care," Lee said. I wondered if he really believed we had two rooms. Probably not.

When we hung up, I stood and looked down the hallway to the bedroom. Lynn stood there, hands on hips, looking at me.

"You don't think it was Marnie shot at us, do you?"

"Oh, God no. She's very competitive about men, she really is. Sure, we play jokes on each other about it and kid around, and down underneath she really is in competition with every woman on earth. But so much that she'd shoot at an old friend—? Hell, no. It was just a joke between us. I'd bet anything it wasn't her."

"It's crazy," I said. "Just crazy."

"Why are we talking to each other the length of this hall?" she asked.

I walked to her and kissed her. She was very good at kissing. I'd expected that. She was also very good at other things. It was a most refreshing night.

32

Something on my ear woke me. It was Lynn, playing with my ear. She also had a cup of steaming black coffee. "Wake up, you glorious hunk of man."

"What time is it?"

"Ten."

"Jesus. Red Yellow Bear would be terribly pleased to know how doggedly I'm pursuing the Tingley murder case."

Lynn laughed and played with my ear some more. I put the coffee down on the stand next to the bed. "You're asking for it," I said, feeling the delightful pressure below.

"I sure am."

I grabbed her and pulled her, laughing, back into the bed. By the time I got to the coffee, it was cold.

After we showered and dressed, we sat at the black table in the kitchen. Lynn had made some more of the coffee the inn provided for guests. We looked at each other in that smug way you do after a good night.

"It was lovely, Al. It was just beautiful."

"It really was."

"I hope, though, you don't get any ideas about the future, like marriage."

"Why would I think of marriage? What are you? Just rich, beautiful, great lover and expert cook, besides being charming, humane, warm and delightful. Who wants to marry someone like that?"

She laughed. When she stopped laughing, she said, "I mean it, though. You're wonderful, Al. You really are. It's just that I can't make any commitments. Don't want to. We were a couple of people who got shot at and were frightened. It was the most natural thing in the world that we fell into each other's arms. We did it because we were

alive. I'm glad we did. Am I ever. I feel great." She
stretched and yawned.

"I wanted to ask you something," I said. "I hope you
don't mind."

"Anything."

"You know that picture of you and Lee that's in the
room I'm using at your place?"

She nodded a bit uncertainly. "I think so."

"Well, it's strange. It looks like you married each other."

She burst out laughing again. "It would have been better if we had," she said. "You have no idea how much
better it would have been. Actually, it was taken on our
wedding day."

"What?"

"Do you really want to hear about it?"

I nodded.

"I told you we were brats, conspiratorial brats. Well,
we eloped, both of us, to southern Oregon. Lee with Annie
and me with Orlando."

"Orlando?" I questioned the unusual name.

"Yes, goddamn it," she started to laugh. "Orlando
Ponce. Wouldn't you know? Any woman who marries a
guy named Orlando Ponce deserves a bad marriage."

I found myself laughing with her.

"We barely knew them. Orlando I'd met in Eugene
when I was going to the U of Oregon. Lee had met Annie
briefly somewhere. I think they'd shacked up a couple of
nights. None of our friends knew them. We thought we'd
spring a great surprise on everyone. So we set it up, Lee
called Annie. I think she was in Corvallis at the time—I
don't know. And I called Orlando, and we set up a ren-
dezvous in southern Oregon. Both Lee and I had money.
Mother was already dead and had seen to it we got some
directly from her will. So down we went, without telling
anyone. It was another of our little jokes. We'd come home
married to people no one had ever seen. So we got married.
Lee married Annie in Ashland, Oregon, and Orlando and
I stood up with them. An hour later, I married Orlando
in Medford, and Lee and Annie stood up with us."

"You must have surprised everyone when you got
back."

"We didn't get back. I called Daddy to tell him the news,

and he was furious. He told us to not come back. Lee got on the phone and tried to reason with him, but he wouldn't budge. He told us to stay away but permanently. Well, we knew he'd cool down finally, but to play it safe we went to San Francisco. Orlando and I lived in Sausalito. Lee and Annie—what was her name—Barzeletta, I think— lived in the city. The marriages lasted a short time. Theirs lasted four months. Ours went on for five. I was pregnant with Mike when Orlando left." She started to laugh again. "Can you imagine it? Orlando Ponce, for God's sake."

"Where is he now?"

"This is really fantastic. The last I heard, he was in Albania."

"Albania." I started to laugh again.

She almost burst a seam saying, "Running a frog farm."

I started to be infected by her laughter. I couldn't stop laughing. We howled.

Punctuated by laughter, her next statement broke me up so bad I started to cramp: "Can you imagine telling anyone your former husband is Orlando Ponce who now runs a frog farm in Albania?" We were shaking with laughter. Tears were running down my face.

"Jesus, you couldn't make it up," she said. "They'd have to believe you."

Finally, I stopped laughing from exhaustion. "Where's Lee's wife?"

"Off in the East somewhere, Kentucky, I think." She laughed a final burst. "Orlando Ponce, who runs a frog farm in Albania."

"I understand it's hard and dangerous for Americans to get into Albania."

"I heard that, too. I don't know how he did it. Maybe he didn't. It's just what I heard from a guy who knew him. That was years ago. Maybe it was a damned lie. But isn't it a great story?"

"It sure is. Did you come home then to have the baby?"

"Oh, God, no. Daddy wasn't over his anger. Lee stayed in San Francisco until I had Mike. Then we came north. We figured the baby would soften Daddy."

"Did it?"

"Oh, yes. Once we were here, Daddy took us back. He

was a real softy, Daddy was. He died three years later. Mike could talk by then."

It took us two hours to drive back to Portland. We both felt very good. It rained all the way. I loved it. We only get about twelve inches a year in Montana.

33

When I told them about the shooting at Cannon Beach, Petrov seemed interested, but Mrvich passed it off. "I go along with that deputy," he said. "You weren't followed. The gunner wasn't trying to hit you. I'm sure it was one of those rustic nut kids having what he thinks is fun. Anyway, we can check Marnie Tingley's whereabouts if you want."

"I guess I'd like it if you would," I said. "I'm not sure about it. And Marnie did know where we'd be. She didn't have to follow us."

"Yes, but why the hell would she deliberately miss you? What's to gain?"

I felt dumb. I had no answer.

We had ordered five dishes—roast pork to start things off. Mrvich and Petrov collaborated on the order. They knew the menu at the Republic very well. I felt safe in their hands. My stomach felt especially safe. Rick Petrov was dipping a piece of roast pork into some hot Chinese mustard. When that was finished, he dipped it into the sesame seeds and put it into his mouth. He washed it down with tea.

"He told the cops, all right," Petrov said when the tea had washed down the mustard heat from his mouth. "Medici. He told the cops about the fight with Desk. But the cops didn't tell the DA."

"Why not?"

"You know why not. I hate to tell you guys this, but a lot of cops, and I mean a lot, decide who they want to be guilty and then build the case against that guy."

Mrvich bit his lip and nodded. I had to agree; Petrov was right. I'd seen that all too often when I'd worked in Seattle.

"The cops wanted Medici to be guilty. If something came up that showed he might not be, they kept it quiet. That's why there's so much antagonism between lawyers and cops."

"One of the reasons," Mrvich said.

"Yeah, OK. Anyway, the prosecutor went into court not knowing about Desk. When Matthew produced him, the case was shot."

"I know what you're saying about cops is all too true," Mrvich said. "I've seen it again and again. Dopes who work on the good guy-bad guy theory. But there are a lot of cops who don't. A lot of us just want the guilty to pay. When you get some punk off who everyone knows is dangerous as hell, that doesn't do the world any more good than cops hiding evidence."

Before Petrov could answer, a chunky Chinese waiter started bringing some fine-looking food to our table. Beef and tomato. Shrimp and greens. Roast duck. Some kind of chow mein. The last dish he put down was chicken with cashew nuts. The weaknesses of law enforcement could wait. We dug in.

I was sure they'd had the argument before. They were obviously the best of friends and respected each other a great deal.

After he'd finished his first plateful, Mrvich said, "We got all the stuff in. Everybody was in Portland when Tingley got it, except Marnie Tingley. We can't establish where she was. Everybody else connected with the Koski case was here, Medici, Robbins, Clueridge, the Hammers."

"The Hammers?"

"You wanted me to check on everybody, didn't you?"

"Sure. But I knew they were here. I called them a few hours after the body was found. Tingley had taken them to the plane the day before."

"Right. We got a photostat of their tickets."

"Very thorough."

"And Rasmussen was in Buffalo."

"Very, very thorough. What's with Tingley?"

"We just can't get anything for sure. Her maid was off

that day. The doorman can't remember back to that day
for sure."

"If she drove, she'd need two days, and without much
sleep if she killed him at six A.M., or whenever it was. It
was about then. A green car with Oregon plates got gas
in Plains about eleven A.M. A woman was driving. Marnie
has a green car. It's possible. I found out from Lynn that
Marnie is given to a lot of deep feeling about losing men
to other women. I've met her, and I believe it. Tingley was
interested in Lynn Hammer, I think. If she's an hysteric
like the doctor suggested, well—" I let it trail off. I wasn't
sure where any of this was going.

34

Sometimes I'd won-
dered why women don't have a skid row. It's like men
reserved destitution and defeat for their exclusive use. I
wondered if most women weren't too strong to become
derelicts, if derelictions required a weakness seldom found
in women. Sometimes I wondered if there weren't just as
many women derelicts as men, but they stayed inside and
didn't put it on public display. Sometimes I wondered if
women weren't too weak to resist prevailing values and
so couldn't risk demonstrating failure. Sometimes I wondered why I did so goddam much stupid wondering.

Mrvich and I were walking slowly east on Burnside
Street. One place we went by, a dirty little coffee shop, a
guy in a white apron was pushing a guy with a dirty, torn
coat and a week's beard out the door and yelling, "I'll get
you thirty days, you fucking bum."

The man in the dirty, torn coat finally let himself get
pushed into the street and walked away muttering. It was
the usual skid row: small business places, most of them
closed; empty shops; a café here and there that never
served anything more complicated than a fried-egg sandwich; a mission, and the men who looked as aimless stand-

ing still or crouching in a door as they did walking. Some men bent their heads as if there might be money on the sidewalk and they didn't want to miss it. Others bent their heads for deeper reasons. Some tried to walk erect, hoping the cops wouldn't notice they were drunk. We crossed Fourth, and I could see the Republic, where we'd eaten just last night, a couple of blocks north. How close these men were to that good food and how far, farther than just the lack of money.

Mrvich hadn't come along because there might be danger. Skid row is usually one of the least dangerous places in town. They are all scared of you, especially if you look like you could pass in other parts of town. Mrvich had come as guide and as official authority. He thought I might need both. Lips get awfully tight on skid row.

"Where's the Eagle?" Mrvich asked a man sitting in the doorway of a closed store. The man shook his head and vaguely waved us out of his life forever.

A black kid, looking not more than twenty, came along. "Murv," he said. "Long time no see."

"Randy. How's it going?" The kid didn't look skid row. He was reasonably well dressed and shaven, and his eyes were alert.

"Nothing doing, Murv. Not a thing."

"Seen the Eagle?"

"He's up at Moore's, drinking coffee." The black kid pointed up the block behind him.

"Hang in there, Randy."

"Right, Captain."

After the kid moved on, Mrvich said, "Narcotics detail. I don't know what in hell he's doing here. These guys can't afford dope."

"Seemed to know the place. Seemed awfully young."

"He's older than he looks. He knows the place, all right. He knows the whole city better than any guy on the force—the downtown area, anyway."

We found a coffee shop with an old sign, black letters on white. The black letters weren't solid, and the white wasn't white anymore. It said, Moore's Eats.

The Eagle turned out to be an old man. His clothes said skid row, but his eyes said better. He was one of those guys you see on skid row who enjoys life there. His eyes were receptive and keen. His beard was three days, maybe. It didn't look like a lot of beards on skid row. He just looked like a man who hadn't shaved but would. A lot of others looked like men who hadn't shaved and might never.

"Mrvich, for Christ sakes. Big John Mrvich." The Eagle stood up and pumped Mrvich's hand. "Where in hell have you been, Murv?"

"Eagle, I was so incompetent, they promoted me to get me the hell out of the way so some real cops could do their work."

"No shit? That's great, Murv. I didn't know what had become of you. How long has it been?" He gestured to the table.

"Eagle, I want you to meet Al Barnes. He used to be on the Seattle force with me years ago. Now he's a sheriff in Montana."

"Pleased to meet you," the Eagle said. He gestured again to the table after giving me a friendly handshake, and we sat down. Mrvich asked the sad-looking man behind the counter for a couple of cups of coffee. "You need another, Eagle?"

"No. No. Thanks, Murv."

"Eagle, how's the neighborhood?"

"Changing," the Eagle said a little sadly. "Really changing, Murv. It used to be we had the place to ourselves. Now they're putting in clubs, good eating joints, stuff like that, right on the fringes. At night, well-dressed people on their way to hear some music or to get some cocktails and a good dinner pass right by the bums. Makes the bums feel lousy. It's the same old problem: encroachment. Christ, Murv, there's no place in this fucking country where you can live your life anymore. I mean, you can't even live like a harmless bum and be left alone. It's hard to live anywhere. If some goddam big corporation isn't tearing down something in your backyard, the fucking government is building a freeway through your front yard. They've got two bars for the swells within two blocks of here. Posh places. Buck and a quarter a shot and waitresses with lots of leg in silk who cut your throat if you don't leave at least five bucks on the table. Can you imagine the kind of people who pass through here at night all dressed up? Makes the bums feel like shit."

"I agree more than you know," Mrvich said. He turned his big, rugged face to the window and looked out into the street where a bum was shuffling across, managing to dodge the cars coming down Burnside. Mrvich looked sad.

"I mean," the Eagle said, "can you think of one fucking place that's stayed the same for over ten years? One?"

"I know," Mrvich said. He finally overcame his preoccupation with change and loss and said, "Eagle, are you still up on the personnel here?"

"Try me."

"Harry Bird?"

"Big Heart Mission on Third. Sleeps in the back on one of the cots there."

"How do you do it, Eagle?"

"A mayor has to know his community," the Eagle said.

Mrvich tucked a bill into the Eagle's shirt pocket. It looked like a twenty, but it was one of those quick exchanges that happen so fast in cities you might miss it if you weren't looking for it. The Eagle nodded his thanks. "Don't stay away so long next time, Murv."

"I'll try not to," Mrvich said. I tipped my hand in salute to the Eagle. He was sitting there alert to the next possibility when we left.

It was only a short walk to the Big Heart Mission. The heart may have been big but the mission was tiny, no more than a hole in the wall. It might have been a shoe repair shop once. About twenty chairs were set up facing a lectern, where I assumed someone led some singing of hymns now and then. An old woman with a warm smile came out from behind some cloth that was meant to be curtain but looked like an old bed sheet, hung on a wire that stretched from wall to wall. "Hello, Murv," she said. She gave Mrvich an affectionate kiss on the cheek.

"Sadie. Long time." He held both her hands in his. "You look beautiful."

"Eat your heart out, Jacqueline Bisset," she said and laughed. She might have been seventy.

"Sadie, is a guy named Harry Bird here?"

"Sure, Murv. He's sleeping in the back."

The back turned out to be another small room into which somehow about fifteen army cots had been squeezed. Harry Bird wasn't sleeping. He was sitting on the edge of a cot with his bedding thrown about behind him. He was pale and small and over fifty. He had small hands and small wrists. He also had the shakes.

He'd already managed to get dressed, except for his shoes and socks. His shoes, with curled-up toes and white blotches on the brown leather, sat under his bed. His socks were in them. Harry Bird wore baggy brown trousers that looked too big for him, a black shirt that seemed to be of foreign manufacture and frayed yellow suspenders. The yellow was as frayed as the elastic.

"Oh, shit, I feel awful," he said and motioned to us to sit down without even asking who we were or what we wanted.

John Mrvich showed him a badge. All Bird did was nod.

"My friend here is a cop, too. He wants to ask you some questions."

"OK. OK." Bird nodded. "You got a drink?" He might have been saying it to anyone. He probably was.

"I'll get one," Mrvich said; "be right back. Anything special?"

"Make sure it has alcohol," Bird said. "I'm particular." He shuddered with the chill peculiar to hangovers. His pale eyes watered with the sadness of a man who is physically small and has always been aware of it. His hair could have been called brown if it had any color at all. There wasn't much of it.

"Mr. Bird," I said, "at one time did you write editorials for a newspaper called the *Seaside Beacon?*"

He shrugged. "Sure. What of it?"

"I'm interested in this one." I pulled a photocopy from my pocket and unfolded it in front of him. "It got a murder trial switched from Astoria to Portland nineteen years ago."

He read it. "What lousy work. My best was on sewage disposal."

"Did you write it?"

"Christ, I don't know. Nineteen years ago?"

"Don't you remember writing it?"

"No, I don't. But—" He stared at the editorial again.

"Yes, Mr. Bird?"

"Well," he kept looking at it. "Necrophilia? Jesus Christ, necro-fucking-philia. How about that?" He put his trembling right hand to his head and brushed what little hair he had back. "Necrophilia. Shit, that's evil," Harry Bird said.

John Mrvich came back and handed Harry Bird a bottle of apple wine. Bird fumbled with the cap and put the bottle to his mouth. He took at least a fourth of it. "Oh, shit, that's good. You're a good guy," he said to Mrvich. "Got a cigarette?"

I offered him a cigarette and lit it for him. He started to relax a little. His hands were steadier. One drink, one cigarette and a lot less fear.

"It's very important to me, Mr. Bird. Did you write this?"

Harry Bird seemed to consider for a while. Finally he said, "No. I remember it, all right. I didn't write it. It was handed to me, and I was told to put it in the paper just like that."

"Who handed it to you?"

"The guy I worked for. I told him it was shit and might get us into trouble."

"Was his name Leo Colobrite?"

"Yeah, that's him. Leo Colobrite. He's a son of a bitch, a real male cunt." He swigged some more wine.

"Did Colobrite write it?"

"Colobrite? That fuckhead couldn't scratch his name in the tide flats with a stick. He couldn't write shit."

"Well, who did write it?"

Harry Bird looked around the room as if someone might be listening. The only other person in the room was an old man in a corner bunk who wasn't listening to anything. "You won't tell anyone I told you?" He looked at me, then at Mrvich. We both shook our heads, and I put up my hands in a perish-the-thought gesture.

"T. T. Armstrong wrote it."

"T. T. Armstrong? Who's that?"

"He's the guy owned the *Beacon*. He was *the* boss, understand. He owned a hell of a lot of other things, too. He owned half of Seaside at one time."

"Did you know him?"

"Saw him once, that's all. The *Beacon* was just a sideline with him."

"Do you have any idea why he wanted this printed?"

"Sure, I do. He wanted the trial fixed, I mean, moved."

"How do you know that was his motive?"

"Well, figure it out. Inflammatory shit like that. What in hell did he care about Clatsop County except as a place to invest his fucking money? All that shit about the outraged community. The out-fucking-raged community, for Christ sakes. He lived in Portland up in those fucking West Hills somewhere and drank champagne and looked at the fucking mountains with his rich friends."

"Why do you think he wanted the trial moved?"

"He didn't want that kid to burn. What's his name?"

"Victor Medici."

"Yeah. Medici. He'd killed a sixteen-year-old girl, and the natives were restless for shit sure. They'd have burned his ass in Astoria. The kids had been raising hell every year for a while—Christ, a couple of years after this we had the Seaside riots—and this was the chance to burn one of their asses."

"Yes, but why would T. T. Armstrong want Medici to get off? What's the connection?"

"Shit, I don't know. Maybe Medici was a friend of his."

By now he had the bottle half done. I handed him a five.

"Thanks very much, Mr. Bird."

"Think nothing of it. I sure appreciate the wine and the money."

We stood up. "Tell me something, Mr. Bird," I said. "If you don't mind. How come a newspaper man with some ability, well—"

"How come I ended up here?"

"Yes. I guess that's it. I mean you don't seem—was it the editorial? Did you feel you helped get a murderer off? Or was it a woman or—"

"No. No. None of that. I love to drink. I'm not rich. This is the only place I can drink and not work. I hate work almost as much as I like to drink."

The air seemed unusually fresh outside. Something was breaking. But what? Mrvich gave me the answer.

"You just hit pay dirt," he said. "The late T. T. Armstrong was in construction with a man named Ross. Armstrong-Ross Construction. Ring a bell?"

35

Vic Medici's dark suit looked hand-tailored, possibly in Rome. He was darker than I remembered him. Maybe he'd found lots of sun in Los Angeles. He smiled, but Mrvich didn't, and Medici's lips tightened ever so slightly. I had known Mrvich for so long I never thought of him as being tough, but he was. He was a tough city cop, a lot tougher than Medici, and Medici seemed to know it.

Mrvich spoke in a hard voice. "Who paid for Art Matthew nineteen years ago, Vic?"

"I don't know, Murv—"

"Captain Mrvich, goddamn it."

"Sorry, Captain. I really don't know who paid Matthew. He just took my case. That's all I know."

"You ever hear of a man named Sy Ross?"

"Don't think so."

"He was Marnie Ross' father."

Medici went silent.

"How did you feel about Robin Tingley?"

"Like I told Sheriff Barnes here, Captain. His testimony helped me so I had no grudge—"

"I don't mean that. I mean before the Koski mess. When you were all running in a pack."

"I don't know, Captain. He was OK, just another guy, a kid like the rest of us."

"Well, not exactly like the rest of you, Vic. He had some guts for a kid. I mean real guts. He put you down at a dance, didn't he?"

"Robin? He never put anyone down. He was a gentleman. Even a bit stuffy sometimes for a kid."

"Gentlemen put people down," Mrvich said. "Some of them are real experts at it."

Medici didn't say anything.

"He never put you down at a dance in front of other

151

people? Never suddenly pointed out you were the unpol-
ished son of a garbage collector who couldn't solve anything except with your fists? You must have been sensitive
about it. You were traveling in a hot set—Tingley, Marnie,
the Hammers. Just being there said you wanted something
'better,' in quotes. Candy Koski got in because she was
beautiful, and you got in because you were a star football
player. You were in with the swishies, but one of them,
Tingley, was a smart swishy for his age. He sensed your
weakness. When you offered to fight him at a dance, he
humiliated you for it. It must have hurt. Does it still hurt?
Enough to pay someone to kill him?"

"Come on, Captain. I don't know what you're talking
about." Medici had regained his cool. He pushed a gold-
plated cigarette box at Mrvich. The underside of the open
top was inlaid with a photo of a lovely, young, naked blonde.
"Cigarette, Captain?"

He lost his cool right away when Mrvich said, "If you
didn't kill Candy Koski, why do you pay her surviving
mother and brother five hundred dollars a month? Sounds
like conscience money to me."

Medici showed a lot of emotion trying not to show any
emotion. "I give them—" He stopped. Then he grew sullen.
"How do you know that?"

"I trailed your boy on a hunch," I said. "I saw the
payoff."

Medici looked at me like he didn't like me.

"Why do it? And why do it anonymously?" Mrvich
asked. "Did you kill Candy Koski in a jealous rage and
then years later, when you got some adult conscience, trace
her family and start some cash atonement? You were
raised Catholic. Some things last a long time, given the
right past—like guilt."

Medici looked at his hands. He raised them. "See these
hands? They beat a lot of guys up, but I swear they never
killed anyone."

"Stop the fucking dramatics, Vic. Did you kill Candy
Koski, then plead with Marnie Ross for help, convince her
you didn't and have her talk her father into getting you
a good mouthpiece?"

"No, Captain. Honest."

"Why did a rich guy like T. T. Armstrong, who was Sy

Ross' business partner, plant an editorial in the *Seaside Beacon*, which he owned, and get your trial switched to Portland where Matthew could get you off? You seem to have an awful lot of influence working for you for such a poor slob."

"I don't know anything about any editorial. No one told me about that." Then he brightened. "Captain, maybe they liked football. I had a scholarship to Oregon for sure, and lots of people are nuts about football. Did Ross and Armstrong—is that right, Armstrong?—did they go for football? That's a possibility, isn't it?"

"Knock it off, you slimy little bastard," Mrvich roared. Medici almost melted. Mrvich's voice scared me, too.

"Honest, Captain. I swear I didn't kill anyone. Sure, I paid the Koskis. I had them traced and found out they were really sad people. I was starting to coin it. Sure, it was conscience. If I hadn't taken her out there, she'd still be alive. I loved her. When I found her dead, I damn near died, too. I tried everything I could think of to save her."

"You sure did," Mrvich said sarcastically. Jesus, he could be merciless.

"You told me before you had an idea who killed Candy Koski," I said. "Could it have been Marnie?"

Medici didn't answer.

"Tell us, you bastard," Mrvich said. "Who was it and why all this bullshit to get you off the hook?"

"Captain, believe me, I don't know. I was scared, just a kid facing a murder rap. This smooth lawyer shows up. He's all I got. I had to trust him. He knew what he was doing. I never paid him a cent and don't know who did or why. It was all so damned mysterious. I was a kid in a jam and grabbed my chance when it came along. Matthew was my chance. I didn't ask any questions."

"All right." Mrvich stood up and leaned across Medici's desk. "Listen to me, you rotten little punk. You're into a lot of shady stuff. It may be legal but you can be squeezed, even with good lawyers. You got at least four ex-cons working for you that I know of. If I find out or even suspect you're lying or withholding, I'll squeeze off a lot of the cash flow for months. I may even get a court order to audit your books. Even if you're clean, you'll feel dirty and a hell of a lot poorer for a while."

Medici looked hard at Mrvich and said, "I'm not lying, Captain. I know what you can do to my operations if you want to."

"You fucking well better," Mrvich said.

36

I had to be careful. I couldn't let anything go unchecked. First I went back to Dale Robbins' place. He still had two girls, both bare to the waist. They weren't the same two girls. One was black, and gorgeous. The other was Oriental. She was bouncing evidence that not all Oriental girls are small-breasted. He was as classy as the first time, a real charmer.

Robbins couldn't remember the incident at the dance. He had never heard of Armstrong. Then I drove to the home of Joyce Cuddles Bebar Clueridge. If anything, she was more repulsive. She wore a long, vivid, orange gown that showed her figure off in all its lumpiness. The gown went with the hopeless pink walls about like Joyce Clueridge went with the human race.

She didn't remember the incident at the dance. She'd never heard of T. T. Armstrong.

But I did get something. The sullen maid, Mary, stepped outside with me when I was leaving. "Can I talk with you for a minute?"

"Please."

Her face was still sullen, a mask of hostility she'd been wearing too long to take off now. But her manner had thawed.

"You seem like a good man, Mr. Barnes—isn't that it?"

"Yes," I said as pleasantly as I could, "that's right. Barnes."

"I got something to tell you. I helped Lila get her job with Marnie Ross Tingley. Marnie called her for help. She doesn't see Mrs. Clueridge much socially, but Mrs. Clueridge calls her once in a while just because Mrs. Tingley has money. Mrs. Clueridge is impressed with folks who have money."

"It fits," I said, and Mary laughed slightly.

"Well, this time, Mrs. Tingley wanted a maid, and she called Mrs. Clueridge. I guess she figured if Mrs. Clueridge could find a maid, she would be able to help Mrs. Tingley find one. Lila's my niece. I spoke up for her."

"I see." I waited. I knew there was more.

"Well, it was strange doings over there at Mrs. Tingley's. First, she wanted a maid who was young and pretty. She made that clear. I've been talking with Lila, and she wants to see you. I told her you were a nice man. I think you should talk to Lila, Mr. Barnes. I told her she ought to talk to you. It's really weird. But she'd better tell you."

"I really appreciate this, Mary."

"It's my duty, Mr. Barnes."

"I'm sorry you have to work for her," I said and pointed to the house.

"I'm the only one who would. It's hard for me to get a job because I look so sort of angry all the time."

"Aren't you angry all the time?"

"No, sir. I'm a deeply religious woman, and I find happiness in my religion. I don't know why my face is like this. It always has been. But no one else would work for Mrs. Clueridge, so I got the job."

"Mrs. Clueridge doesn't deserve you, Mary. She deserves to have the Frankenstein monster for a butler."

Mary laughed again. Even when she laughed, her eyes held what I had thought was anger. People fool you. I felt good driving back to the Hammer mansion.

37

"And now you know what those fucking Republicans are thinking of doing?" Yellow Bear growled over the phone. "They're thinking of running an Indian against me, Rudolph Tough Otter."

"Rudolph Tough Otter?"

"That's right. They figure they'll steal an idea from us and run their own Indian."

"I didn't know there were any Indian Republicans."

"Don't kid yourself. There are all kinds of Republicans, even human Republicans."

"Is Tough Otter a good man?"

"He's Indian, isn't he? Christ, as if I didn't have enough trouble. Sanderson is still missing. What is it, four days now? Pop Powell is in the hospital with a hernia, and you're in Oregon investigating the wrong murder. Swell. If the crooks of America ever hear about the police coverage in Sanders County, they'll be migrating here like geese. I'm putting in twelve-hour days minimum and driving all over the fucking place. Get the hell back here."

"Wait. Listen, Red. I'm getting close. I just feel it. A bunch of stuff has busted, and people are starting to talk."

"Look, if you're getting close to solving the Tingley job, OK. Cause I want the bastard caught. But if it's that other murder, forget it. I'm deputizing drunks and elk just to keep the peace. The teenagers are going wild here and down in Plains. Now, just how the hell close are you?"

I gave him the full report. When I finished, he said, "Shit, that's not close to finding Tingley's killer. You're just fucking around with that other business. Goddamn it, get the hell back here, Al."

"Did you check the Marnie Tingley photo with Mitter?"

"Yeah. No go. The kid couldn't identify her."

I finally talked him into letting me stay two more days. It was easy. Like getting Jimmy Carter drunk.

Next, I called Arlene. We purred over the phone for a few minutes. Then she said, "When are you coming back? I really miss you. I need you."

"And I need you, but I'm onto something."

"Are you getting laid down there?"

"Sex orgies every night," I said.

"You bastard." We kissed over the phone. That's not sexy enough, and you have to wipe off the mouthpiece afterward.

Then I called Marnie Tingley's number. Lila answered.

"This is Al Barnes. Your Aunt Mary said you might be willing to talk to me."

"Yes. I can." I waited, but she didn't follow up.

"Where would you like to meet me?"

She gave me an address. "Can you find that?"

"I'm sure I can."

"How about four, day after tomorrow, Mr. Barnes? It's a black district. Does that bother you?"

"Depends on the district. Is it a rough black district or a nice black district?"

"It's OK. I wouldn't ask you there if it wasn't. But I don't dare talk here. Mrs. Tingley might come in."

I said I'd get there by four, day after tomorrow. I went out of my room and found Lee at the far end of the house in the study.

"Hello," he said. "How's it going?"

"Better, I think. Where's Lynn?"

"Out shopping with Marnie. They go shopping once every so often. I'm trying to find a few minutes' relaxation before a four o'clock conference this afternoon. We're debating buying this mill in Eureka. God, but business is complicated."

"I wouldn't know."

He settled back into the deep leather chair. "It's funny how I got trapped in it just by inheritance. I had some dreams, believe it or not. I wanted to be a doctor. Maybe a surgeon. An eye surgeon, perhaps. Did you ever want to be something else?"

"Yes. I wanted to be a poet."

"Really? God, there are so many these days. Isn't that a funny thing for a cop to want to be?"

"Not necessarily. My friend, John Mrvich on the Portland force, is a poet, and so is a friend of his, Rick Petrov, a defense lawyer. They've both published books of poems."

"I always thought poets were sort of ethereal," he said. "You know, sort of mystical and other-worldly."

"I don't think many are," I said, "but then, I don't know many. I think it has more to do with ways you feel about yourself and the world, something like that."

"Well, I never wanted to be a poet, but I often think of getting married and having children. It would be nice. But somehow I got so involved learning the business and staying involved with it that the years just flashed by after my first marriage. I suppose Lynn told you about that?"

"Yes. Said it lasted only a few months. She told me all about Annie and Orlando Ponce."

"Yes, Orlando Ponce, for Christ sakes. Did she tell you about Albania and the damned frog farm?"

"That, too."

"Isn't that a gas? A novelist would give his eyeteeth to dream up something like that. His publisher would no doubt throw him out."

"You might be able to help me with something," I said. "It's something that happened at a dance when you were in high school. Lynn told me about it." I told him about the confrontation between Tingley and Medici. "The trouble is, I can't find anyone else who remembers it. Medici says it never happened."

"It happened, all right, but if Lynn said a lot of people saw it, she's not remembering it right. It was a quiet business, not really a scene. I saw it, and so did the girl I was with. Marge Appleton. We both saw it, and it's pretty much like Lynn says, only it wasn't any giant public humiliation for Vic. Just a brief exchange that maybe six people overheard."

"By the way, I'm sorry about Marge Appleton. You went with her, didn't you?"

"Oh. Yes. We heard about it when it happened. What a sad business. It really makes you feel old when someone you knew in high school dies." He stared at the floor for a while. "We went together for about a year, maybe more," he said. "Marge Appleton."

38

Two hours later I got a call. Mycroft took it, and I went to the phone in my room. A familiar voice said, "Barnes, Vic Medici speaking."

"Al Barnes here." I heard Mycroft hang up his extension once he heard our voices.

"Listen, I liked you. You got me in big trouble, bringing that captain up here. He's a tough guy. He's given me trouble before."

"What could I do? You're starting to look like a possible for two killings, and I needed help, big help. He's got authority here and plenty of clout."

"OK, OK, I know you're a good cop and doing your job. Whether you know it or not, I think murder stinks, too. But look, I can't risk the tough heat Mrvich is apt to put on me. I got a couple of big deals pending, and he could queer them for me. I'm thinking it over and decided I'll level with you. I admit you got a right to your suspicions, but you're in the wrong ball park. I'll even admit Tingley humiliated me once in front of some people at a dance. But I got something a lot hotter than that for you. I'll give it to you if you get Mrvich off my back."

"He's not on your back."

"He could be, and I can't risk it."

"I'm not sure I could influence him," I said. "He's a tough cop."

"Well?"

"OK. I'll try *if* the info is good enough."

"It's very good."

"What is it?"

"Oh, come on. Not over the phone."

"Why not?"

"You'll see when I tell you. Why not meet me here at

the office around ten? I got some important business with
my esteemed VP at nine-thirty. It shouldn't take too long."

"Is it about Marnie Ross Tingley?"

"No comment. See you."

Mike Ponce, looking bigger and more handsome than
ever, joined us for dinner. But his teenage charm couldn't
save the meal. The food was good as always, but Lynn was
cold, and Lee was preoccupied with the Eureka deal and
left three times to call his lawyer (I think he said lawyers)
about this or that point about the plant purchase coming
up. I mentioned I had to go see Medici about the case just
to have a get-away excuse handy. Instinct told me my time
there had run out. I don't care to stay in strange homes,
and I'd been there for more than a week. My social clock
was running down, and the alarm was about to wake with
a voice saying, "Time to move on, Mr. Barnes. Thank you
for your stay here." The case was buzzing around, and
Marnie Ross Tingley kept coming up for the Koski killing
and for her husband's.

I got away from the table as soon as I could and went
back to my room and called Red. He was in a foul mood
and growled brief answers over the phone. Nothing yet on
Manny Sanderson. I'd better get my ass back there. Rudolph Tough Otter was using his job as deputy to get
around the county and charm the natives for the next
election. He was so far off form I decided not to call Arlene.
She might be, too, and that I didn't need.

39

A fall fog had started
down by the river and was edging up toward the Ironfast
Building when I parked the blue Mercedes. The night was
one of those depressing Pacific Northwest nights when,
though it isn't cold, you feel cold. A night when most everyone stays home because the damp and the fog and the
black night make you feel that home is the only place life

could survive. The streets seem deserted with or without people in them. Everyone talks in hushed tones, and if someone is having a good time, it seems an intrusion, even a violation of the law, some ancient tribal law that says people must obey the prevailing mood of weather.

I didn't see anyone outside the Ironfast Building, and when I stepped in, I was certain I was the last person who would ever be there. My footsteps came back at me off the walls. The slight delay of the echo didn't make the place seem cheerier at all. That night the Ironfast Building housed the ghosts of a hundred horny businessmen and a hundred secretaries who had been vivacious and seductive and a host of salesmen who had come and gone. They were all dead and all here, come back to watch their favorite dumb detective, Al Mush Heart Barnes, who didn't even know for sure what case he was investigating.

The elevator door was pulled open. I stepped in and pushed the button. The door slammed shut like a cannon. Why is it, when you know you are alone in a building, the sounds amplify themselves? Maybe sound likes an audience of one. Maybe I'm flipping out.

The elevator stopped, and the door slammed open. I walked past the receptionist's desk and pushed on the door that opened the big woman. My steps had become nothing on the white shag.

The door swung open easily, as if it had been waiting all its life for my push. Even from the top of the hallway, I could see him. His door was open, and he sat behind his desk, his head tilted back awkwardly with his mouth wide open. The light from the lamp on his desk glittered from one of his teeth. I knew he was dead by the time I reached the door.

I went to the body. Without touching it, I could see he'd been shot at least twice, once in the chest and once in the stomach. The wounds were hard to see because he was wearing a dark suit. But I saw them, all right. I'd seen people shot through dark clothing before, and through shower curtains and bathrobes, and windows and doors, and once through the glass window of an iron lung.

So Vic Medici, self-styled tough guy and, in my books, pretty decent guy, had gone with no chance to say goodbye. His hands were on the arms of the chair as if he were about to stand up. They were skinned and raw around the knuckles. One knuckle seemed to be broken. Had he hit the guy who'd shot him?

In front of him lay several pieces of paper with figures apparently written with the felt-tipped pen on the desk. They were written in big, slashing, black markings, as if in anger. One sheet had $4 \times 12 = 48 \times 500 = 24,000$. Another had the figure 500 written straight down the page, over and over. One sheet had only the figure 24,000 written in huge, angry marks and followed with a big punctuation mark. A fourth sheet had $4 \times 12 = 48 \times 1000 = 48,000$.

I put a handkerchief in my hand and was reaching for the phone when I was aware someone else was there. I stopped and tried to swallow the lump in my throat. An even bigger lump in my stomach wouldn't let the lump in my throat go any further down.

T. Curtoise Lamarr was standing in the doorway I'd just come through. His office door hadn't been open when I'd passed—or had it been? I'd been so concentrated on Medici I hadn't really noticed. I assumed Lamarr had just stepped out of his office. He had a revolver, and for a moment I was sure he was going to shoot me. I ducked behind Medici's desk and got my gun out fast. I peered over the top of the desk and watched Lamarr.

He never tried to raise the gun. He was dressed in yellow that night, solid yellow of various shades. The irrevelant thought crossed my mind that yellow shoes must be hard to find. He wasn't really all yellow because a huge red stain that centered around his abdomen had spread about eight inches in diameter right through his coat. His eyes were puffed, and the skin around his face was badly cut. One of the gashes would have stopped any professional fight. He was so far gone, he couldn't lift the gun. I stood up.

He leaned against the doorway and stared at me with final eyes. I walked toward him, watching to see he didn't try to raise the gun.

"Found out—he—eyes—gun—beans for dinner—gummo—" He fell into my arms. He had been hurt for the last time. Now I could find some sympathy for him, and it was too late. It wouldn't do him any good at all. He was heavy, and I let him down as easily as I could.

I called Mrvich at home and told him I'd feel easier with the Portland police if he were there. He said he'd try to bring Petrov, too.

40

John Mrvich took his time coming after he'd called his own men. By the time he and Rick Petrov showed up, I was telling my story for the fourth time to Detective Second Class Lou Bodlouie. Lou Bodlouie wasn't impressed by my badge or my friendship with Mrvich, which I'd made a point of telling him about. I decided Lou Bodlouie was a pretty good cop, and I hoped from now on to admire his work from a distance. Mrvich showed up and rescued me, finally. He and Rick and I went to his office to drink some coffee. The lab technicians were still working when we left. It must have been nearly one A.M.

I was feeling lousy.

"I killed them," I said. "If it wasn't for me, they'd be alive."

"Don't blame yourself," Mrvich said. "Christ, how could you have known?"

"How could I have missed it? Those clothes, that car. I knew he couldn't afford those on his salary. He took five hundred right off the top every time he delivered to the Koskis, and Medici didn't know. What kills me is that Medici trusted him that way."

"Sometimes," Rick Petrov said, "bright guys have blind spots. He may have figured a sissy jerk like Lamarr wouldn't dare cross him."

"And I told him," I said. "That's how he found out. Shit."

"No. I told him. Remember?"

"Yeah, but I told you."

"The way it looks now," Mrvich said, "is Medici beat

Lamarr up. You're right, Rick. Lamarr was a sissy. Always had been, and a *big* sissy. Physically, he was big, maybe over two hundred pounds, but no muscle, no coordination. He'd been beaten up by guys half his size a lot of times, a big blubbery kid who had been the punching bag of the schoolyard. When Medici was beating him up, it must have brought back a lot of old humiliations. He couldn't take it anymore. He shot Medici, then gunned himself, rather than face jail. A poor guy like that. You can imagine how he'd do in jail."

"Jesus Christ," I said.

"Oh, hell, Medici would have found out, anyway, sooner or later," Petrov said. He was trying to make me feel better. I appreciated it. But I didn't feel better.

"We're pretty sure the beating took place in Lamarr's office. That's how it looks," Mrvich said. "We think Medici called him down to the office late when no one would be around. He confronted Lamarr in Lamarr's office just as Lamarr got his overcoat off. The coat's there. Medici accused him of stealing from him. By the way, we think Lamarr figured the Koskis were so sad and crazy that five hundred would seem plenty to them, so he could pocket the other five hundred, and Medici would never find out."

"Only he did find out," I said bitterly. "I told him, through you."

"Then Medici told him he was through and started thumping him. We think Medici left him on the floor, probably in pain and maybe crying because again he was suffering at the hands of someone smaller. Medici probably told him to get out as soon as he could pull himself together. Then Medici went into his office to wait for you, Al. But Lamarr had a gun. He had had enough humiliation for a lifetime. He got the gun, walked into Medici's office and shot him. Then he walked back into his own office and thought about it for a minute, then shot himself. He must have been lying there in pain when you went by his door and tended to Medici. He came out, and you know the rest."

"Don't blame yourself so much," Petrov said.

"Look. The guy was making thirteen thousand a year. Medici told me that. Those clothes. That car. Where in hell did I think he was getting the money, from income tax rebates? Shit, anyone would have wondered."

"Don't forget," Mrvich said, "Medici didn't wonder. Some people are so absurd, you just can't mistrust them."

"You should be Jewish," Petrov said to me. "Then you can have guilt all the time, even when you aren't guilty. You can have other people's."

I looked into his sad eyes, and I caught the wisdom and genuine sense of absurdity on his face. I couldn't help it. I started laughing. He made me feel a little better, after all. Or maybe I had to do something, and laughing was easiest then, if not appropriate.

41

Mrvich called at eleven the next morning and gave me the lab report and the medical examiner's report. His version looked solid. The gun had killed both Medici and Lamarr, and Lamarr had fired the gun, according to the evidence. It was already in the books: murder and suicide.

I tried to stop kicking myself for having tipped Medici to Lamarr's skim, but it wasn't easy. The most comforting thought I could find was that Medici, not necessarily as trusting as I am, hadn't suspected it, so even if I had no smarts, I had an excuse.

Now I had an unpleasant task to take care of. If people were paid in proportion to the unpleasantness of the job, cops would be the highest-paid people around. Well, maybe some doctors, too. Mustn't feel too sorry for myself. On the other hand, damn it all, this was a dirty business.

I drove north to Vancouver under a sky that was dotted with high, small clouds, but west I could see far off a blacker, thicker kind of cloud moving east, if it was moving at all. I wasn't sure. Most of the trip I just dwelled on what was ahead, how I could put it some way that would cause the least hurt. I didn't find in all the remarks I rehearsed the magic phrase that might make it easier.

The last house with the old paint that may have been yellow once stood alone again at the end of the last block of the last street of the last settlement in the West—not true, maybe, but you could believe it. The dark sky was closer now.

Robert Koski answered the door. "Who are you? Coo coo coo."

"Don't you remember me, Robert? I'm Mr. Barnes. We danced together, and you gave me some wine."

His sudden, childlike happiness burst on his face in a smile you'd have to call beautiful. "Why, it's Mr. Barnes. Mother," he called, "Mr. Barnes is here. He danced with us."

"Have him in, Robert," Madeline Koski's voice came from the living room. We passed through the old parlor with the sheet music of another time yellowing on top of the piano.

"Mr. Barnes has come to see us, Mother."

Mrs. Koski grinned her brown teeth at me and winked. "Why, Mr. Barnes, how nice of you to come. Please sit down. Robert will get you a nice glass of wine."

"I'm sorry, Mrs. Koski, but I can't have any wine today. I've brought you some bad news." I was trying to get it over with as fast as I could.

"Bad news. Good news. We all need new shoes," Robert said.

Both of them seemed dressed exactly the way they had been on my first visit. I felt they must always be dressed like that.

"Robert's crazy," Mrs. Koski said and winked again. She sat on the dingy couch, her splotched, heavy legs making their sad way to her rolled-down stockings. Robert stood near the door. Mrs. Koski added, "Aren't you, Robert?"

"Not crazy," Robert said and pouted.

"Mrs. Koski, I'm sorry to tell you this, but Mr. Lamarr won't be bringing you any money anymore."

"Why, Mr. Lamarr always brings us money. Mr. Lamarr is very nice, isn't he, Robert?"

Robert said, "Nice ice mice price."

"I'm sorry, Mrs. Koski, but Mr. Lamarr is dead."

Madeline Koski took it in slowly. Finally, she bent forward and looked at the floor in defeat. I had the feeling she'd looked at the floor like that many times before. Not this floor always, but some uncarpeted floor someplace. Same sad, bowed head. Jesus, why torture myself? I found myself saying, "Mrs. Koski, I don't know if I should tell you this, but Mr. Lamarr didn't give you his money. The money came from Mr. Medici." I don't know why I said that. I think I didn't want the wrong dead man getting the credit.

"Victor Medici?" She raised her head. Her eyes were unfeeling. Too much hurt too many times. She was numb, beyond reaction, and I felt selfishly grateful. It made things just a bit easier.

"Yes. He's dead, too. He felt bad about Candy, and when he found out where you were—"

"Candy. Candy. Is Candy here?" Robert's eyes were shining with a child's hope.

"Candy's dead, Robert," Madeline Koski said tonelessly.

Robert started to cry. "No more Candy. No more money. Not so funny. That's just dandy."

"Oh, shit, Robert," Mrs. Koski said without feeling.

Robert started to chew on his hand. Tears kept rolling down his face.

"I'm terribly sorry," I said. "Mr. Medici was a nice man in his own way, and I'm sure he didn't kill your daughter. He just wanted to help you because of the loss. A lot of people—" Jesus, I was babbling. I said weakly, "I'm sorry."

"How did they die?" I was surprised it was Robert who asked.

"In a car wreck," I said, not knowing why. Then I wondered if they heard or saw the news, TV, radio, newspaper. I'd not seen any in the house. Then I had to get out of there. Robert was crying again. "Well, I'm sorry but I must go."

"Can't we dance?" Robert asked. He was happy again, that fast. "We had such a nice dance last time, didn't we, Mother?"

"It was very nice, Robert," she said in the same flat tone.

I'd made up my mind not to cry this time, no matter

what. "Sorry, must be off." Christ, I was trying to sound
breezy.

"Won't you come and dance with us again, Mr. Barnes?"
Robert asked. "You'll come back and see us. Won't you?"

I couldn't see that another lie would hurt anything.
"I will, Robert. I'll come back and bring some nice wine
someday, and we'll dance. Just the three of us."

Robert started to dance by himself. Madeline Koski had
gone back to looking at the floor. I walked through the
parlor. Just as I opened the door, I heard a terrible wailing
sob. I couldn't tell which of them had done it. I shut the
door, and the dark air of the afternoon with rain threatening felt good in my face. It felt very good, the air, the
outdoors.

I noticed the white
foreign sports car parked about a hundred feet back of
mine. I crossed the yard of tall weeds and grass. The white
car looked new and hopelessly out of place in the drab
neighborhood of run-down old homes separated by empty
lots of fern and weed. No one was in the car. I was curious.
I walked to it.

Rain was not just a possibility. The air was thick with
dark threat and cool. The wind moved the weeds slightly.
The dark sky was overhead now. Rain was a certainty.

The white car turned out to be a brand-new Maserati.
I went to the driver's side and looked in the window. The
mileage indicator said 437 miles. I chilled as the air dark-
ened even more. I walked to the rear of the car.

The plates were new Oregon plates. The license plate
bracket said: "Italiano Imports, Portland, Oregon." I felt
very alone and so did something I would have done had
someone been with me. I shrugged to show indifference.
I stepped back to the left and took one step toward my car.

A voice I'd not heard for a while said, "You always were a softhearted son of a bitch."

I looked up. Standing next to my car, about a hundred feet away, was Manny Sanderson. He pointed a revolver at me and grinned. He pulled the trigger. A dog barked just before the gun barked.

It was all reflex. I couldn't move that fast again if you offered me any prize I wanted. I jumped on the trunk of the low sports car and rolled back onto the ground. Maybe the dog's barking had ruined his aim just enough. I still can't believe he missed at that distance, or that I moved so fast I caused him to miss. But there I was behind the Maserati on the ground, my gun out, and I inched toward the right rear of the car. I could hear him coming. The gravel crunched under his feet. He seemed to be coming still on the left side of the car. I crawled forward as quietly as I could.

Then it occurred to me that he must have thought he'd hit me, and that my sudden dive to the right had seemed to him my final reaction to the impact of the bullet. I was alongside the passenger side of the car now. I could see his feet on the other side of the car.

"Al? Are you dead, Al?" His voice seemed full of amusement. "Too bad, Al."

I shot him in the left foot. He screamed and fell. I was up and moving around the front of the car. He was sitting on the gravel, and as I came around the car he tried to twist around to get off another shot. I kicked him hard in the elbow of his right arm. The gun fell to the gravel. Then, for the next few moments, I became someone I didn't like.

I let out all the hate I'd built up against mean cops over the years. I hit him on the head with my gun. I kicked him twice in the right kidney. He started to moan. I kicked him in the small of the back and for a moment thought I'd paralyzed him. I didn't care.

The rain started. It seemed to bring me back to my senses. "Get up, you bastard," I said.

"I can't, Jesus. My foot." He was rolling back and forth in pain.

"Get up, goddamn it."

"I can't, honest. I can't." He talked through clenched teeth.

"Then crawl, goddamn it. You bastard. You tried to kill me. What the hell for?"

He just moaned.

I fished in his jacket pocket and found the keys to the Maserati. I put my gun against his left ear. "Crawl, goddamn it. Crawl to the car."

It took him a good two minutes. During that two minutes I found some handcuffs on him and wondered why he'd kept them. Then I supposed he still thought of himself as a cop. By the time he reached the car, the rain was getting serious. I unlocked and opened the door and dragged him up to where I could cuff him to the steering wheel. I couldn't cuff him without going around and opening the passenger door and reaching across the seat. I left him cuffed to the steering wheel, his body half out the open door on the driver's side. Rain hit him from the belt down.

I walked back to the Koski house and just went in without knocking. Mrs. Koski was still on the dingy sofa, looking at the floor. Robert was sitting on the floor with his face to the wall. Without looking at me, he said, "No more money, not so funny. Mr. Barnes has come back, Mother."

"Yes," Mrs. Koski said. "Was that you shooting, Mr. Barnes?" She sounded like she didn't care.

"Part of the time," I said. Do you have a phone, Mrs. Koski?" I was sure they didn't.

She surprised me. "Yes. It's in my bedroom off the kitchen."

I didn't even bother to ask her permission to use it. I went out to the kitchen and found a door next to the stove. I walked in and groped for a light switch. I didn't find one. Then I remembered how old-fashioned the house was. The room was very dark, and I waved my hand around until I felt a string. I pulled it.

The room was dark because it had only one small window, and that was covered by the green pull-down shade. The bed was unmade and had no sheets. The light was not very bright. I calculated the bulb at forty watts, but it was a harsh light the bulb gave off. I could never remember a light both harsh and dim before.

The phone was a surprise. It was an elegant, gold

French phone that went with the house like the Maserati outside went with the neighborhood. Well, everything seemed out of place now. I called the cops. It turned out we were several blocks beyond the city limits, so the operator put me in touch with the sheriff. I told them what had happened and walked outside to wait.

Sanderson looked very still. His body was still mostly out in the rain that by now was steady, his head under the roof inside the car. I went around to the passenger side to get a better look at him. His face was buried in the seat cushion.

I lifted his head. The bullet hole in his head looked neutral and neat. The bullet hole in his throat looked obscene.

I went through his pockets and found his wallet. He had seven one-hundred-dollar bills and a couple of twenties, four ones. In his wallet I found a page torn from a small notebook. It had two telephone numbers on it. One seemed familiar, but I couldn't place it. The other bore the letters H. M. C. I put the piece of paper in my own wallet and put his back.

I went to my car and slipped into the back seat to wait. The rain got very hard. In the few minutes I'd been in the house, someone had come by, stopped, walked around to the passenger side of his car, looked right at him and put the two shots into him. Then had simply gotten back into his or her car and driven off. Very cool. Very cold.

I started to shake. The rain had nothing to do with it.

43

The next five hours were grim. It took a dumb deputy named Flanner almost an hour just to unravel my story. While I was telling it, I wondered that anyone would believe it. We made calls to Thompson Falls, Montana, and to Portland. The sheriff himself showed up after two hours had gone by and seemed

a bit more understanding, or at least capable of understanding. Mrvich's replies to the calls, as well as Yellow
Bear's, helped a lot.

My gun checked out OK, of course, and they let me keep
it. My answers stayed pat. No, I hadn't heard the shots.
No, I hadn't noticed the white Maserati trailing me from
Portland. Yes, I was working on a murder case myself.
No, I hadn't heard the shots. What was all this about
Medici and Lamarr and the Koskis and money? Can we
try that again? No, I hadn't heard the shots. What kind
of a detective can't spot a white Maserati tailing him? No,
I didn't hear the shots. No, I didn't hear the car drive away.
Maybe the killer came on foot. Like hell. No, I didn't hear
the shots.

Rick Petrov showed up before eight and acted like he
was licensed to practice in Washington. The sheriff didn't
think to question it. They released the Mercedes. I trailed
Rick back to his house. He put a wondrously strong scotch
in my hand about ten seconds after we entered the front
door.

Rick's wife turned out to be an elegant, tall woman
named Winnie, rather quiet and most pleasant. She served
me a quiet, pleasant and most elegant steak after I'd polished off three scotches, and I chased the tender meat down
with some tender, imported beer.

Rick and I kicked it around for an hour or so after I
finished dinner. Finally, in desperation, Petrov said, "Oh,
shit. I know. The masked avenger who dispenses swift
justice just showed up on the appointed hour and did the
bastard in."

It wasn't very funny, but he always seemed to know
when I needed a laugh.

After I quit laughing, I said, "I want to move out of the
Hammer place. I don't feel very comfortable there anymore." Then I remembered the piece of paper. I got it out
of my wallet. He handed me the phone when I asked if I
could use it.

I dialed the first number. Lila's voice said, "Marnie Ross
Tingley's residence."

I hung up.

I dialed the H. M. C. number. A voice said, "High Mountain Club." I hung up again.

"Tell me about the High Mountain Club, can you?"

"Money," Rick said. "Lot's of money."

"Could Marnie Ross Tingley be a member?"

"Oh, sure."

"Could Mrvich get me in there tomorrow?"

"Sure. If not, I can."

"Really?"

"I've had a couple of rich clients, not many, but a couple. I'm very good in the courtroom, and they feel they owe me."

"I'm sure they do."

Then Petrov dropped one on me. "I almost forgot. Mrvich called me to go get you, and in all the excitement, I forgot to give you a message he had. He said to tell you Marnie Tingley wasn't in Montana on October sixth. She was shacked up with a guy at the Benson Hotel."

"That would be worse news if Sanderson hadn't come into the picture," I said. "She could have killed her husband without moving. I'm almost convinced she did. Who was the guy at the Benson?"

"Murv gave me a number for the detective who checked it out. Wait a minute." He rummaged around and found the number. "Detective Hogan."

I got Hogan on the phone after ten minutes of tracing him through four numbers.

"Barnes? Yeah, Murv said you might call. The guy signed the register Mr. and Mrs. Randall Cleaver. I don't think that was his name because he paid in cash, and from the descriptions I got he was the credit card type. I talked to a desk clerk, a bartender and two bellhops. The guy was tall, maybe six two, handsome, in his forties, everything you need to impress some women, including a touch of gray at the temples, for Christ sake. He was maybe a bit arrogant, thought he was hot shit after a martini or two. One of the bartenders didn't like him at all. I almost forgot. After he sat at the bar, his Mrs., who is, I'm sure, Marnie Ross Tingley, came in and they moved to a table. A waitress served them. She liked him. He left her a fat gratuity—that's a tip to us slobs."

"How can you be sure the woman was Tingley?"

"Showed a photo I picked up from the Portland newspaper, the *Oregonian*. She used to be on the society pages now and then, but not in the last few years. Her life seemed to get more private."

"We might say that. Thanks much, Hogan."

"Anytime."

Rick offered to put me up if I was serious about leaving the Hammers'. I was serious about leaving the Hammers'. The Petrovs were more my style after all. I could use Winnie's '72 Chevy. They had a spare room that was smaller than the Los Angeles Coliseum. Finally, it was plainer and easier, more comfortable. Opulence, even if tasteful, bores me after a few days. It would be a relief to leave a place where I no longer felt welcome. And the most uncomfortable thing of all was that I was closing in on Marnie Ross Tingley for at least two and probably three murders, and Lynn Hammer was close to Marnie.

We did it all in less than two hours. Rick trailed me to the Hammers', and I dropped off the Mercedes with no regrets. I'd started to feel conspicuous driving the thing around town. I picked up my things, told Lynn how much I'd enjoyed staying there, thanked her and asked her to thank Lee, who seemed to be out.

She made it easy. I'd expected that since she was a gracious woman. But I thought I detected some sense of relief. That didn't surprise me, either. I really had been there too long.

I couldn't tell her I was closing in on her old friend. But even as I was leaving, I was still the dick.

"Lynn, you mentioned Marnie visiting you in Montana last summer. Tell me something. Did she meet Manny Sanderson when she was there?"

"Did she ever. She had him panting at the starting gate. He took her to lunch a couple of times, I remember." She laughed. "I have to admit, Marnie is pretty good with the boys."

I decided not to tell her Sanderson had been killed a few hours before, but I didn't know why. I realized I didn't feel as close to her as I should. I didn't understand that, either. She'd find out about Sanderson soon enough.

"Look. I probably won't see you again before I leave, but I'll see you next year in Montana." I took her hand. "It really was fine, you know."

"For me, too. I just hope Arlene doesn't find out about the Tolovana Inn."

"If she does, maybe we can be buried side by side."

Rick drove me back to his place. We got there around eleven. It was what you might call a rich, full day. I slept like a gunnysack full of live eels.

44

The High Mountain Club turned out to be an old estate that had belonged to some high muck-a-muck back in the early part of the century. Probably some guy who cut down all the trees he could find, sold them, used the money to start a prostitution empire, then retired, perfected his manners and entertained only the best people. The approach was too much. A white gravel road wound gracefully through very tall cedars and alders and firs. I can't remember seeing more magnificent trees. It took about three minutes to reach the mansion from the gate. My '72 Chevy seemed out of place. I didn't feel like a fixture myself.

I had two "ins," one from Mrvich and one from Petrov. I'd decided to use Petrov's. Petrov's "in" was an invitation from an old member named Byron Oswald. Rick had defended him once from a charge of stock fraud. Petrov told me Oswald had been innocent beyond doubt and wouldn't have been charged had not the D.A. been two weeks from a mental breakdown when he filed charges. Not only had Petrov proven Oswald's innocence in court, he had managed to point the finger at the guilty party right in the courtroom and had been called Perry Mason by his colleagues for a year or so after the trial. Happily, the nickname hadn't stuck.

The mansion was huge but sedate. Inside, it was quiet. The closest thing to a guard was a good-looking, middle-aged man who sat at a desk inside the hallway. The walls were dark panels of some kind of expensive-looking wood and highly polished. The good-looking man wore a dark suit, and he graciously asked me if he could help me. The place was too confident to bother with suspicions. I had the feeling the members didn't worry about anything. They assumed that this was exclusive in a way understood by all.

The man at the desk directed me to Mr. Oswald, who was in a room I suppose you'd call a study. A big study. Around twenty-five deep leather chairs were placed so that people could sit apart and not notice each other. I found Byron Oswald deep in one of the chairs, a small man with a kindly face. He was reading a book of poems by William Stafford. I liked him immediately. His hair had been blond once but was now a wispy silver and quite fine. His gentle face said life had been good to him, and when it hadn't he had learned something.

"Mr. Barnes." He gripped my hand, and his eyes sparkled. "Mr. Petrov said you would be coming to see me. Please sit down." A leather chair had already been pulled next to him, and I assumed I'd been expected since they were the only two chairs close together.

"I see you're reading William Stafford," I said. "Do you like his poems?"

"Oh my, yes. He's one of my favorites. I came from a small Midwest farm myself, came West many years ago and settled. So Mr. Stafford's poems speak specially to me."

"Me, too, Mr. Oswald, and I'm strictly big-city west coast until I moved to Montana."

"He lives here, you know, not far from here. I had the honor to meet him once. A lovely, mild-mannered man. One of my nieces was a student in his class, and she's very fond of him. Have you met him?"

"No. I heard him read once in Seattle years ago. I've never forgotten it. I wanted to be a poet myself once."

"Really. And instead you became a policeman. What an unusual diversion."

"Well, I could have kept writing but didn't. You can be both. A friend of mine on the Portland force is."

"I tried once myself but instead became a financier," he laughed quietly. "What can I do for you, Mr. Barnes?"

"Mr. Oswald, I wonder if you could tell me a bit about the club. Do you know all the members?"

"Oh my, yes. We only have about sixty. I don't know some of the new ones very well."

"Is Marnie Ross Tingley a member?"

"My, yes. A lifetime member. Her parents bought her a membership years ago. Sy Ross and Elaine. Both dead, alas. Well," he sighed, "time for everyone."

"Mr. Oswald, I realize you're obligated not to talk about the other members to a stranger, but I'm investigating three murders and—"

"Good lord. Really?"

"Yes, sir."

"Heavens." He looked a bit depressed. I had the feeling moral failure always depressed him.

"Might I ask you some questions, Mr. Oswald? It's very important to me. If you feel you can't answer, I'll understand."

"Surely no one in the club is suspected?"

"I'm not sure who is suspect at this point," I said. It seemed as close to being honest as I could be and still not cause him alarm.

"I understand," he said. I doubted he did.

"You mentioned Marnie's parents. Can you tell me about them, anything at all?"

"Sy? Sy was a nice man. He made a lot of money, and he gave much to charities. I liked Sy"—then he laughed— "except on the squash court."

"Why didn't you like him on the squash court?"

"He was so serious. Had to win at all costs. You'd have thought he was playing for his life. He usually won, too. The only time I beat him, he stormed off the court. It took him an hour and three drinks before he could bring himself to speak to me. Elaine wasn't much different."

"Mrs. Ross?"

"Yes. She was club tennis champion for years, and she played with a vengeance. Once, she slammed a forehand into the face of her opponent who was crowding the net. Poor woman couldn't have been more than a few feet away. She was stunned and needed a few minutes to recover, I remember. Elaine stood there coldly, waiting. Offered no assistance and acted as if her opponent was an enemy in some war. She seemed impatient for the poor woman to get up so she could continue the game. Later on in the locker room, I understood she apologized. Would you care for a drink, Mr. Barnes?"

"No, thanks."

"It's about time for my crème de cacao. That's all I can take anymore, and the doctor limits me to one a day." He signaled ever so slightly with his hand. A waiter was there almost immediately with the drink. "I do wish you'd join me, Mr. Barnes."

"Well, a scotch would be good."

"Ah, splendid. Hal, bring Mr. Barnes a scotch. Ice and a bit of water?"

"Fine." The waiter, young, dark and with dignity, walked off. "I take it you found the Rosses' competitive attitude strange, Mr. Oswald?"

"Well, naturally you run into it, but theirs was so advanced it seemed just a bit out of place here at the club among friends—I'm sorry, Mr. Barnes. I'm afraid I'm just a stuffy old man. Forgive me."

"You seem awfully nice to me," I said with meant feeling. Hal put my scotch beside me on the small table.

"You're nice, too, Mr. Barnes. I always assumed the police were crude and tough."

"There are all kinds. A lot of cops have to be tough. They deal with tough people."

"I'd thought being a policeman would make one jaded about people, look for only the worst in others."

"It affects some that way over the years, and they start looking at everybody with suspicion. But others are like me. I've found over the years that the big, big majority of people are fairly decent. They just want to be left alone and to get along. For me, it's given me a pretty positive view of people."

"That makes me feel good," he said. He tipped his glass toward me. I returned the toast.

"Do you have a membership list, Mr. Oswald?"

"I suppose we do. I've never seen one but"—he gestured again—"Hal, do we have a typed list of the members here?"

"Yes, sir. We do."

I said I'd like to see it, and Oswald nodded Hal on his way to get it.

"Murder is terrible, isn't it, Mr. Barnes?"

"The worst."

"Do you know, William Stafford somewhere says 'our lives are an amnesty given us,' or something like that. When you murder someone, you break their amnesty. You take away their right to stay out of war—isn't that what that means?"

"I'm not sure," I said. I felt embarrassed because I wasn't sure what Stafford had meant by that, though I liked the line. Hal handed me the list. "Would you excuse me for a moment, Mr. Oswald?"

"Surely, Mr. Barnes."

I went down the list. What amazes me is that there are so many rich people, and no one knows who they are. Except for Marnie's name, none were familiar, but one other I hadn't expected. Randall Clueridge. Randall Clueridge? Randall Cleaver?

- "Do you know Randall Clueridge, Mr. Oswald?"

"Yes, but not well. He's one of our more recent members. A handsome fellow, financier, I believe, like me."

I didn't bother to correct him, but I doubted Randall Cleaver was anything like him.

"Does he come here often?"

"Oh, yes. He practically lives here. He's usually in the bar."

"How about his wife?"

"His wife?"

"Yes, Joyce Clueridge."

"I don't believe I know her," he said diplomatically.

"Is he here now?"

"I'm sure he is." He gestured, and Hal came. "Hal, is Mr. Clueridge in the bar?"

"Yes, sir, he is."

I made some polite good-bye gestures, thanked him to a point of what I thought he would find good taste. As I was leaving, he said, "I hope you catch your murderer, Mr. Barnes."

"Even if it's someone in the club, Mr. Oswald?"

"Especially if it's someone in the club," he said.

I decided not to hug him, but it took some effort.

45

The bar was in keeping with the club, quiet, polished, dignified. Four women were drinking at a table, three of them smart and not very good-looking. The fourth was attractive but in some cold, forbidding way. The same expensive-looking wood paneling stretched around the walls. Afternoon light came through a tall window at the far end of the room. The bartender looked like he taught history at Harvard. It was as different from the bar in Dixon as a bar could be. I decided if I wanted to drink more than one, I'd take Dixon.

I knew who Clueridge was without being told. He was standing at the bar, the farthest of three drinkers standing there. The nearest two were chatting. Clueridge seemed to be drinking alone. He had a martini in front of him. His skin was dark from a sunlamp tan, and he had a touch of gray in his sideburns and also high on his temples. He was a good-looking man, but his black eye seemed absurd in this setting.

I introduced myself and told Clueridge why I was there. He didn't seem surprised. His manner was cold and disdainful, as if I hadn't cleaned his toilet to suit him.

"I've heard of you," he said. He made it sound like he'd heard of me along with Heinrich Himmler.

"From your wife or from Marnie Tingley?"

He didn't ruffle easily. "From both, as a matter of fact."

"Perhaps we should move to a table," I suggested gently.

"What the hell for?" he said belligerently.

"Well, I'd like to ask you some questions, if you don't mind."

"Hell, yes, I mind. How would I know anything that could help you?"

"Please, can't we talk where we can't be heard?" I felt awkward. I knew some of the others could hear us. He was playing to the audience, and this was his stadium.

"No, Burns or Barnes or whatever your name is, we won't move anywhere." He even looked around for appreciation. I was getting tired of this.

"Please, Mr. Clueridge, it would be far less—"

"Please, Mr. Clueridge. Please, Mr. Clueridge—Jesus, the servile were born to it," he said. With that he almost bowed. "I like it here at the bar. You ask your damn questions, and if I feel like answering, I'll answer. If I don't, you'll be thrown out of here on your ass."

I upped my voice a few decibels. "Very well. On the night of October fifth you took a woman who was not your wife to a room at the Benson Hotel. She's been involved with three people who have been murdered. If you'd rather talk to Captain John Mrvich of the Portland police, then I can—" He waved me quiet.

"Perhaps we should move to a table," he said.

"I like it here," I said loudly. "While you were still shacked up in the Benson with this woman on the morning of October sixth, her husband was being killed with an axe about five hundred miles away in Montana." Though my back was turned to the others, their eyes were on the back of my head and on his face. I felt them on my head. I saw them burn on his face. He walked away from the bar toward the far wall and sat down at a table. For a moment I thought I might yell at him across the room. The bastard deserved it.

I ordered a scotch and carried it down to his table.

"OK. I went with Marnie to the Benson," he said sullenly. "What of it?"

I didn't say anything.

"We've had something going on and off for years. You've met my wife so you can appreciate my problem, which can get very sexual at times. It isn't just looks, mind. Joyce makes Marnie look like Mary McCarthy when it comes to brains."

"How did you get that black eye?"

"Oh, that. I got mad on the golf course and threw a club and it bounced right back up and—"

"Please."

"Well?"

"Another boyfriend?" He nodded and looked out the window. I went on, "How about a guy who isn't your type,

sort of primitive? Near albino with blue eyes like an Alaskan husky, cold, no facial expression?"

Clueridge looked at his hands. They didn't shake. "I
didn't even know him. He came up in a parking lot downtown and flattened me. It was damn unexpected. Just
walked up and bam. I was on the ground, stunned, and he
said, 'Stay away from Marnie, you son of a bitch, or I'll
kill you.' He showed me a gun. I should have known."

"Known what?"

"Known she had someone like that around, and others,
too. I know what she is. But she gets under my skin, and
I can't help it. She's good in bed and—"

I waved away his need to go on. But he went on.

"She's wild. All kinds of kinky impulses. I know it's no
good getting tangled up with a broad like that, but, shit,
she comes in here looking like a princess. I just can't lay
off. Her maid is our maid's niece so I couldn't risk taking
her to her place. We used motels, hotels. I just can't afford
a divorce."

"You mean you don't want to part with what your wife
might get."

"Something like that." He waved for two more drinks.

"You needn't worry about your assailant. He got one
bullet in the head and another in the throat yesterday in
Vancouver."

"B.C.?" he asked hopefully.

"Washington."

"Can I be suspected? I suppose I can."

"Have an alibi?"

"For the whole day?"

"Early afternoon. Say around one-thirty, two."

"I was at lunch with some business associates. You can
check."

"I know, but I won't. I don't think you knew Sanderson
was dead until I told you. I'll take the names of your lunch
partners just to look like a good cop. Anything else about
Marnie?"

"I don't think so. I'll bet her maid can tell you plenty."

I wrote down the names of the people he'd had lunch
with the day before and left. On my way out, I found a
telephone on a shelf. It looked private enough. I called
Mrvich and asked if he could find out two things. One,

where Marnie was yesterday, early afternoon, and two, did
the phone company have a record of any calls on her phone
to or from Montana a few days just before October 6?

46

The sales manager
at Italiano Imports was named Grazenhouse, a big, florid
man with a big, florid smile. He had been acting cheerful
so long, he had become cheerful.

"What can I do for you, Al?" He pumped my hand like
the pump might not work and he would be without water
forever.

I told him what I wanted.

"White Maserati, sure. About a week ago. Strange guy
with blond hair that was almost white and spooky eyes.
Came in and asked about the white Maserati in the window. I was a bit leery. Didn't seem like the Maserati type,
exactly."

"What is the Maserati type, Mr. Grazenhouse?"

"There aren't many," he said.

"Please go on. Sorry to have interrupted."

"Well, he asked if he could take it out for a spin. Christ,
a brand-new Maserati. What in hell did he think he was
buying, a used pickup? I tried to be polite. I said that
Maserati buyers usually knew what they were getting,
and I must have insulted him because he gave ma a bad
look. Spooky. Spooky. Spook. Spook. Spook. Like he could
kill me without feeling anything. We don't get many like
that here at good old Italiano Imports, Al, you can be sure.
By the way, I noticed you drove up in an old Chevy. You're
not by any chance in the—"

"Sorry, Mr. Grazenhouse. Wish I was."

"Niente fortuna," Grazenhouse said and laughed.

"Did he ask the price?"

"Not exactly. He sat in the driver's seat for a moment, shifted gears and then just said he'd take it."

"Just like that?"

"Exactly. I took him to the office and sat him down to talk terms. I didn't much care for him, but we don't sell a Maserati every day. But when I said, 'Now about financing, Mr.'—and he said 'Sanderson,' and I said—"

"He gave you his real name?"

"Was that his real name?"

"Yes."

"He paid cash. He pulled out a big, big wad of money and paid cash. I couldn't believe it. I've never seen that happen, and I've been selling cars for twenty-five years. At least, not for a new car and sure as hell not for a new Maserati."

"How much was the car?"

"Thirty-four thousand dollars."

"And he gave you that in cash?"

"*Che strano,* hey, Al? Paid in one-hundred dollar bills, three hundred and forty of them. I was disappointed, naturally."

"Why?"

"Well, we make a lot of money on financing, on the interest, you know." I waited. He seemed to get flustered for a moment. "Well, there it is. He signed all the papers, and we made arrangements to register the car in his name. We mailed the papers to the state so they could forward the title to him and—"

"He must have given you an address, then."

"Oh, yes. Otherwise, the state wouldn't know where to mail the title, you see."

"Can I have it?"

"Sure. *Certimente,* Al." He called a secretary through a speak box. "Vivian, give Al here the address for Sanderson, Manfred Sanderson, the guy who bought that white Mas for cash."

I walked out, and Vivian handed me the address. Grazenhouse's fleshy arm was about my shoulders. "Al, if you're ever ready for a classy Italian car"—he gestured toward the gleaming models on display—"don't forget to call me. We're here to serve."

He walked all the way to my car with me. "Well, thank you, Mr. Grazenhouse. You've been a big help."

"It's just plain Grazy to my friends," he said.

"Well, thank you, Grazy." And that cheerful old Italian Grazenhouse was waving and crying *"Ciao"* as I drove away in Winnie Petrov's Chevy.

47

Sanderson's address turned out to be a motel called the Nickel Inn. It was hidden away in a fairly nice area of town, one of those places that probably has a steady clientele because it's not on any main arterial. Mrvich was there ahead of me, and one of his detectives was going over the room.

"We traced his address through the state," he explained. "I figured he'd bought that white Mas and so it would have to be registered. And look what we found." He pointed to the bed where a lot of money was spread out. "Over twelve thousand. He kept it inside a shirt in the drawer. Sort of risky, but I suppose he didn't want to bank it for fear of arousing suspicion. He probably intended to take off soon."

"What's it look like to you?"

"Well, you can forget about Mrs. Tingley for the target practice at the beach. She was here that day, all day, with Sanderson. They got sloshed in the house bar that afternoon. She's starting to come unglued. Her hands fluttered like birds when my boys were questioning her. I'm sure the local cop was right. That was just some nutty kid trying to scare you. That shit goes on a lot in the sticks where kids got guns and loads of boredom.

"But now the going gets good. She can't account for yesterday at all. Says she was out driving around. Also, she phoned Sanderson three times in Montana after she got back, the last time October fourth. She also phoned her husband twice, last time on October fifth, one day before he got axed. Also, Sanderson phoned her on the fifth."

We sat quietly for a few minutes. Finally, I said it. "I think she killed Sanderson and her husband and, years ago Candy Koski—I mean, she paid Sanderson to kill her husband and to kill me. When Sanderson missed me, she was waiting in the wings. It seems impossible I had a white Maserati on my tail and missed it, but it looks like that's what happened. I was just so damned preoccupied with giving the bad news to the Koskis, I missed it."

"I'm with you," Mrvich said. "Too much points to her. She must have figured you were getting close. She could have learned you'd discovered Medici and Lamarr from the newspapers. It was in there, all right. And she must have surmised that Medici either was about to or did say something that pointed to her for the Koski killing. Well, we know her father got Medici off. Why? For silence, maybe. That makes sense. He gets the editorial planted through Armstrong, gets the trial switched, gets the fancy lawyer, saves whatever conscience he has, saves his daughter's ass—because she must have told him Medici was innocent, and either he guessed the truth or slapped it out of her or she just flat out told him. Then, years later, alone—I mean husbandless—she finds a dirty, brutal guy in Montana who'll do anything as long as she puts out her ass and money. She pays him to kill her husband in revenge for her bruised little ego, and she pays him to kill you when she fears you are on the trail, getting way too close. But she's driving backup. When Sanderson misses, the moment you're in phoning the cops, she drives up and shoots him twice while he lies there helpless, cuffed to his steering wheel. Now he can't finger her if he's caught. There's just one problem."

"What's that?"

"No proof."

"Oh, yes. That."

We sat a while longer. Finally, I said, "Her maid wants to talk to me. Maybe I can get proof."

"Go, oh, master detective," Mrvich said sullenly.

48

I was glad I had the Chevy instead of the Mercedes. The blacks paid no attention when I parked. The district was no slum, either. Nice older houses lined the streets, most of them with a lot more character than more recently built suburban homes. The few people in the street seemed uninterested in a white man in their neighborhood.

Lila's house was a heavy green color, frame, with four wooden steps leading to an open porch, Midwest style. Lila answered my buzz.

"Come on in," she said matter-of-factly, as if this was something that had to be done.

The house was comfortable and homey. The furniture was old and useful. The carpet was old and useful. The floors were meant to be walked on, the chairs to be sat on. We walked through the living room and into the kitchen. A young black man was sitting at the table. He had a drink in front of him, either gin or vodka. I spotted the bottle on the drain: vodka. He seemed very cheerful. I guessed his age at twenty-five.

Lila didn't bother to introduce us. She was wearing tight slacks and a black and white nylon blouse and looked awfully good. She motioned me to a chair. "Want a drink, Mr. Barnes?"

"I guess not," I said. "Thanks, anyway."

She sat down and looked right at me. Up close, I could see she was truly beautiful. Her features were soft, almost exquisite. She got right down to business.

"You're investigating Mr. Tingley's murder, aren't you?"

I nodded.

"She wanted him dead," Lila said without fanfare.

"Did she tell you that?"

"Lots of times, when she was drunk. She gets real, drunk, Mr. Barnes. She gets drunk, and she says things like, 'He can't leave me. No man leaves me. I'll kill him for it. I'll kill him if it's the last thing I do.'"

"How did she react when she found out he was dead?"

"She was disappointed."

"Disappointed?"

"Yes. She acted as if she hadn't gotten what she wanted for Christmas. She's very weird, you know, and not nice. Sometimes when she gets drunk she starts to rave how she hates all men. But for someone who hates them, she sure doesn't throw any of them out."

"She has lots of men?"

"Does she ever. Sometimes she has three lovers in three days, bang, bang, bang, like that. It's hard on me."

"How? I mean, does that mean you have to leave?"

"No. No. It's a big apartment. You didn't really see it all. It's huge. It costs her eight hundred a month."

"How is it hard on you, then?"

"Well, Mr. Barnes, she's really weird. I got hired because I'm pretty. And when she's bringing a man up, I have to be real pretty. I have to dress up in one of the sexy costumes she got for me."

The young man giggled. "She's real sexy, Mr. Barnes."

"I can see that," I said. Lila flashed a smile that would have started the battle of Troy all over. The young man giggled some more.

"I have to try to turn the guy on," she said flatly. "I'm supposed to come into the room often and sort of parade around without looking like that's what I'm doing. You know, let the guy get a look at me several times."

I was getting confused. "Let's see, you—" I caught myself. I wasn't sure what the next question should be. Finally, I said rather feebly, "Why does she do that, Lila? Do you know?"

"I didn't for a while. I just thought she wanted the guy to be stimulated, you know. To be turned on so she'd get a good night out of it. But that didn't make much sense. I mean, a woman wants to do her own turning on. So I did like she told me. I didn't mind. I'm young, a lot younger than her, and I'm pretty and like to dress up and get looked at by men. So what was the harm of it?"

"I see. It does seem odd, like she was setting up some competition deliberately."

"That's it exactly, Mr. Barnes. That went on for a while. Then it got rougher. The next morning, after the guy had left, she'd lord it over me."

"What?"

"She'd say things like, 'You tried your best, you bitch, but you can't top me,' things like that. As if I'd really wanted the guy, when all the time I was only showing myself all dolled up because she asked me to. I had to listen to her gloat about her victory while she ate breakfast. 'I sure don't let any bitch get ahead of me, not even a lovely hunk like you,' she'd say."

"What did this have to do with her husband, if anything?"

"Well, she thinks her husband left her for another woman. She says it lots of times when she's drunk. She says, 'That bitch stole my husband,' things like that."

"Does she have anyone in mind? Do you know who she's talking about?"

"No, she never mentions anyone."

"Could it be Lynn Hammer?"

"Oh, no. Lynn Hammer is like a mother to her. Lynn Hammer is a nice lady. Sometimes, when Mrs. Tingley gets really wild, sobbing and swearing revenge and all that, Lynn Hammer comes over and quiets her down. And Mrs. Tingley often calls Lynn Hammer when she's lonely or needs someone."

"And you don't know who this woman is that Robin Tingley is supposed to have taken up with?"

"To tell the truth, Mr. Barnes, I don't think there is any other woman. I think he just couldn't take her anymore and split. That's what I think."

I sat back and looked at her. My mind seemed to be grabbing at this and that and not quite coming up with anything. I supposed I'd better ask the big one:

"Lila, do you think Mrs. Tingley killed her husband?"

"Mr. Barnes, I think she could have, yes."

The young man got up and fixed himself another drink. He said, "Sure you won't have one, Mr. Barnes?"

"Oh, OK, I guess I will. Light, though, please. What's your name, by the way?"

"Marvin Green," he said. Then he added proudly, "I'm her boyfriend," and pointed at Lila.

"And a very lucky boyfriend," I said. He handed me a vodka and tonic.

Lila said suddenly, "I hate her, and I hate myself for working for her and letting her whip me."

"What?"

"That was the next thing, Mr. Barnes. After she'd been shacking up all night with a guy, she didn't feel satisfied just lording it over me. So one day she asked me right out. She said, 'Lila, I want to whip you with a belt.' Well, I didn't know what to say. The guy had just gone home, and she was drinking coffee, and she told me that it would make her feel better if after she had a night with a man, she could whip me. I said, 'Mrs. Tingley, I don't want to take any whipping from you or anyone else,' and she said. 'To the victors all things,' or some shit like that. And then she offered me three hundred dollars to take a whipping. Well, three hundred bucks is a lot of money for a few minutes of pain. I got friends who get beat up by their husbands for nothing. So I let her. I felt lousy about it, but I let her. She says things like, 'This will show you, no one steals a man from me,' while she's hitting me with this belt. One month, I made thirty-six hundred dollars by taking twelve whippings."

"Jesus Christ," I said.

"You know that a lot of rich whites use blacks to play out their kinks. I always thought it was disgusting when my girl friends did it. And here I am, doing it because I want the money."

"I've known a case where a white man has done it," I said. "I never ran into this before."

"She gives me cash so I don't have to pay no taxes on it," Lila said. "But, God, Mr. Barnes, I feel so damned cheap letting her do it, that white bitch laying her belt across me like that."

"So it's a cycle," I said. "She gets a guy up to her place. You parade for him like you're trying to win him for yourself. She lays him. The next morning, she beats you like she's a conqueror. Like you've been in some contest, and she won, and you get punished for daring to have competed with her."

"That's it. And it's all in her mind, Mr. Barnes. The whole thing."

"Have you known about this, Marvin?"

"Sure. She's my girl. She tells me everything."

"Well, don't you feel lousy about it, too?"

"It won't last much longer," he said. "We got enough saved up to buy our own house. I got a job, and we're going to get married. Then Lila's getting the hell out of there."

"I sure am," Lila said.

49

We got to the Ming Arms by six. It was dark and rainy. The doorman asked if Mrs. Tingley was expecting us, and Mrvich said no and flashed his badge, and we went up.

She didn't try to work on us. I suppose she saw how grim we were. This was the part I hated, the confrontation. I wish I could be like Nero Wolfe and just sit and figure out the case and have somebody else get the confession, make the arrest, break the hearts, ruin the lives, while I grew orchids and swilled beer.

She was dressed in tight, ultraclean slacks. They rippled on her, and they hugged her every contour. They were still great contours, still in perfect proportion. Her off-white sweater looked like it had cost seventy dollars. It fitted her contours, too, all of them. I wasn't having any of it.

We sat down and faced her. She crossed her legs and relaxed. "What do you want?"

"I want you to confess to three murders and save us the trouble of finding more evidence," I said.

"Oh." Her face started to contort. I thought she was going to cry. "I didn't kill anybody," she said, and her voice turned high and whiny in mid-sentence.

"Let me talk for a minute. Let's go back nineteen years. One problem with a lot of rich people is that they are winners. They win and win, and winning becomes an obsession. It gets so important that the game itself doesn't matter. If they think they might not win, they rig the game. They're a bit like people who cheat at solitaire.

"Your father was one, I think, and your mother, and they passed on their warped values to you. Nineteen years ago your father found out his daughter had killed somebody. I don't know how he found out. Maybe you told him. It doesn't make any difference. You had to win. When you saw there was a chance you might lose, in this case might lose Robin Tingley to Candy Koski, you killed her."

"But I didn't," she whined. "I didn't. I was too small to kill her that way."

"You don't have to be big to strangle someone. All you have to do is get a towel around her neck and hold for four seconds. That's all it takes to render someone unconscious. After that it's easy, providing you're dedicated enough." I'd almost said "vicious" instead of "dedicated." "Robin wasn't really important. Just winning. He must have realized that, after years of being married to you. That's why he finally took off. Daddy, seeing his little girl had done a no-no, and seeing that someone innocent might have to pay for it, rigged the game. He always rigged the game so everything would come out right, just the way he wanted it. He wasn't about to lose his daughter to the nasty old authorities for the murder of a girl from a miserably poor family, a girl who had the good luck—scratch that—the bad luck to be beautiful. A girl who at sixteen suddenly found she had what her family had never had and what yours had always had, power.

"She had power over the male. She could turn them on. She could interest any man in her. She had it. It was unfair, wasn't it? A nobody from a family of losers about to win from someone in a family of winners. About to win Robin Tingley, maybe, if she wanted him. So you saw to it she didn't win.

"And then Daddy saw to it you didn't lose. He had his business partner plant a dumb editorial in a newspaper he owned. He may even have gotten Art Matthew himself to write it, I don't know. He hired Art Matthew, your father did, to take Medici's case. The game was rigged. Medici would get off. Your father wasn't all that bad. He wouldn't

see Medici hang for his daughter's crime. With the help
of the editorial, Matthew got the trial switched to Portland;
then he destroyed the opposition. All winners in your
world. Matthew. Mr. Ross. Armstrong. You. Even Medici,
though he never knew what was happening, really. Matthew told him to keep still, told him just what to say in
court, and Medici believed him. He had to. He had no
choice. But he must have guessed the truth."

"It isn't true. It isn't. I didn't know anything about all
that." She stamped her foot like a little child about to be
punished for something she didn't do. Tears were forming
in her eyes, and her face was dissolving.

"Save it, Marnie," I said, more to bolster my own sense
of righteousness than to correct her. I wanted to believe
her pain was an act, at least long enough to finish.

"Then the day came when Robin had had enough. Why
no children? You screw like a mink. I'll tell you why, even
if it's only a guess. You couldn't risk losing that perfect
little figure—"

"Do you think it's perfect?" she asked, sniveling.

"Oh, for Christ sakes," I said. "Give it a rest. Look, if
you lost all those ideal little lines by doing something as
natural as giving birth, you might not be able to win anymore. You want to do to every man what Candy Koski
could do. You play games with Lynn about who's most
successful at turning on this and that guy. She told me so.
But with you it goes a lot deeper, doesn't it?

"Talk about rigging the game. It must have been unbearable when he left you. The last thing you would admit
is that it was your fault. That kind of reason never would
occur to you. It would make you a loser in your own right.
No, you invented another woman. Then, to make up for
that one game where you lost to another woman, even if
she doesn't exist except in your knotty little mind, you
rigged a game where you would win again and again. It
didn't matter to you that it was fantasy. You found a beautiful young girl to be your maid. Then you made her play
out your fantasy. She was supposed to be after your men,
every one you brought home. And you were supposed to
win, over and over. Finally, just sadistically rubbing it in
to your so-called competition wasn't enough. You had to
show her you were a winner. She had to submit to your

whippings after every night you spent in the sack with the man you won, in quotes, won from her.

"Of course, to make it work, you had to find someone who would take a lot of shit. Who better than a black?. They're used to taking a lot of shit. They've been in practice for a long time. And she would need the money you paid her to take your shit. Whites—well, you could have found someone if you'd tried hard enough, somebody poor and lovely, or just plain masochistic. But why bother when it's so easy to find a black who needs the money?

"But it didn't work. Those things never do. Somewhere you must have known that the rigged little game wasn't taking care of that one time you were a real loser. And you must have known in your clearer moments, if you have any, that it was all unreal. Lila didn't want your men. She only had to act as if she did. You must have known, even while you were rubbing it in verbally or later when you were beating her, that it was all a sham. You weren't winning a thing. Lila is fifteen to twenty years younger than you are, and she's a stunning girl. If the game hadn't been rigged, you'd have been laid about as often as the Pope. Lila could win in any fair competition hands down, unless you were competing for a racial bigot. All she did it for was the money."

"No. No. No," she whined. "I would have won."

"Bullshit. You couldn't even wipe out once one fantasy with another. Finally, it got unbearable."

"You can get a lawyer if you want to," Mrvich put in.

"I don't want a lawyer," she sniveled. "Please make him stop saying these awful things about me."

"I'm not his boss," Mrvich said rudely.

I went on. "Then, in a trip last summer to see the Hammers and probably to beg your husband to come back, you met the perfect hit man. And then came a series of axe killings to hide in. You offered him your delicious little blonde body, and you offered him money. And he took it, and he killed your husband for you. Sanderson really went for you. He'd do anything for you. He even knocked Clueridge on his ass in a downtown parking lot when he found out you put out for him, too."

"He did?" She looked almost dignified for a moment, revived by Sanderson's dedication to her. Christ, on top of everything, in spite of killing three people, she was shallow. What a mess of a woman. Woman, hell. Little girl. Spoiled little girl. Dangerous little girl.

"You paid him with sex and money, and he axed Robin. You wanted Robin dead. You even said so in front of people. Only, Sanderson couldn't duplicate the insane butchery of a crazy young woman in Orofino, Idaho—or else he got scared off. Anyway, he only hit Robin twice. Once he realized my boss and I weren't buying Mary Lou Calk for Robin's murder, he decided to take off. So he disappeared. But he had someone to run to. You. He had plenty on you, and in his own rotten way he loved you.

"Then you decided to have him kill me. You were afraid I was getting close. I'm not clear how you knew, but what difference does it make? You couldn't lose. If I killed Sanderson, you'd be off the hook. He couldn't testify against you. If he killed me, I'd be off the case for good. The only way you could lose was if we both survived. And for a moment we both did. So you backed up your boy. When I was in phoning the police from the Koskis'—"

"The Koskis?"

"Yes, goddamn it, the Koskis. That's where they live, in that dilapidated old house in the middle of nowhere, the house you drove by after parking a couple of blocks away with Sanderson's new white car in sight. You found him cuffed to his steering wheel, but alive. You shot him twice and drove off. No one was around. You got away with it. He was dead and couldn't talk, couldn't point to you."

Marnie stared at us, her face bloodless white.

Mrvich tried his terrifying best. He stood up and said in his most officious manner, "You'll make it easier on yourself some if you confess." He was everybody's father for that moment.

She did a lot of things. She howled. She stamped. She whined. She howled over and over that it was all untrue. She even called Lynn for help.

But she didn't confess.

"What in hell are you doing?" Lynn asked me when Marnie handed me the phone.

"What in hell do you think we're doing?" I said frustrated. "Peeling grapes for the wine festival?"

"I've got a lawyer on the way," Lynn said. "Damn it, Al. You can't push my friends around."

"Fuck the lawyer," I said.

But we left before he arrived. We didn't say a word on the way to Petrov's place.

50

Mrvich and Petrov and I had a good-bye drink at the airport. I was in no mood for the festive, but I appreciated their being there. They seemed like the most supportive friends I could find in a world where rich women get away with murder.

I didn't even see the mountains on the way home. I kept dwelling on all the details of the case, wondering how I could have missed the skim Lamarr was pulling on Medici, how I could have missed a white Maserati on my tail, how I could have failed to crack a vile murderer who had about as much character as a hungry hamster.

Arlene met me at the plane. Two hours later we were in bed, whatever is left over from two hours after you drive from the Missoula airport to Plains.

A week later the letter arrived from Mrvich.

> *Dear Al:*
> *Well, you were right. The enclosed will tell the story, or most of it. I'll fill in the rest. Now don't start blaming yourself. She was such a tortured mess, she had no way out other than this. What's more, she was bloody dangerous to all of us. A few things the article doesn't cover—*

I interrupted his letter to read the xeroxed news clipping. It was dated, Portland, October 27.

WEALTHY LOCAL HEIRESS
SUICIDE IN PARKING LOT

Marnie Ross Tingley, wealthy Portland heiress and socialite, was found dead in her car in the Lloyd Center parking lot this morning at approximately 11 A.M., apparently a suicide. Police said she left a note but refused to divulge the contents. Some of Mrs. Tingley's friends said she had been upset recently. Her death follows her husband's by just three weeks. Mr. Tingley, who was estranged from his wife, was murdered in Plains, Montana, on October 6. The crime remains unsolved.

Marnie Ross, daughter of Sy Ross, wealthy contractor who died some years ago, attended Lincoln High School and later the University of Oregon. Like many of her well-to-do friends, Marnie Ross shunned the wealthier schools in the East.

Her only surviving relative, Dr. Ralph Tingley, a brother-in-law and practicing psychiatrist in Portland, refused comment. Dr. Tingley will handle the arrangements.

I went on with Mrvich's letter.

I put Lou Bodlouie on it. He's the best I got—I believe you met him at the Medici-Lamarr business—and he declared it a suicide a couple of days later. One thing bothered him—the silver nitrate test was inconclusive—she was wearing gloves when she did it. But you know what a lousy test that is. We've both seen cases where the nitrate test meant nothing.

But here's the clincher. The same gun killed Sanderson. Absolutely. Bodlouie took it to Vancouver, and we dug the slugs out of the storage there, and sure enough. Same gun. The coroner's report supports Bodlouie. The gun was fired no farther than an inch from her head. Angle of entry checks out OK.

By the way, the inscription and signature are definitely in her handwriting. Well, old friend, this wraps it up for sure. Now, damn it, you softhearted slob, don't sit up there in the tundra and blame yourself. You just solved three murders, not counting those other four in Montana and Idaho. And, damn it, don't blame yourself for the Medici-Lamarr business. That

wasn't your fault either. Write me a letter. By the way,
if you ever need a job, etc. etc. etc.

Fondly,
Murv

I looked at the xerox of the suicide note. It was typed,
except for the inscription at the end and the signature.

My Dear Friends Who Survive Me:
I'm sorry to go this way, but I can no longer live
with what I've done. Years ago I killed Candy Koski
after she'd made a play for Robin. She was a lovely
girl, and I was jealous and afraid I'd lose Robin. I
strangled her with a scarf, then beat her with my fists
after she was dead. No one came in. It took just a few
minutes. I covered my fists with makeup to hide the
bruises. Once the police arrested Medici, they didn't
bother to check the rest of us. Detective Barnes knows
my father helped Vic get off because he knew Vic
hadn't done it.
I begged my husband to come back to me, over and
over. He turned me down. I finally hired Manny
Sanderson to kill him and make it look like one of
the axe killings I read about in the Portland papers.
The last time I called Robin and he rejected me, I
told Manny to go ahead with our plans.
When Manny didn't kill Detective Barnes, I was
watching from a distance with field glasses. The
moment Barnes went in the Koski house to phone, I
drove up, got out, shot Manny twice and drove off.
Most of you have been wonderful to me. I wasn't
worth it. I've been sick for a long time. I only hope
you can find forgiveness in your hearts for me. Please
know I wanted always to be a far better person than
I turned out to be.

Then, handwritten in ink at the end:

Still with a deep, deep love,

Marnie

When I was a boy, I once heard a guy with a hangover say he felt like a million dollars worth of shit. It seemed funny to me when I heard it the first time. It didn't seem so funny now.

A few days later, the letter from Lynn Hammer arrived.

Dear Al:

I just can't let you sit up there thinking I'm mad at you for what happened or in any way hold it against you. Marnie was an old and close friend, but she had terrible problems. I'd nursed her through so many lousy spells, and I'd heard her threaten to kill Robin many times. I don't know what her suicide note said, but I was sure she was headed for trouble. She had been for a long time. I was mad at you the night you and Mrvich went over and accused her of all those killings. She told me about it. But the longer I thought about it, the more sense it made.

She got withdrawn after that, sullen and depressed. I tried to talk her out of it, but she just sat in her apartment and stared at the floor or out the window. Once she said to me, "I've done terrible things, Lynn. Terrible things." But she never told me what things she'd done that were so terrible. Naturally, I was shocked when I read about her suicide. I couldn't believe it. At least her agony is over.

Next summer when we come up, we must get together. It is just no good going over all this again and again. We are still alive, and we must go on and leave this miserable business behind us forever. I still feel about you the way I did at Cannon Beach—I don't mean as a lover, just as a good human being. I don't blame you at all for what you did. And I don't want you to blame yourself. I want you to be your sweet self, old Mush Heart himself, when I see you next summer.

Love,
Lynn

I appreciated her concern. And her reassurance helped. Some days, I didn't think about any of it. Other days, I thought of all those dead people and my part in it.

Well, I thought, at least it's over. Now if I can get over it.

And it would have been over, too, if I hadn't gone to a baseball game the next summer.

THREE

51

April is the cruelest month, my ass. Oh, I know rebirth is an illusion, and we are getting older no matter what the lilacs say. But in Montana the months that break their promises aren't nearly as cruel as those months that keep theirs.

November kept its promise. So did December, and January, and February and March. Five straight months of lousy promises and all kept. It snowed. It snowed and blew. It froze. One night in December, it hit minus thirty in Plains. Then it warmed up for a few days. Then it snowed. It blew. It froze. Some fields remained buried in snow for over four months. When I say it warmed up, I mean it almost got to thirty above.

Montana winters can put you to the test. Married couples find they spend more and more time together inside until each decides to find time with somebody else. Cabin fever is hard on marriages. In Missoula, the divorce rate is twice the national average.

About half the scheduled flights never land in Missoula during the winter. You can go ice fishing or skiing, but I've never cared for skiing, and ice fishing is seldom any good.

Arlene and I went once to Rainbow Lake, and the wind lifted snow from the ice and sent white walls of doom down the lake at our throats. No bites, and stinging tootsies in two hours. We retired to her bar.

Arlene and I had a fight. I suppose it was my fault. I'd gotten moody, dwelling far too frequently on those dead people in Portland and my part in it. The fight helped a little.

Mary Lou Calk had been returned to Idaho by the time winter had set in. Her two brothers found money for a good lawyer, good because he had connections with the Idaho state government. Somewhere, talks went on between Montana and Idaho officials behind thick, closed doors. Later, motions were filed, and finally Idaho assumed jurisdiction. Mary Lou had gone to Idaho State Hospital for observation, as they say, and hadn't come out yet. I suspected she'd never stand trial.

I got to know Arlene's daughters a little better, since the hard winter kept them home more than usual. They were genuinely sweet girls, full of hope for their futures, filled with ideas of romance and adventure. They asked about some of my cases and I told them, sparing them the more hideous details. I didn't tell them about Vic Medici and T. Curtoise Lamarr and Marnie Ross Tingley.

The mill workers may have talked to each other on their way into the mill, but from where I watched from a distance, they seemed silent and glum. The new plant manager Lee Hammer had sent up from Portland had the personality of a spoiled cod.

There were a couple of pluses. Rudolph Tough Otter turned out to be a charming guy, too much so for Red Yellow Bear. Now Red was worried that with his charm and his chance to contact so many citizens on his job, Rudolph Tough Otter had an even better chance of beating him in the election. Red Yellow Bear spent much of his time trying to talk Rudolph Tough Otter into becoming a Democrat. But while Tough Otter may have been giving Yellow Bear cause to worry, he was a big plus for the rest of us. Replacing Manny Sanderson with Rudolph Tough Otter was like replacing stale beer with Jack Daniels.

Red Yellow Bear went to Reno for a law enforcement conference. Both Tough Otter and I volunteered to go on bended knee, but Yellow Bear growled his most sadistic laugh and bought a new sports coat and tie in Missoula, which he showed us with a gleam in his eyes and sadistic remarks about the good-looking, unattached women in Reno. He left me in charge of the office in Thompson Falls, not wanting Tough Otter to have any more advantage in the next election. Under-sheriff Pop Powell had complications from his hernia operation.

"You'll come back with a dose of the Blackfeet clap," I said.

"What's the Blackfeet clap?" asked Yellow Bear.

"It attacks Flatheads," I said.

"Then it's bound to die soon," he said.

That was as witty as anyone got that winter, except for Tough Otter. Running the office in Thompson Falls was as exciting as watching a replay of *The Great Knute Rockne* on television. Crime hibernated for the winter.

52

April is the cruelest month, my ass. That year it was anything but. It all broke in April, broke one day for good. Oh, sure, we'd had a couple of false starts, but one day spring was in every odor that came on the warm air from the west. Birds. Flowers. The trees didn't do anything. They do their thing late in Montana. But we had no doubt that winter was over. You could see it in Arlene's face. You could see it in other faces, too, but I liked it best in hers.

We could still get snow. We could get snow until July, and even then. But it would be nothing. It would fall and disappear almost at eye level before it hit the ground. If it fell at all. Winter was over. I almost shouted one day in the streets: You are all washed up, winter. Turn in your jock.

When the ice broke on Rainbow Lake, Arlene and I went there and and caught those trout that wouldn't bite when we had ice fished. I prepared them, and Yellow Bear and Tough Otter came down and helped us eat them. We chased them down with the best white wine we could find in western Montana, which wasn't the best you can find most places, but it worked.

Then some teenagers had a meeting. Arlene's daughters told her about it, and she passed it on to me. Some smart tough guy, an undeclared but recognized leader, told the others that if they didn't want a cop like Sanderson back in Plains, they ought to hold things down just a little. If they wanted a nice guy like Al Barnes (old Mush Heart himself) on the job, they had better have fun but not set the town on fire. That made me feel good, too.

And so we ushered spring in and helped it along with bourbon and loving and fishing and smiles. The jokes got better in the bars. And around the end of May, Lee and Lynn Hammer arrived with Mycroft and moved into their house a couple of miles downstream from Plains.

Lee and I shook hands, and Lynn and I embraced. Arlene never guessed about our night the year before in Cannon Beach, and Lynn and I never mentioned it in our great wisdom. Arlene and I had lunch with them a couple of times at their place. Mycroft was still on the gate when Lee was home. And Mycroft hadn't changed a bit. You need a few constants in a world of change, even if they are absurd.

By June, I'd caught over forty trout. Arlene and I talked briefly about getting married. Yellow Bear was getting nowhere trying to talk Tough Otter into becoming a Democrat. The mill was doing so well they hired nine more workers. The long winter was long gone.

53

I love baseball. I can't remember when I didn't. When I was a kid, I played baseball every chance I got. I played park league baseball. I played American Legion baseball. I played high school baseball, and I even rode the bench for part of a season at the University of Washington. The only time I ever got in a college game was as a pinch hitter against the University of Oregon. You may not believe this, but the Oregon pitcher was named Walter Johnson, and he hit me in the thigh with a fastball. It hurt so damned much I couldn't run and had to have a pinch runner. This Walter Johnson threw hard, too. That was my college baseball career.

I played in the city league in Seattle, and after I joined the police, I played for the Seattle police force for several years. I played a fair second base but a much better outfield. I was a pretty good hitter but had a bad time with

inside fastballs. One thing I regretted about moving out
of Seattle was that now they had a big league team. The
Yankees came to town and the Red Sox, all the American
League clubs came. And so here I was, sitting in Plains,
Montana.

I tried to catch the weekly games on TV. Baseball is
the one game I can enjoy watching, even if I'm the only
person in the stands. That's not true about football or
basketball, at least for me it isn't. Those games need the
crowd. Baseball needs nothing but baseball.

Years ago, Missoula had had a pro team. I think both
Gil McDougald, the old Yankee, and Jim Kaat, the pitcher
who, last I heard, was still with Philadelphia, had once
played on that Missoula team. But that Missoula team
was long gone. The closest pro ball was in Great Falls, and
it wasn't as far to go west to Spokane. They don't play
high school ball in Montana. The only baseball to be seen
for many miles is American Legion ball in Missoula. Even
the University of Montana dropped their team a few years
ago to save the budget for football, I was told by one of the
locals.

So one Sunday I drove down to see Missoula play Havre.
Arlene had to tend bar that day, and at breakfast I'd seen
the game announced in the Sunday *Missoulian*. I got into
town early enough for lunch at a drive-in and got there
in time for the last of infield practice. Only about six people
were in the stands, but by game time about a dozen more
had arrived.

One couple that came, I took special note of the woman.
She was a sleek little blonde and looked as fresh as the
ocean. I couldn't stop looking at her. I paid no attention
to the guy with her. Then it struck me that I'd seen the
woman before. It was Mrs. Bailey. I confirmed that finally
by looking at the man. Sure enough. Shelly P. Bailey.

I moved down a couple of rows and sat beside them.
"Hello," I said.

"Why, it's Sheriff Barnes," Bailey said, and he shook
my hand and introduced me to his wife, as if some formal
introduction was necessary.

"I remember you," Johnnie Bailey said and gave me a
great smile.

"I didn't know you were interested in baseball, professor," I said.

"Not professor," Shelly Bailey said. "It's Shell to my friends."

"Did you ever play, Shell?"

"He played shortstop for Harvard," Johnnie put in and looked at him with eyes so filled with adoration, I felt sorry she ever had to wash his socks.

"I did," Shelly said. "Two years, first team. Started every game. And I followed the Phillies at home."

The more I knew about Professor Shelly P. Bailey, the more I liked him.

"How's the job?"

"They're keeping me on for another year. If I survive next year, I'll have tenure. I'm thinking of writing a book on Rilke—he's a German poet," he added, not unkindly, just to make sure he was communicating.

"I know," I said. "Believe it or not, I studied the Duino Elegies in college at the University of Washington. I don't remember much. He's the only foreign poet I ever studied."

"Really. That's great. Did you major in lit?"

"Creative writing. I didn't finish. I'm a poet who didn't write poems good enough."

Shelley laughed, "Aren't we all? Listen, I'm teaching the Elegies next fall. Why not drop in if you get a chance?"

I said I would try, and I meant it. I felt I had a lot better chance of learning something from Bailey than I did from Professor Wolfgang von Schmidt. God, he had been a rotten teacher. He made Rilke about as exciting as *The Barretts of Wimpole Street*.

The game was badly played for two innings. Missoula made two errors and Havre three. By the beginning of the third, Missoula led four to two, and no runs had been earned. The pitchers toiled away hopefully.

One interesting and confusing thing about the Havre team was that they had two players who looked just alike. At first I thought they were twins, but they weren't. In fact, they were no relation. Just one of nature's freak coincidences.

One was named MacKensie and the other Swenson. MacKensie played first base, and Swenson played right field. Swenson wore number twelve on his uniform.

MacKensie was number three. I couldn't tell them apart, but I gathered that Swenson was the better hitter. He batted cleanup, while MacKensie hit eighth in the lineup.

As the game went on, I could see why Swenson was hitting cleanup. He had driven in two runs with a single and a triple and had scored once. MacKensie was hitless by the first of the seventh, the last scheduled inning. A lot of seven-inning ball is played in Montana American Legion.

In the first of the seventh, Missoula was leading seven to four. Swenson led off the inning, and he picked on the second pitch, a low fast ball, and drove it far out of the park. It seemed to reach the height of its arc at the fence, and it fell a good 400 feet from home plate. It was a real blast. That made it seven to five. The next batter popped up, but the shortstop lost the ball behind him, turned the wrong way and the ball fell safe. That brought the tying run to the plate. The number-six hitter fanned. The number-seven hitter lined a single into center. MacKensie stepped in, his number three looking stark on his uniform. As a game gets close, players' numbers always seem to get more vivid.

Well. Tying runs on. One out. The game was getting interesting. I had no idea how interesting it was going to get.

MacKensie took one pitch outside for a ball. Suddenly the Missoula manager appeared from the dugout, waving his arms and calling time. He started for the plate. The umpire took off his mask and waited, hands on his hips.

The Missoula manager reached the plate and made a gesture with his hand. The umpire gestured with his mask. The Missoula manager gestured again. He seemed to be talking fast, and he wasn't happy. The Havre manager joined the discussion. Gestures became more animated.

The base umpire joined the discussion, which was beginning to look less like a discussion and more like the beginning of trouble.

"What the hell is it?" I asked nobody in particular.

"I don't know," Shelly Bailey said, "unless—"

The Havre bench had emptied and had come to the plate. The Missoula bench and the players in the field had crowded around. The Havre manager shoved the Missoula manager. The Missoula manager shoved the Havre manager back. We couldn't hear what they were saying, but we could hear their voices getting louder and louder. The Havre manager took a swing at the Missoula manager. He missed and decked the umpire. The umpire threw the Havre manager out of the game while still sitting in the dirt.

The Missoula manager decked the Havre manager while the Havre manager was still arguing with the umpire who had stood up again. A riot started. Players started throwing punches. A couple of town toughs who had been drinking beer behind the fence near the Missoula dugout joined in. They were doing pretty well, the two toughs, when the cops arrived. The baseball players, like most I've known, were lousy fighters, but the two toughs were having a ball, dropping Havre players with crisp right curves and left hooks. The cops stopped the fight and took the two toughs away in one of the squad cars. The umpire forfeited the game to Missoula. I was disappointed. It was like seeing *Hamlet* shut down by the fire department for ordinance violations before the last act could be staged.

Shelly and I soon found out why from one of the other fans. Swenson and MacKensie had switched uniforms behind a screen of players in the dugout. Swenson had been hitting in MacKensie's place. I never did find out how the Missoula manager detected the switch. MacKensie and Swenson looked the same to me.

Shelly and Johnnie Bailey and I walked to our cars together. "Did you ever see anything like that?" I asked.

"Never. Not that I can remember," Shelley said. "I've seen a lot of baseball, and that's got to be the first time that's happened."

By the time we reached my car, we were laughing about it. Just as we were saying good-bye Shelly said, "What's funny is they must have been doing that all season when the situation was right for it. This is the first time they got caught."

That night I came up out of a restless sleep with my eyes so open the dark bedroom seemed illuminated by floodlights.

54

The next morning I was on the phone. I ran up some awful bills that day. Red Yellow Bear never complained about them later. By Thursday I had all I needed. I drove to Thompson Falls and sat alone with Yellow Bear for a half hour. I told him what I knew and what I didn't know but suspected.

He said nothing while I talked. He didn't even look at me. He looked out the window and rolled an unlit cigar around in his mouth. When I finished, all he said was, "Shit, let's go." We drove back toward Plains.

Mycroft was at the gate, so I assumed Lee Hammer was home. Mycroft came out of the guard shack and said, "Whom do you wish to see, sirs? Mr. Hammer is quite busy and Miss Hammer is—"

"Open this gate, you stuffy son of a bitch, or I'm going to shoot you in the balls," Red Yellow Bear said. I never heard anything sound more meant. Mycroft opened the gate. While he was doing it, Red Yellow Bear stepped out of the car, walked to the guard shack and ripped out the telephone. "You stay right here. If you don't, when I find you I'm going to cave in your fucking skull." That sounded meant, too. I could tell by the slight crack in Mycroft's composure that he intended to stay there.

We dove toward the house. I motioned Yellow Bear to stop about two hundred feet away where huge ponderosas partially hid the car. "I'll go around in back. Give me just a couple of minutes. Then you knock." He nodded.

I made a wide circle through some willows and mountain ash trees and a few jack pines. I came up from behind the house and looked in the back door window into the kitchen. I saw no one. I tried the door. It was unlocked. I slipped in as silently as I could. The house was still.

Red Yellow Bear started pounding on the front door. I stood next to the refrigerator and waited. A door I couldn't see opened back on the hall to my left. I flattened against the refrigerator so anyone coming down the hall would miss me unless they looked sharp right as they passed. I heard Lynn's voice say, "God, somebody's here."

Then I heard Lee say, "Who could it be? Where's Mycroft?" The voice sounded like he was still in a room off the hall. Lynn passed me. She was naked. She went toward the front door. She passed out of my line of vision. I heard her say, "God, it's the sheriff."

Then Lee passed me. He was naked. He stopped where I could still see him, his back to me. "God, Lynn, yell something. Stall him. We'll get dressed." He turned and saw me. A wave of hatred passed over his face. "What the—"

Lynn came up behind him. She saw me now. She let out a scream they must have heard in Billings. She started to cry and wailed over and over, "Oh, my God. Oh, my God."

Lee was staring at me with such hatred, I felt my pulse weaken. I put my gun on them. I didn't say anything. I motioned them against the wall. I walked around them, keeping my gun pointed at them and my eyes on them. I opened the door and let Yellow Bear in. The hatred in Lee Hammer's face was so vivid, I felt a hundred times stronger when Yellow Bear stepped in.

"All right," Yellow Bear said. "First, let's get some clothes on. Both of you down the hall." They led us to a bedroom. "You," he said to Lee, "you throw her clothes out here and get your own on while I watch you. You," he pointed to Lynn who was sobbing and wringing her hands, "go down to the other bedroom and dress. Barnes, you watch her."

When they were dressed, we sat down in the front room. Lee looked less angry now, just cold. Lynn had stopped sobbing. She was beginning to go frigid, too, taking the cue from her brother.

Red Yellow Bear said, "I'm placing you both under arrest. You know your rights because you're rich. You can call a lawyer if you want."

"And just what might I ask are we being arrested for?" Lee asked. His voice sounded like Mycroft's a little. "Incest?"

"There *is* a law against it," Yellow Bear said, "even in lonely old Montana. And you can't screw sheep here, either, despite all the old jokes, at least not legally."

"Oh, Al," Lynn said. "I know it's awful and wrong but in this day and age—"

"It's not awful and wrong necessarily," I said. "It's just illegal. In this day and age, you said? OK. In this day and age, what? In this day and age I don't care if you screw your pet weasel or have a *ménage à trois* with the ghost of Charles A. Lindbergh."

"That's what I mean, exactly," Lynn said with some hope in her voice. Hope? Or desperation? "I mean, it's not like we were really criminals."

"Well, maybe it just seems that way because between the two of you, you've managed to murder six people."

Lee looked terribly angry. Then he looked at the floor. Lynn said, "Oh, Al," as if saying, "Oh, Al," made some difference.

"You said it very well in Portland. Conspiratorial brats. Jesus, were you ever, and you kept right on. You threw things in my face and dared me to catch on—like putting that wedding photo in my room at your place in Portland. And how did you put it? You couldn't make it up. Wasn't that it? Well, the hell you couldn't. You did. You married each other twice, once in Ashland, then an hour later in Medford. Getting fake credentials was easy, but I'm not even sure you needed them. In one marriage, Lynn was Annie Barzeletta—in the other, you, Lee, were Orlando Ponce. Then you moved to San Francisco long enough to have your baby. You probably took two residences. Your mother was already dead, and she'd left you scads of money. It just kills me you had a wedding picture taken and showed it to people, put it on display. What did you do when someone visited from Portland? You must have said Annie was in Los Angeles if they visited Lee, or Orlando was in Salt Lake if they visited Lynn. It only took a few months. You were probably already pregnant when you got married. What a great joke. Go ahead and have the baby and laugh at the world. And if he had to carry a name you'd made up, why, that was a joke, too. He wouldn't know the difference. His 'Uncle' Lee would be his father in everything but name."

"But a brother and sister can't have a big healthy kid like Mike," Lynn said weakly.

"The hell they can't. What's to stop them? Any brother and sister can have a perfectly healthy baby. Oh, if you keep doing it in a family for generations, you start getting into problems. But on one shot? No real risk at all. Talk about arrogance. They ought to issue a new citation—the distinguished arrogance cross—and give it to you two.

"So you lived in San Francisco long enough to have the baby, invent two early divorces and come back to Portland. I'll bet no one even came down during those few months. Your father, even."

"And," Lee said, "where, may I ask, is the proof of all this?"

"In the mail. It should arrive tomorrow. By the way, I even found out from a prof at the University of Montana that Barzeletta means joke or gag in Italian. What a great time you were having. What fun. But no one checks such a wild story, do they? Well, I did. First, no one named Orlando Ponce ever attended the University of Oregon, or has ever been issued a passport by the State Department. So your phony ex couldn't be in Albania, could he, even if he existed. Then I had John Mrvich get ahold of that wedding photo. He got a court order and entered your house. The caretaker had to let him in. He took the photo to Ashland personally, as a favor for me. You lucked out there. The JP who married you was dead, and his wife was senile and unreliable. But the JP in Medford, a woman named Jackson, is still alive and very sharp. She remembers you very well. She thought you were a fine couple. Almost perfect, she told Mrvich. She was sure the marriage would last because you both looked so much alike already, the way married couples do after years of living together— that was the way she put it. And all the murders, except for Candy Koski's, were to hide your big secret that started out as a joke you were playing on the world at large. Why Candy? Well, I imagine she turned you on, Lee, like she did all the other boys. She was a real threat. You going around with another girl—was her name Marge Appleton?—was just so much show. But you must have been jealous of your sister even then because she was often dateless, a sort of fifth wheel, the second girl for Dale

Robbins. It all fit. He liked two girls, anyway. Shit, at that age you get by with all sorts of complicated arrangements, and no one thinks much of it. Then you, Lynn, seeing Candy Koski was a real threat, killed her one night at that wild party in Cannon Beach, strangled her with a scarf, I imagine, the way it says in that phony suicide note of Marnie's. That would be just one more touch, wouldn't it? The rotten thing is, you aren't even smart murderers. You just had a lot of luck going your way, and every manipulation you tried worked, almost. I think you killed Candy Koski because even then you were already having relations. You killed her out of sexual jealousy. Then you got your father to put in the fix via T. T. Armstrong because you didn't want Vic Medici paying for something he didn't do. You were lucky there, too. Armstrong and Marnie's father were business partners. When I uncovered that, it looked like it was Marnie's father who put in the fix and Marnie who had killed Candy Koski. But it was your father who put in the fix. I don't know how you got him to do it. I don't much care. But you were all part of a gang of wealthy people living in West Hills, and I just found out your father knew both Sy Ross and Armstrong. A nice man named Oswald told Mrvich. Had I been on the ball, I would have asked him myself when I talked to him, but it didn't occur to me because neither your father nor you were ever members of the High Mountain Club."

"I suppose you can prove all this," Lee Hammer said. He was still being snotty, but some confidence had left his voice.

"I don't have to. I can prove enough when the time comes. I'll tell you what else I can't prove. I can't prove that you threw Marnie and Sanderson together. I can't prove that Robin Tingley saw in Lynn a wife he'd like to have, and when he started to make his move, he found himself mysteriously blocked. Then one day he saw the truth. His brother said he should have been a psychiatrist because he had great insights into people, but he was too stuffy. I can't prove that you paid Sanderson to axe Tingley to protect your secret because you knew Robin Tingley was outraged. He was a man of propriety, a nice man, really, but all of a sudden a threat. Sanderson blew the job and only hit Tingley twice. He must have told you our plan to chase down very tall women in the West, that someone who was disturbed was running about, killing men with an axe, and you saw your chance to bury one more murder among the rest. Only you had bad luck there. We actually caught the killer. I'm sure Sanderson never believed you would, and he told you so. In addition to the newspapers, you had inside information. No, I can't prove it."

"And what else can't you prove, oh, great detective?" Lee Hammer said. He was almost beginning to enjoy this now, but not quite.

"You told me a lie, Lynn. You said Tingley had testified against Medici in the trial. But, actually, his testimony helped Medici. True, he was a prosecution witness, but Art Matthew arranged it that way. Then he could cross-examine, ask leading questions and take full advantage of the situation. The D.A. wasn't very bright, and he fell for it. Everything Tingley said worked to Medici's advantage, everything. You were trying to give me a motive for Medici to kill Tingley. It wasn't a very good motive, but you weren't being a real top-notch master criminal, just someone trying to throw suspicion on somebody else.

"And I can't prove that, either. But somehow Medici knew about you two. I don't know how, but he knew. That's why he wouldn't tell me over the phone when I was at your place. He insisted I come see him so he could tell me in person. I wonder how long he knew or if he ever connected your little game of run-around-the-bedroom with Candy Koski's killing? I doubt it. I told you I was going to see Medici, and after I left you called Sanderson. You got word to Sanderson to get to Medici first, and then you really got a break. By luck, when Sanderson got to the Ironfast Building ahead of me, Medici was beating up Lamarr because Lamarr had skimmed twenty-four thousand dollars in four years off the money Medici was sending the Koskis out of sympathy. I'm not sure how it happened, but I'd guess, after Medici had thumped Lamarr good, he went back to his desk. Sanderson walked in and shot him. Then Sanderson went into Lamarr's office and found Lamarr beaten up on the floor. He must have been groggy. Sanderson forced the gun into Lamarr's hand, turned it into his body and pressed Lamarr's finger on the trigger. Lamarr was too dazed from the beating to put up much resistance. He was babbling when he died, and nothing he said made any sense except one word: 'eyes.' He was talking about Sanderson's eyes, which were weird and which everyone noticed. He must have looked up and seen those strange eyes just about the time the gun in his hand was being fired into his body. No, I can't prove it, but I know enough about people to know that when a guy has taken a lot of crap in his life and has developed some fantasies to escape to, he usually relies on those fantasies. He doesn't suddenly shoot someone who has humiliated him in some way he is used to. He has other outs. Lamarr had been beaten up before by smaller but stronger and better-coordinated men. Why should he suddenly turn killer over this one? He was no killer.

"And I can't prove that, earlier at Cannon Beach, you'd set me up for the big shooting scene, then suggested it might be Marnie. The two of you. By the time Lynn and I called you in Portland, Lee, over two hours had passed, easily enough time to get back. You made no attempt to hit me or Lynn. It was all a phony to try to suggest Marnie was getting desperate. You weren't thinking very clearly. After all, Marnie might have an alibi. By a lot of luck and a bit of manipulation on your part, she later turned out to look awfully good for her husband's killing. I never did understand that shooting business at Cannon Beach."

"And you can't prove any of it," Lee Hammer said. "Very good, Detective Barnes." Lynn was looking out the window, biting her lip. Red Yellow Bear was looking at both with no sympathy.

"If you were really bright, you might have covered your tracks better. Why I didn't think of the transmitter, I'll never know. That's how Sanderson trailed me to the Koskis'. You planted a transmitter in your car, my car, the Mercedes. The receiver was built into the radio on the Maserati. Now, I can prove something. Mrvich found the transmitter. First, one of his detectives, a guy named Bodlouie, found the mark the transmitter left on the underside of the frame. Even a Mercedes gets dirty underneath. You attached a transmitter underneath the car. It was held there by a magnet, and it was battery-powered. We have it. When I brought the car back late that night and moved out, you removed it after I left, maybe even the next day. There was no hurry. Then you did a careless thing. You didn't throw it away. You just put it in a box in the carport with some other things, screws, a couple of files. Bodlouie traced it to a shop called Radiomotive. The guy there remembers you both because you were both there when you bought it, and you even told him a white Maserati was coming in shortly afterward, and you paid him to install the receiver in the radio. We found the receiver, by the way. The white Maserati is still being held in Vancouver. The guy at Radiomotive remembers you, and he remembers Sanderson. He also remembers the thousand dollars you gave him to keep quiet. It's very hard to keep quiet when Lou Bodlouie is questioning you.

"You trailed Sanderson when he was trailing my signal, and he probably knew it—you may even have told him you'd be there, in case anything went wrong. Something went wrong. One of you had to drive up and shoot him twice while he lay there helpless, cuffed to the steering wheel of the Mas. Now you were free and clear, except for Marnie. But you were five corpses to the good now, and when I mistakenly tried to shake Marnie down, I played into your hands. I was sure she was guilty. When she didn't crack, I thought she was innocent or tougher than I thought. I'm not sure how you got her to sign the confession, but let me guess. I think she signed the confession before it was written. 'Still with a deep, deep love' is a funny way to sign a suicide note. You could make her do anything. You controlled her like a mother does a small child. You may have told her if she would inscribe something nice at the bottom, you'd type a nice love letter for her. To whom? Hell, what difference would it make? Or you may have challenged her to a little contest one night when she was drinking. You took turns seeing who could sign the most provocative inscription on a letter. She might have signed a dozen sheets of paper, trying to beat you at the little game you'd made up." I could tell by the way Lynn's lips tightened that I'd hit it. She said nothing. Lee was sneering at me. I didn't like it.

Then Lynn said, "You're very close, Al."

The silence got thick. The sneer left Lee Hammer's face. He just looked at his twin sister with wonder. Red Yellow

Bear looked at her with disdain. His disdain was worse than most disdains. It was the disdain of a red man who had never had an easy life for a white woman who had never had anything but an easy life and who had made it hard. It was the disdain of a man who played by the rules when he had license not to for a woman who had no excuse at all for breaking any of the rules, and who had broken them all.

Lynn said from far off somewhere, "We started when we were sixteen, and from the first moment it was beautiful. Can you understand it? It was beautiful. And we swore we'd keep it always."

"Shut up," Lee said.

"Why, why should I?" Lynn said, resigned. "Just for once, let's tell the world we love each other more deeply than any people ever loved because we were born together. And we killed for it."

Lee shrugged and looked away out the window.

"After I killed Candy, Lee told me he'd only been teasing me about her. Once I'd killed for our love, it seemed to make that love more binding than ever. And to think I'd never had to. He'd only been teasing. And yet, once I'd done it, he knew how deep our love really went. A few years later, we planned the wedding bit. You guessed it all."

Lee was looking at the floor. He seemed totally depressed. All rage, all contempt had vanished.

"What I don't get," Red Yellow Bear said, "is how you got away with it, I mean the masquerade, all those years. You must have fended off some people. You're both attractive, rich and, when you aren't running around killing people, charming. A lot of people must have been interested in you."

Lee took it up, finally resigned. "We played it for the two hurt divorced slobs for a while. When that ran out, we played too busy. It wasn't easy, especially for Lynn. Robin Tingley really wanted to divorce Marnie and marry Lynn. You're right. He saw what was going on. And Medici, too. But that was nearly twenty years before Robin caught on. He found us one night after a party at our place. Father was out of town on business, and we threw a real wingding of a party. When we thought everyone had left, we started making love right on the living room floor, all alone in that big house. Only we weren't alone. Vic had passed out in the study in one of those deep chairs, and we hadn't seen him. He came in on his way out of the house, and there we were. He never said a word about it after that. When Mycroft told us you'd had a call from him and you mentioned you had to go see him, we both got scared he was going to blow the whistle. I called Sanderson who had come down from Montana, and he went. It happened just like you said. We paid him off. I didn't like Sanderson much, for what that's worth."

"Oh, Jesus Christ," Red Yellow Bear growled, "let's take them in while there's still a few people left alive in the nation."

"I'll get my jacket," Lee Hammer said, still depressed and resigned. He went around the corner and down the hall toward the bedrooms. I looked at Lynn Hammer, and she stared back at me without much life left in her eyes. She seemed dazed, on the verge of some final capitulation, as if she were about to surrender a great battle, the final battle of a long war.

Then it struck me Lee Hammer was out of our sight, and that sweet little old man in Seattle flashed on. I turned and yelled, "Red!"

Lee Hammer came around the corner fast. The pistol in his hand was pointed right at me. If all Indians could draw and shoot as fast as Red Yellow Bear, the cowboys wouldn't have had a chance. The gun seemed to appear in his hand as if I were watching it happen on spliced film. The noise would have started a revolution. He shot Hammer through the chest before Hammer could fire a round. Lee Hammer died before he hit the floor.

Lynn rushed to his side and started to hold his head in her arms. She wailed and moaned over and over, "My darling brother. My lover." She was beyond tears. We let her play it out until she was drained. Finally, she turned and said, "You didn't have to kill him, you goddam Indian."

"The fuck I didn't," Yellow Bear said.

We took her out in handcuffs after Yellow Bear phoned for the meat wagon. We picked up Mycroft and handcuffed him on our way out.

As the car hit the highway, I said, "Tell me something. Was your father really angry when you told him about the marriages?"

"We made that up, too. He told us to come home right away. We told him we'd be home soon."

"Didn't he try to visit you? I mean, to see your spouses?"

"We put him off. Once I had to beg him not to come. He wasn't in real good health. He was forty-three when we were born. We lucked out. He was just ill enough not to try the trip. When he thought he could make it, I told him we'd be home soon, not to try because it wouldn't be very long. By then, he believed we were already divorced."

"Tell me. Did he know you killed Candy Koski?"

"No. Only Lee and I knew. We convinced him Medici was innocent. We begged him to trust us, and he did. He went to Armstrong and got the rigged editorial planted. They were good friends. You guessed that, too. God, you did an awful lot of guessing, Al." Her face still sat white from the shock of her loss, but normal conversation was coming out of her mouth. It was like we were discussing a movie we'd seen last night. It gave me a creepy feeling.

"Sure, I guessed. But I had the transmitter. I mean, we had it, the cops in Portland. I still can't figure why you left it in your carport."

"We were sure we'd beaten you, once I decided to kill Marnie. I figured—we figured—the suicide note would take us off the hook for good. We thought for sure no one would look inside the Maserati radio for the receiver. I mean, who looks inside a radio long as it's working?"

"You weren't very bright, just brash as hell when it came to putting the world on."

"How did you guess so much?"

"I saw a baseball game," I said. I hope it still sounds cryptic to her when she recalls it.

We didn't say anything for a couple of miles. Finally, Lynn said in a dead voice, "The Cannon Beach thing wasn't exactly like you said. I used it to throw suspicion onto Marnie, but that was just a last-minute idea. We set you up for the evening with me. Then Lee thought better of it and decided to scare you—he was jealous because I was going to spend the night with you. I didn't know it was him shooting. He miscalculated. He wasn't thinking straight. The shooting just drove you deeper into my bed. The bed was our idea together. The shooting was Lee's alone. He told me about it later at home. Lee killed Sanderson. He sent Sanderson to kill you because he was still jealous. We never thought you were that close. We just set up the bedroom scene at Cannon Beach to make sure you'd never guess about us."

"What I find hard to believe is you'd kill so many friends—God, Robin Tingley and Marnie were longtime friends of yours. I can't believe you'd be that cold."

"Remember that sonnet of Shakespeare's—'Let me not to the marriage of true minds admit impediments. Love is not love which alters when it alteration finds'—or something like that. Ours was a marriage of true minds. We could not admit impediments, not even in the form of other people. I could kill Marnie, and Lee and I could pay to have Robin killed, because we were protecting the greatest love in the world."

"I'm not sure that's what Shakespeare had in mind when—"

Red Yellow Bear interrupted me. "Shit," he said. "A few months back I had a great piece of ass in Reno. How do I know my piece was better than yours or anybody else's? You got some machine that measures ecstasy?"

"I suppose it never crossed your animal mind that there's more to human love than just sexual fulfillment," Lynn said with what slight prideful disdain she could manage.

"Yeah, I know," Yellow Bear said, "but that's the part you can't talk about."

55

Two things still bothered me. One was the boy, Mike. Damn it, kids are just too sensitive to the situation at home. He must have known, must have wondered at the relationship of his 'uncle' and mother. A letter from Mrvich helped settle that.

Dear Ace Detective Barnes:

I hope you're doing OK now that the excitement has died down and you're back to issuing citations for spitting in public. One thing that bothered me about the whole business was the boy. I suppose it did you too. Well, I went out and talked to him just to satisfy my curiosity. You'll have to admit it seems unlikely he could have grown up in that situation and not guessed something.

So I interviewed him and would you believe it, he did know. I mean he knew they were lovers and he guessed his uncle was also his father. So I asked him, point blank, "Didn't it bother you at all?" And know what he said? Jesus, I'll never forget it. He looked right at me and said with a slight sneer, "It's not so hard when you've got lots of money. Nothing else matters that much." May the Lord help us, Al. Christ, no shame, no sense of regret, no psychic scars at all. Does money make people that tough? You tell me. I never saw anything, or heard anything like that.

Hope you get down again, soon. Maybe I can catch some fishing with you next year up there. Meanwhile, if you crave big city police work again—

as always,
Murv

The other thing that bothered me was me. My pride wasn't hurt that the Hammers had fooled me so badly. But it hurt to think what the case means about me. I know I want the world to be better. Does that mean when I meet people who seem to be making it better, I'm so attracted to them I can't see what they really are? Was I too easily taken in by money and gentility? I'd seen it happen to other cops. Respectability is one hell of a great disguise. Sometimes I told myself, oh, Mush Heart, they were just lucky, gutsy amateurs. They would have fooled anyone up to a point. But I wasn't sure I hadn't over the years developed some weakness peculiar to those who look too much for the best in people. I took a vow I would develop smaller eyes. But I knew I couldn't keep it. The best I could do was not fall too fast for the next person I met with that easy dignity of having grown up in the chips.

56

Mary Lou Calk remains confined to the Idaho State Hospital.

Lynn Hammer is serving a life sentence in the Oregon State Prison for the murder of Marnie Ross Tingley.

The Ross fortune, depleted somewhat by attorneys, went to Dr. Ralph Tingley.

Mycroft is serving time in the Oregon State Prison as an accessory to murder.

Arlene and I decided not to get married.

The mill was sold by the Hammer estate and soon after fell into receivership and was torn down. You can see it today, lots of lumber and debris, if you go to Plains.

Red Yellow Bear beat Rudolph Tough Otter by 479 votes. That's a good majority in Sanders County, Montana.